AFTER THE DREAM

But there was no room for sentiment in the professional life of a woman forging ahead. Kate returned her mind to the decision that still had to be made and went to make herself some tea, thankful that she had opted for an Aparthotel whose accommodation included a minature kitchen, though she had so far made little use of it.

While she waited for the water to boil, her thoughts again began veering back and forth. Why was she still hesitating about accepting Goldman's offer? Featuring in a documentary to be networked worldwide was an opportunity most journalists would grab. The trouble was that the man and the offer went together. During filming Kate would be glued to Goldman's side, and given the antipathy he aroused in her . . . There was also that inner voice saying, "Don't do it," to which logic could not be applied. monition.

About the Author

Maisie Mosco is the author of eight best-selling novels, the most recent of which was *The Waiting Game*. A former journalist, she turned to fiction in the sixties, writing initially for radio and theatre.

MAISIE MOSCO

AFTER THE DREAM

NEW ENGLISH LIBRARY
Hodder and Stoughton

Copyright © 1988 by Maisie Mosco
Manuscripts Limited

First published in Great Britain in 1988
by New English Library

First New English Library paperback
edition 1989

British Library C.I.P.

Mosco, Maisie
  After the dream
  I. Title
  823'.914   [F]

  ISBN 0-450-50250-3

Printed and bound in Great Britain
for Hodder and Stoughton
paperbacks, a division of Hodder and
Stoughton Ltd., Mill Road,
Dunton Green, Sevenoaks, Kent
TN13 2YA (Editorial Office:
47 Bedford Square, London
WC1B 3DP) by Cox & Wyman Ltd.,
Reading.

In memory of CAROLA EDMOND,
editor and friend.

Acknowledgements

Carolyn Caughey, for editorial advice. Rita Eker, for assistance with research in Israel.

Friends of the Soviet Jewry Education and Information Centre, Jerusalem, for guidance regarding Soviet immigrants.

The many Israelis of all shades of opinion whose conversation contributed to the theme of this novel.

"A change came o'er the spirit
of my dream."

Byron

PART ONE

CHAPTER ONE

Kate Starling's first impression of Israel was far removed from the biblical image of the Holy Land. Though she had not expected to be transported from Ben Gurion airport to her hotel astride a donkey, her preconceptions were irrationally at odds with rattling along in a cab, pop music blaring from its radio, to a city where the trappings of the fast food era were visible on all sides.

She had arrived in Tel Aviv late and gone directly to bed, travel weariness ensuring that she would sleep soundly. This morning a cacophony of traffic noise had awakened her. From the balcony, a rosy haze softening the lines of the rooftops foretold that this would be an unseasonably hot day. On Kate's left, beyond the seafront road, she could see the ocean gently lapping the shore. On her right was Hayarkon Street, where bumper-to-bumper vehicles were reminiscent of the London rush hour.

She turned from the petrol fumes rising to her nostrils and sipped the freshly squeezed orange juice on her breakfast tray. Was the waiter who brought it a Jew, or an Arab? Kate had wanted to ask him, but it could be a touchy question – not that the assignment her paper had handed her wouldn't be peppered with them, she was reflecting when the telephone rang.

"Welcome to Israel, Kate!" a bubbly voice greeted her.

"Oh, it's you, Barbara—"

"Who were you expecting to hear from?" Barbara Ross inquired.

"I thought it might be Ferdie, calling to check up on me."

"Why did I greet you like an Israeli would, when I'm a Londoner like you?" Barbara asked herself.

"Perhaps because you're Jewish and I'm not," said Kate, "and it probably proves that even the Jews who don't live here are proprietorial about Israel. Wouldn't you agree?"

"If you mean we all feel we have a stake in it, why wouldn't we?" Barbara replied. "But who is this Ferdie you just mentioned? A new man in your life?"

Kate wanted to laugh. As always, Barbara's conversation was more like an inquisition. They had first met on a flight to Moscow, and in retrospect it seemed to Kate that she had passed much of the journey satisfying Barbara's curiosity. Was that really no more than a year ago? A year in which Kate had wrought drastic changes to her life, and during which she and Barbara had become firm friends.

"Sorry to disappoint you, Barbara," she said, "but Ferdie is the paper's features editor, and a crusty old bachelor describes him. With what my assignment here will cost in expenses, he's entitled to ring up and keep me on my toes."

"If what you write is half as good as your article about what went on in Moscow, it will be money well spent," Barbara declared.

It was through Barbara and her husband Howard that Kate became embroiled with a refusenik family in Moscow; with Irina Smolensky and her child, whose harrowing circumstances had brought Kate face to face with the cruelty and cunning of the KGB.

Twelve months later, she wondered how she had had the nerve to pit her wits against them, and could still not recall the events of that week without a shudder. In April 1986, the outlook for people like the Smolenskys had seemed as bleak as the Russian spring. For vast numbers, despite Mr. Gorbachev's "glasnost", so it remained. But campaigning had finally achieved Irina Smolensky's release to the West. She was here in Israel.

Would Irina's little boy remember the woman who had briefly fostered him after his mother's arrest? Or had his

4

finally being snatched from Kate's hotel room blotted out the few days of care and cosseting she had given him?

"Did you manage to find out where Irina is living?" Kate asked Barbara.

"It wasn't difficult, Kate. The Soviet Jewry Centre in Jerusalem keep tabs on their own immigrants and help them as much as possible – which, apart from handing out bare subsistence allowances, I regret to say the government doesn't. And frankly," Barbara added, "I wouldn't blame Irina if she felt, after all she's been through, that when she finally got to Israel she'd been warmly welcomed and then been dumped."

Kate was taken aback. "What on earth do you mean, Barbara?"

"You'll see when you visit her. The place they've put her in is in Upper Nazareth and somewhat off the beaten track. Are you thinking of hiring a car?"

"I'll need one to cover my assignment," Kate replied.

"You'll probably need an interpreter, too," Barbara said. "But before you start out on your travels, why not spend today lazing on Herzlya beach, with Howard and me?"

Kate did not require too much persuading.

"Bring your bikini," said Barbara before ringing off.

While taking a shower, Kate contemplated the depth and breadth of her assignment, which was only now seeping through to her. She had gone into Ferdie's office to suggest writing a sequel to Irina Smolensky's story, and had emerged with the instruction to make it part of a series of articles about Israel forty years on.

Kate's piece about Irina's plight had got her the job she now had on a national daily paper. Till then, she'd been a part-time columnist for a local weekly – and straining at the leash to prove herself capable of more, she recalled while soaping her shoulders. What was the leash but her marriage?

Kate had got back from Moscow and after greeting her family had gone immediately to her typewriter, burning to set her experiences on paper. Her husband had followed her

5

and asked what the hell she thought she was doing. Kate could still see the outraged expression on his face, and remembered her own effort to keep her voice pleasant.

"I'm a writer, aren't I, Alun?"

"You're a wife and a mother, too!"

"And I've always put that first, but I'm not going to any longer," she had heard herself say.

A blinding row had followed. Long-held resentments neither had known the other nurtured shot forth from both of them. When the torrent of words was over, so was their marriage. Kate had known in her bones that her increasing disenchantment with her life could lead to this, but hadn't anticipated reaching in a flash the decision she did.

She looked up and saw her children standing in the doorway, and it was them whom she addressed.

"Your father and I are going to separate."

Alun added, in a tone that displayed his acceptance of the inevitable, "Your mother wants a life of her own, kids. She always has."

Kate had wondered, since, if Alun's knowing that the woman with whom he was now living was waiting in the wings had contributed to the way he had taken it. If you waited a long time for a man, and finally got him, he could count on being all in all to you, she reflected now. But did the man exist who could be that to Kate Starling? Probably not. And Calvin Fenner, with whom she'd shared her Moscow experience, and one night of passion, had doubtless had a lucky escape when Kate afterwards realised that what she felt for him wasn't love.

Calvin's being an American had since served to keep them apart. Was he still hoping Kate would change her mind and marry him? Seeing her in the helpmate role that went with the word "wife"? The tall, slender blonde looking back at Kate from the mirror while she dressed would soon be thirty-five, and it had taken her fifteen years of her life to find out that she wasn't the kind a man could be content with.

Though the rest of what was said on the evening her

6

marriage capsized was by now a blurred memory, recalling her children's initial distress brought an ache to Kate's throat. How could it not, when she loved them so dearly? Nor had the speed with which they afterwards adapted to their mum and dad splitting up eased her conscience.

Kate's own parents' divorce, some years ago, would have been for her a good deal more shattering had it happened when she was still a child. In the days when broken homes weren't the norm, she reflected while brushing her hair. But for Emily and Jason it must seem rather like joining a club – a comfort to them, perhaps, but not to their mother!

Kate had spent that night at her typewriter, fired by the injustice of Irina Smolensky's situation, compassion for Irina's little boy stirring within her, the professionalism of which she had always known herself capable serving to temporarily blot out the crisis in her own family.

As if, she thought now, I had to complete that important task before letting myself think of the future. Daylight was filtering into the room when the final paragraph was written and Kate had paused only to make herself a cup of tea before going out to mail her article to the first of several editors who, one after another, chose not to find space for it. The fate of Soviet Jewry had not then been the political bargaining point, nor the topical issue, it had since become.

Eventually, Kate's friend Audrey, a highly successful journalist, had pulled some strings and got the article published, after which Ferdie had called Kate and offered her a job. Though Audrey had advised her to stay a freelance, a steady job was what Kate had wanted.

She left her hotel room clad in jeans and a tee-shirt, oblivious to male heads turning to look at her when she emerged from the lift and strode through the foyer, the first of the notebooks she would fill still pristine in her large, canvas shoulder bag. On the beach she'd be soaking up impressions, as well as some sun, and that would apply wherever she went from now until her assignment was completed, she thought, getting into a taxi.

7

But steady job indeed! With me in the Middle East and the kids in London. Would they mind their mum's lengthy absence? Ferdie had said she could have as long as it took to gather her material. Kate stemmed her guilt. The alternative to the career she now had was the half-measure one that helped sour her marriage. What Alun had said to the children was true. Kate did want a life of her own. And Emily and Jason were fine in their gran's care. When Alun departed, Kate's lonely mother had been only too pleased to move in with her, and before Kate left for Israel had made a moving little speech about how good it felt to be needed again.

The taxi had crawled its way out of the jam on Hayarkon Street and Kate gave her attention to the bustling pavements of the narrow thoroughfare into which the driver had turned.

"This must be the busiest part of the city," she remarked when they halted at a traffic light.

He glanced at her with a smile. "If this is what you call busy, just wait till we reach Dizengoff!"

"What is a South African doing driving a cab in Tel Aviv?" His accent was unmistakable.

"If this were China, and you asked what a South African was doing driving a cab there, it'd be a good question," he replied. "But in Israel? And addressed to a Jew? When my father could no longer stomach South African politics, where would he bring his family? Israelis and proud of it is what we are now. The only thing is, I don't like what's happened politically here in recent years. Nor do a lot of other people. The religious fanatics, though they're the minority, have got the rest of us by the throat – and that includes the government. Are you here on vacation?" he inquired.

"Yes," Kate lied. If she told him why she was here, he'd be careful what he said.

The taxi had joined the traffic on Dizengoff, where the pavements were so thickly populated Kate wondered if perhaps Tel Aviv's spring sales had begun this morning.

8

Men whose garb seemed of another age were visible among the throng, their black frock coats and heavy brimmed hats out of key with the modern scene.

"But that's Israel," the driver replied, when Kate remarked upon it. "An ancient people that's turned itself into a modern society. Speaking for most of us, that is," he added. "But there are whole enclaves who have done the opposite. Turned the clock back for themselves and would like us all to do that. My parents and my brother live in Jerusalem, where what I'm talking about is rife, but I moved to Tel Aviv. I couldn't stand it."

"Couldn't stand what, exactly?" Kate led him further.

"Well, let me put it this way," he said crisply. "How would you like to be made to feel like a pariah in your own country because you won't toe the religious line? If you're getting the impression I'm an atheist, I'm not. But I think the traditions that are part of Jewish family life should be there to enjoy, not to throttle people with. It's how I was raised, and it's what I want for my kids. This is Dizengoff Circle, by the way," he said, negotiating the vehicle around what seemed to Kate a garish architectural monstrosity atop a raised paved area lined with benches.

She caught a glimpse of the people of all ages sitting around, or standing in groups, and of others crossing the curved walkways which flanked the Circle.

"You should see the Circle at night," said the driver, "when all the weirdos meet up here."

"Does Tel Aviv have a drug scene?"

"It's a cosmopolitan city, how wouldn't it?"

But Kate was still having trouble shedding her expectations of the Holy Land.

When they reached Herzyla, Kate cast her eye on the glistening sea, then turned to look at some mellow stone houses nestling against a wooded landscape. Though vehicles were speeding along the road, compared with Tel Aviv this was a haven of quietude.

"Where would you like me to drop you?"

9

"Here will be fine. I feel like stretching my legs and will manage to find my way to the address I'm going to."

He got out of the car to open the door for her, eyed her appreciatively, and said with a grin, "To me, your legs seem long enough."

On arriving at her destination, a large bungalow whose exterior, creeper-clad, blended perfectly with the environs, Kate found Barbara and her mother-in-law in a shady arbour at the far end of the broad flagstone path.

"How did you get here, Kate? On the back of a tortoise! I expected you for coffee, and it's now nearly lunchtime."

She came to greet Kate, looking, Kate noted, her usual glamorous self, not one of her brilliant red locks out of place, and her voluptuous shape accentuated by a candy-pink jumpsuit, walking sinuously in high-heeled sandals that made Kate feel frumpish in her flat ones.

"I came by cab," Kate replied.

"All the way from Tel Aviv? Are you mad? I thought perhaps you'd got on the wrong bus. How much did it cost you?"

When Kate told her, Barbara let out a shriek. "That cab driver took you for a ride in more ways than one. It ought not to've cost anything like that much. Didn't he have the meter switched on?"

"I was too preoccupied by his conversation to notice," said Kate as they joined Barbara's mother-in-law at the family-sized circular table that filled the arbour.

Barbara paused only to introduce them before saying to Kate, "It's a good thing you intend hiring a car, or your paper would go bankrupt from you taking taxis and paying whatever you're asked!"

"One would think that my daughter-in-law was money conscious," said Mrs. Ross with a smile.

"And if I didn't know you better, I'd think that was a crack like your son sometimes makes to me," said Barbara. Without a smile. "Would you like some homemade lemonade, Kate, since it's long past coffee time? I'll go and get us some."

"Barbara is never still for a minute," Mrs. Ross remarked in her absence. "And oh what a terrible worrier she is. Now you're here safely, Kate, she'll be able to concentrate on worrying about her children being out with their granddad for the day!"

"Did Howard go with them?" Kate inquired.

"Why would he do that on holiday, if he can have a day off from them? My son is taking it easy on the beach, where Barbara said you and she are going to join him."

"But I seem to have delayed us doing so—"

"Don't let that bother you," said Mrs. Ross comfortably, "a nice, quiet snooze on his own, in the sun, will do my son no harm. Since he took over his father-in-law's business, Howard works harder than he'd have had to if he'd gone into his dad's. It still breaks my husband's heart that Howard, his only child, refused to."

But Kate could imagine why Howard had refused. On first acquaintance, he had made little impression upon her, but she had quickly recognised his independent spirit and his appetite for challenge. It was the latter that impelled him to give up his job at the UN in New York, where he and Barbara were then working as interpreters, and take the helm of her father's textile company after it was willed to her.

Whilst Kate sat admiring the garden, its sweet-smelling fragrances heavy in the air, she was aware of Mrs. Ross surreptitiously studying her.

"Barbara told me you're here to write about how it seems to you the dream has turned out," Mrs. Ross said as her daughter-in-law came to set on the table a tall pitcher clinking with ice cubes.

"What dream are you talking about, Mother?" Barbara inquired.

"You forgot to bring the glasses," Mrs. Ross observed, "in your rush to get back to your friend! Don't you trust me to talk to her, Barbara?"

"If I didn't, Mother, I'd have taken her with me when I went to make the lemonade."

11

Though the tone of their exchange was light, by now Kate had the feeling that there was no love lost between them.

Mrs. Ross waited until they were all three sipping the delicious lemonade, before answering the question Barbara had asked her.

"The dream I was referring to," she said with a faraway look in her eyes, "was the one we all had when I was young. When you couldn't go into a Jewish home without seeing a blue tin box, with JNF written on it. There was a slot at the top to put pennies into, or silver when you could afford it. And I can remember my father putting some money into it every Friday evening, before my mother lit the Sabbath candles."

Mrs. Ross paused reminiscently, toying with the cameo brooch at the neck of her simple, beige linen dress, then she looked at Kate, the expression on her plump, bespectacled face earnest.

"I'm telling you this, my dear, because I want you to know how my feeling for Israel began, though in those days, who would have thought that the dream of there being a Jewish state would come true? There was so much against it ever happening. But week in, week out, families all over the world, like the one I grew up in, went on putting coins into those tin boxes. Every so often, the man from the Jewish National Fund – that's what the initials stood for – used to ring our doorbell. It was usually on a Sunday morning. My parents would invite him in, and we'd all watch him empty our box, to see how much our family had collected since the last time he called. Then he'd take a stub of pencil from behind his ear and write out a receipt."

She drank some lemonade and added with a smile, "I haven't seen one of those indelible pencils for years, everyone uses a biro now. But I can remember the JNF collector's tongue being purple, from licking his pencil point – and oh, the memories of my childhood and youth talking about this brings back—"

"But I'm sure they can't be very interesting for Kate to listen to," said Barbara sounding embarrassed.

"On the contrary," said Kate.

Mrs. Ross went on, as though she had not heard the interruption, her expression still pensive, "Not just of my young years, but of the little house we lived in. Our JNF box was kept on the mantelpiece, next to a photo of my parents on their wedding day. I can still see the brass candlesticks on the mantelpiece, too – the ones my grandmother brought with her when they escaped from the pogroms to England. My mother always kept them shining bright, and so did I when they came to me."

Mrs. Ross emerged from her reverie of times past and said to Barbara, "I want them to stay in my family. To be given to your daughter when she marries, like I gave them to Howard and you." Her pudgy face crinkled with distress. "But you don't use them, do you?"

"Brass doesn't go with my dining room decor."

Kate agreed. Barbara's home was furnished in the contemporary style and the candelabra Kate recalled being on the long, glass table when she was invited for a Friday night dinner had seemed perfect for its setting.

"What you mean is you prefer silver," said Mrs. Ross.

"It happens to be stainless steel, Mother, and also to mean something to me. Howard brought it back from a business trip to Copenhagen and gave it to me the day Danny was born.

"Howard rushed there straight from the airport. They'd just brought me back from the delivery room when he walked into the ward – with a nurse carrying Danny, right behind him. 'Steady on, Mr. Ross! Wait for your son,' the nurse said, and I shall never forget what Howard replied. 'Right now, I only have eyes for his mother'."

Kate's recollection of Alun's visiting her immediately after Emily's birth was somewhat different. She had not yet stopped smoking and was enjoying a cigarette the midwife had lit for her when her long labour was over. 'Any chance of

13

you packing in that noxious habit now there's going to be a child in the house?' was the first thing her husband had said.

Barbara went on, " 'There wasn't time to get you some flowers,' Howard said to me, 'but you can have this instead.' Then he handed me the big carrier bag he had in his hand. Inside it was my beautiful candelabra, wrapped in tissue paper."

"But I still think it's wrong that you don't light your Sabbath candles in my grandmother's brass candlesticks," her mother-in-law said.

They were back at the point from which their thinly veiled altercation had begun. Kate saw a spark of anger flash in her friend's eyes. Barbara had seldom, in Kate's presence, displayed the temperament associated with red hair, but she was riled now, and flared to her mother-in-law, "What difference does it make what I light the candles in, as long as I light them?"

Mrs. Ross's tone remained as even as it had been throughout. "If you don't understand what I've been trying to tell you, and also to tell Kate, you never will, Barbara."

The question Barbara had flung at her mother-in-law had evoked for Kate a picture of Irina Smolensky's Sabbath Eve table in Moscow. Reduced to penurious circumstances by the Soviet authorities' treatment of refuseniks, the family had had to sell most of their possessions, candlesticks included, but that hadn't stopped Irina from continuing her sacred ritual, nor the candles from burning brightly, affixed to a well-scrubbed baking tin.

Mrs. Ross smiled at her. "There's something else I want to say to you, Kate."

Barbara put down her lemonade glass. "For heaven's sake, Mother! Haven't you already said enough? My mother-in-law is concerned about what you might write," she added, "and I've told her that she needn't be."

"As a matter of fact, I'm not concerned any more, Barbara. Though I have to admit that I was at first. Not just concerned, but angry, to tell you both the truth. I thought, what right has someone who isn't Jewish to come here and pass on their opinion of Israel to the world?"

"Hasn't it occurred to you," said Barbara, "that a lot of newspapers and magazines are probably planning features on Israel right now? How this country has survived to enter its fortieth year – which it will next month – is the modern miracle of the Middle East, didn't you know? And since when weren't Jews news!"

"What I do know, Barbara, is that whatever Israel does rubs off on every Jew in the world – but that's another story—"

"And don't let's go into it now." Barbara gave them all some more of the refreshing cool drink, and remarked to Kate, "How my in-laws can put up with the humidity here beats me. Though it isn't usually like this in April. I feel like taking another shower."

"Then why don't you?" said Mrs. Ross. "Today is warm for the time of year, I agree, but I wouldn't call it humid, nor am I uncomfortable. But I'm wearing linen, not that synthetic stuff your outfit is made of."

Antipathy it certainly was. These annual Passover get-togethers under the same roof must be hell for both women, thought Kate. For their men, too. It wasn't surprising that Howard had escaped to the beach, nor that his father had gone off for the day with the children.

Mrs. Ross turned to Kate. "I stopped worrying about what you might write after reading your article about that refusenik family."

"We brought it to show to my mother-in-law, since it was likely she'd be meeting you," Barbara put in.

"And what you wrote would arouse compassion in a stone," said Mrs. Ross.

"But I'm not in the business of arousing compassion. My job is to tell the truth."

"Now I've met you, I feel I can trust you not to distort it," said Mrs. Ross. "And I may as well add that you're unlikely to meet any Israelis – including me – who'll tell you their country is perfect."

Later, when they were strolling to the beach, Barbara apologised for the bickering to which Kate had had to listen.

"Did you have a good relationship with your mother-in-law, Kate?"

"A better one than I had with her son, looking back on it. And we're still friends."

"So did Howard's mother and I used to be. Then everything changed, and I was glad when his parents moved to Israel."

Barbara smiled at a young woman wheeling a shopping cart, who returned the smile and said, "Shalom", as they passed each other.

"That's the customary Israeli greeting," Barbara told Kate. "Also the Hebrew word for 'peace'." She glanced up at the sky, through a fretwork of trees, and added pensively, "But how is there ever going to be peace here?"

"Don't you mean when?" said Kate optimistically.

"The how has to come before the when, Kate – and there's the rub! As you'll discover along with much more when you get going on what you're here for."

"Meeting your mother-in-law was a useful beginning," Kate replied. "She's a nice lady, Barbara—"

"You'd be welcome to take my place in her household, if we weren't going home tomorrow! And what you could have found useful about her rambling on about days gone by—"

"Well, let's say that it gave me a new slant on that hackneyed phrase, 'the Zionist dream'."

Mrs. Ross's memory of the JNF box being part of her childhood had given Kate an insight she could not have gained from any amount of cold facts. Suddenly, the emotive quality Israel had for those who had once only dreamed of its existence was becoming clear to her; and not just for them, but for their descendants born after the state was founded. As though, like the candlesticks about which Mrs. Ross had made such a fuss, love for the land of their forefathers was passed down from generation to generation.

Kate glanced at Barbara, whose expression denoted that she had still not recovered from Mrs. Ross's embarrassing her, as she undoubtedly had.

"About those brass candlesticks – " Kate said carefully.

"What about them?"

"Well – has it never struck you what they represent to your mother-in-law, Barbara?"

"Yes. They're something to get at me about," Barbara replied, as they turned into the coast road and the sea view was briefly blotted out by a new-looking hotel, "since she has never yet come out with what she really has against me."

"That isn't the interpretation I'd put on it."

"But there are things you don't know, Kate." Barbara's tone was now tinged with bitterness. "That it's me, not Howard, whom she blames for his stepping into my dad's shoes. The joke – if I could muster a sense of humour about this – is that I didn't want Howard to do it. I knew he wouldn't be happy in business, nor is he."

They crossed the road and paused to gaze at a scene that lived up to the travel brochure description of Herzlya. Beyond the vast expanse of golden sand, the Mediterranean shimmered invitingly in the heat of the day, its azure swell as if rimmed with whipped cream where it broke upon the shore.

An air force helicopter appeared overhead, shattering the stillness, a reminder for Kate of how fragile the tranquillity of her surroundings was.

"My in-laws say they've got used to those noisy things patrolling the coast," Barbara said as they went on their way. "I'm not sure that I could. Shall you take my mother-in-law up on that invitation she gave you before we left, Kate?"

"Well, it was certainly kind of her to tell me I'd be welcome in her home if I can manage a break from work. Since this is going to be a lengthy assignment," Kate added with a smile, "the time could come when a weekend of being mothered appeals to me. And if her chopped liver is as good as yours—!"

"Did you try making it for your kids yet?"

"No, but I told my mum how to and she produced a very fair imitation."

They chatted of this and that while Barbara led Kate through a car park and downward on to the beach adjoining the Sharon Hotel, where they espied Howard spreadeagled on a towel, his portliness emphasised by swimming trunks, and the whiteness of his skin made to seem the more so by the trunks being red.

"How's that for sexy!" said Barbara, as they halted to step out of their sandals. "And if his dad were with him, Howard would still be wearing the yarmulke that's been on his head since we got here."

"Are his parents very religious?" Kate asked, plodding beside Barbara toward him.

"By my standards and his, yes. But compared with what goes on in that respect in Israel—" Barbara left the rest of the sentence eloquently unsaid.

Howard heaved himself to his feet and kissed Kate's cheek. "Long time no see, Kate! How've you been? Are you enjoying being single again?"

"We're looking forward to hearing what you've been up to," said Barbara, whilst unzipping her jumpsuit and wriggling out of it.

Howard glanced at Kate, who had sat down on the sand to divest herself of her tee-shirt and jeans. "Now that's what I call a nice modest lady. My wife, on the other hand, likes giving a strip show," he declared as Barbara stood revealed in the briefest of bikinis.

Kate adjusted the bra of her own bikini, though there was less to spill out of it than applied to her friend, and replied to the good-natured quizzing she had come to accept from the couple, "If you mean what have I been up to socially, having a social life isn't too high on my list right now."

18

"I don't like the sound of that," said Barbara, "do you, Howard? And for an attractive woman like Kate it shouldn't be too difficult to find a man."

"I'm not on the lookout for one, Barbara—"

"And I could name you some other divorcées I know who started out feeling that way, but they didn't let it stop them from having a good time."

Howard observed Kate's expression and brought the quiz to an end. "What are you, Barbara? An agony-aunt? Why don't you just tell Kate to go and join that admiring circle over there!"

They followed his glance to where some young girls were clustered around a middle-aged man.

"I've been watching him holding forth to them all morning," Howard went on, "and wondering what he's got that I haven't! Whatever it is, it sure isn't visible—"

Kate and Barbara, however, were aware of the man's magnetic charm even from a distance, and exchanged a private smile. Though he was far from handsome, there was about him that *je ne sais quoi* that has women falling at a man's feet – which was literally where the bevy hanging on his every word was now, and he seated in a deck chair, his muscular and hairy legs comfortably crossed, the expression on his craggy face droll.

Kate was thinking that nobody could acquire that burnt brown look from a holiday in the sun, and that he must be an Israeli, when he glanced her way and she got a glimpse of amused blue eyes, before averting her gaze.

When she opened her eyes after fifteen minutes of toasting herself, the man was alone and reading the *Jerusalem Post*. Since that paper was printed in English, maybe he wasn't an Israeli; just the wealthy playboy tourist Howard had, in the interim, assessed him to be.

What's it to you, Kate? she mentally shrugged him off. Then a beautiful brunette appeared at his side and engaged him in what seemed an earnest conversation. Why didn't the bad-mannered devil get up and offer her his chair? Instead of letting her squat in the sand as those girls had, since she wasn't dressed for the beach – and, for some reason, kept darting glances toward the car park.

The woman, who looked about Kate's age, was wearing a dark, tailored suit, and had with her an executive briefcase. Was she the man's secretary? Kate allowed herself a vision of him travelling the world in his private jet, with numerous glorious girls in tow for his pleasure, and the brunette tagging along as the secretaries of such men were known to do.

"What I wouldn't give for her cheekbones," said Barbara, proving herself equally intrigued.

A remark that caused Howard to say from his prone position beside them, "Is that chap still pulling the birds?"

With that, the three of them went to bathe in the sea. When they returned to the beach, the man and his companion were no longer there. By the time they had made their way to the tree-lined square that was Herzlya's most popular outdoor rendezvous, Kate had forgotten his existence.

Though it was now early afternoon, the pavement cafés were still packed with people lingering after eating lunch. Howard was leading the way to an ice-cream parlour, when Barbara tugged his sleeve.

"Your idea of a meal might be a chocolate nut sundae, Howard, but Kate and I would like something more substantial, if equally fattening. A burger and chips, for instance."

Howard said, "What sort of nosh is that to offer a gentile friend for her first meal in Israel if you don't count breakfast?"

"I've heard that the blintzes are something special here," Kate put in.

Howard ushered them toward a café on the opposite side of the square, and said wryly, "Nobody could say it isn't symbolic that the first food we three eat together in the Jewish state is something Russian."

Kate said as they seated themselves at a newly-vacated table, "If you'd let me, Howard, I'd like to buy us some wine, to drink a toast to how things finally turned out for Irina Smolensky."

"That seems to me a good enough reason for a tipple, Kate."

"If we let ourselves forget that Irina's husband is still in the Soviet Union," said Barbara, her expression clouding. "Glasnost or no glasnost, Kate, the gates are still only opened a crack—"

"And my wife," Howard cut in, "is still spending more hours working to prise them wide open than she does cooking me hot dinners."

After the waitress had taken their order, to which Kate had added a bottle of rosé, they continued discussing Barbara's work for the refusenik cause and were still doing so when the wine, and the piping hot blintzes, were brought to the table. The selection of fillings, savoury and sweet, had made it hard for Kate to choose. She and Barbara had finally opted for cheese, but Howard, whose sweet tooth accounted for his girth, had unhesitatingly ordered a blintze filled with caramel nut fudge.

"Before we leave the subject of refuseniks," Kate said to Barbara, "there's something I'd like to ask you that could be a sore point – how do you feel about so many of them, once they're out and reach Vienna, boarding a plane for America instead of Israel?"

"Well, it's certainly a sore point with the Israelis," Barbara replied, "given Israel's need for new immigrants."

"The synagogues and Zionist youth clubs in Britain are going all out right now to get young people to come and settle here," Howard told Kate, "and that's probably worldwide," he added, dabbing some sauce from his chin with a paper napkin.

"Coming to settle here is called 'making aliyah', Kate," said Barbara, "which I may as well tell you, since it's a phrase you'll be hearing a lot from people who've done it."

"And think that every Jew in the world should," Howard added cryptically, "though there wouldn't be space for us all!"

"But returning to the question Kate asked me," said Barbara, "I did have trouble coming to terms with what seemed to me at first a moral defection. Then I thought, the refuseniks are as entitled as I am to choose where they live once they're freed."

"I think what Barbara's saying is that freedom with strings attached to it isn't freedom," Howard capped it.

"And how I feel about it now is that all that matters is for people to be free."

They were raising their glasses to Irina Smolensky's release when Howard said, "There's that chap again—"

The man they had noticed on the beach was threading his way through the tables to a vacant one at the rear.

"Want to bet that he'll shortly be joined by some lovelies?" said Howard.

A few minutes later, Howard had won his bet and Kate and Barbara were laughing at his sour expression. Then a business acquaintance of Howard's came to have a word with him, and said after being introduced to Kate, and learning that she was a journalist, "If interviewing celebrities is in your line, this could be your lucky day!"

"Well, it isn't what I'm in Israel to do," Kate answered, wondering why the cavernous-faced fellow kept winking at her – no, he wasn't winking, he had a twitch in his eye. And an equally nervy laugh.

"I'd better warn you, Kate," Howard said with a grin, "that Mel is known at home as Mr. Fixit."

The kind whom Kate would run a mile from. "Who is the celebrity you mentioned?" she asked him nevertheless.

"Our waitress just told us that Dov Goldman is eating here, and pointed him out to us." He glanced at the man whose success with the opposite sex was a puzzle to Howard, if not to Kate and Barbara.

"And what, apart from the obvious, is he celebrated for?"

said Howard – the man was again holding forth, and his young companions' expressions rapt. "I've never heard of Dov Goldman."

"Well, you're not a film buff, are you?" Mel replied sounding superior. "He's a film director."

"That doesn't surprise me."

Since Goldman's behaviour seemed in keeping with the casting couch image, nor did it Kate. That he thought himself cock-o'-the-walk – and doubtless spent most of his time literally proving it – was very plain. And for the second time that day, it was necessary for Kate to avert her gaze from the impudent stare he was now giving her.

"Goldman is famous in Israel," Mel went on, "and the waitress told us that the two girls with him are a pop-singer duo high in the charts here. I'm going to take my kid to the table to get the girls' autographs. If Kate would like to accompany us, it could lead to her getting an interview with Goldman. Are you staying at one of the Herzlya hotels, Kate?"

"No, I'm at the Tel Aviv Yamit."

"But Kate's having today off," Barbara interceded while ladling more sour cream on to what remained of her blintze, "and you're talking work to her."

"I'm just trying to be helpful."

"And I appreciate your good intentions," Kate lied.

"You'll let me introduce you to Goldman? He'll be impressed when he hears which paper you work for."

"Probably. But accosting celebrities while they're eating a meal isn't my style. And if you don't mind, I'd like to get on with mine."

Even an individual as thick-skinned as Mel could not have failed to take the hint.

"If I'd known Mel was lunching here, I'd have let Howard take us to the ice-cream parlour!" Barbara said with a giggle after he had returned to his own table.

"But Kate got the worst of it, and we owe her an apology," said Howard. "Mel's a hard guy to say no to!"

"Nor does saying no to him necessarily end there," Barbara added. "Shall we tell Kate how and why we came to have our windows double-glazed?"

"Allow *me* to, Barbara! Since I still haven't forgotten the one and only party we asked him to. How he began advising us that double-glazing would change our lives, the minute he walked in—"

"Or how we heaved a sigh of relief when he left early."

"What we hadn't reckoned on," Howard said dryly, "was his having the chutzpah to ask a double-glazing firm to send a rep to our house. The same firm who'd done his own house, needless to say! And once that master in the art of salesmanship was over the doorstep – suffice to say that he left with my signature on an order form. It was Barbara who invited him in."

"I wouldn't have if you hadn't been home and I hadn't had a pan of chips on the hob—"

"Whatever, that was one time when Mr. Fixit didn't take no for an answer," Howard said to Kate, as they watched Mel escort his pig-tailed teenage daughter to Goldman's table.

"But there's no way that *my* little encounter with him can acquire a sting in the tail."

CHAPTER TWO

After the Rosses' departure from Israel, Kate felt totally alone in a strange land, and wondered if she was cut out for a career that could take her so far from home.

She shook off her doubts and approached her assignment systematically, Though she was longing to see Irina Smolensky and little Yuli, she must curb her impatience until her travels took her north.

Today she was going to Jerusalem and had decided to make the journey in one of the vehicles Israelis called "sharuts", which would put her cheek by jowl with people who lived here.

A cab was taking her to Tel Aviv's central bus station, making its way through narrow streets a good deal less salubrious than Kate's impression of the city had hitherto been.

Here were the sights, sounds, and smells of the Middle East. The aroma of unfamiliar spices drifted in through the taxi window. She glimpsed some overflowing garbage bins, and an odour of rotting vegetables joined the heady mixture. A man in an Arab headdress was leaning against a shop doorway – if only they all wore those, thought Kate, she would have less trouble discerning if darkly handsome young men like the cab driver were Arabs, or Jews.

She decided to ask him and was rendered the more confused by his reply.

"I am an Israeli."

"But you could be an Israeli Arab, couldn't you? Isn't that Arab music on your cab radio?"

"You think it is only an Arab who would to that station

tune in? Or that the Jews do not watch the Jordan-TV channel?"

Kate sensed from his tone that he was an Arab. But, as she had anticipated, the question was sensitive ground.

They had reached the bus station, and the driver did not return her friendly smile when she got out of the car and paid him. What this assignment needed was an expert in the nuances of Israeli society. Someone also equipped with more than a basic knowledge of the political scene here.

Since Kate qualified on neither count, she would just have to feel her way. It was then, while crossing the cobbled street to where the sharuts were lined up, that she stopped viewing her assignment as a fact-finding expedition. What Ferdie wanted from her was the human interest aspect he knew was her forte. Her impressions of how the Zionist dream had turned out for the people now living with the reality.

A reality that included an Arab like the cab driver, whose ancestral hatred of the Jews he had seemingly set aside, given his declaring himself an Israeli as vehemently as if he were waving the Jewish State's flag.

Picking her way through the litter discarded by those buying themselves fruit or a snack from the street stalls, Kate recalled reading that bombs on buses, or at the stations themselves, were a hazard of using that form of transport. Yet people went on doing so, and a group of youngsters she could see boarding a bus were laughing and talking as if they hadn't a care in the world. It occurred to her, then, that to live in Israel it must be necessary to acquire a special bravado, and that this possibly accounted for the veneer she had thought hardness in some whom she had encountered.

Kate had expected the sharuts to be minibuses, and several were, but the vehicle at the head of the line was a shabby car. When she reached it, a girl with a Brooklyn accent and curly dark hair popped her head out of the window and said, "If Jerusalem is where you're headed, this sharut is it, and we won't have to wait for a fourth passenger if you don't mind splitting the difference."

26

The girl was beside the driver, who went on reading a newspaper until Kate had got into the car. Already seated in the back was one of the biggest women Kate had ever seen. Though she might once have been pretty, as her retroussé nose implied, she now resembled a monstrous kewpie doll with orange-coloured hair, a painted cupid's-bow mouth and two blobs of red on its cheeks.

Kate addressed the American girl. "I didn't quite understand what you said before I got in—"

"Well, believe it or not, this car is intended to take three in the back, and the guy won't take off for Jerusalem without his full load unless we reimburse him. I guess you never travelled by sharut before, if you don't know that's how it goes."

Kate shook her head and managed not to laugh, since the lady at her side would have equalled two normal-sized passengers. As for there being space for a third person in the back – Kate was squashed into a corner by her balloonlike curves.

She was jolted from her private mirth when a deep bass voice said from beside her, "Me and the girl are willing to split the difference, and I guess you are, so that's okay."

The kewpie doll was a man. And American, like the girl. So much for Kate's assuming that a sharut journey would necessarily be a close encounter with Israelis! But make the most of meeting a transvestite, Kate. All was grist to the mill for a writer.

Sharut fares were payable in advance, and it was the girl who completed Kate's bit of the transaction, since the driver spoke only Hebrew. Possible too, Kate then realised, that her travelling companions *were* Israelis, immigrants like the ex-South African cab driver.

"Do you live here?" she asked the girl after they had set off.

"No, but I'm thinking of making aliyah. Right now, I'm here on a working vacation."

"Can the two go together?" Kate said with a laugh.

"Well, working on a kibbutz is hard, but it's sure a vacation from home. My name is Libby, by the way—"

"And I'm Charlene," said the bass voice incongruously.

A long story then followed of how Charlene had come to Tel Aviv some years ago on holiday, known immediately that it was a live-and-let-live city, and had stayed on.

"You don't miss the States?" Libby inquired, her stiff tone implying her embarrassment in Charlene's company.

Not just embarrassment, disapproval too, Kate detected, though the girl was trying to hide it.

"What's to miss?" Charlene replied. "And I guess we should tell our friend here what 'making aliyah' means."

"As it happens, I know," said Kate.

"But my apologies for not realising you aren't Jewish," said Libby.

"You've never seen a beautiful shiksa before?" Charlene said to her with a guffaw.

Kate thanked Charlene for the compliment.

"But even if you were Jewish," said Libby, "you wouldn't necessarily understand Hebrew. I guess, outside Israel, there are more who don't than those who do. But there are certain words and phrases we all grow up with, and one is that making aliyah means emigrating to Israel."

Kate was reminded of Mrs. Ross's tale about the JNF box – here was another example of what that reminiscence stood for.

"But it wasn't idealistic claptrap that kept me here," Charlene declared, "and I have to say there are things about our society that make me want to puke. Each time I have to go see a man about a dog, or whatever, in Jerusalem, I can't get out of the goddamn place fast enough."

"Couldn't you have found a less sacrilegious way to put it?" Libby said, giving Kate an uncomfortable glance.

Charlene clasped lavishly beringed fingers on the gold plastic holdall that was clamped on his lap. "Come off it, sweetie."

"This lady could be a devout pilgrim going to visit the shrines, couldn't she?" said Libby rebukingly.

"But I'm not," said Kate, "and I'm finding the conversation highly interesting."

Charlene said, "Then let me tell you you're heading for a city where religion is big business. You're going to trip over Muslims trying to sell you bottles of Holy Water, plaster statues of Jesus and Mary, Chanukah menorahs or whatever. And if you're thinking of taking home a gold cross and chain for your mom, the Jewish jewellers are who to go to. If it wasn't so sick, I would think it was a joke. And when I recall the time I once let myself be persuaded to accompany a visiting Californian buddy to the Wailing Wall—"

"That's what the Western Wall gets called by people who don't have respect for it," Libby declaimed.

Charlene went on, "When we got to the Wall – no, first we stood looking down on the scene there, and suddenly, this guy I'm with, he gets an attack of the guilts, tells me it's years since he attended a synagogue service, and he would like to join the throng to say a prayer.

"While I'm trailing him to where it's all happening, I'm trying to recover from the shock, also trying to remember when *I* was last in a synagogue. When we reach the Wall, a little guy accosts him and asks did he have a Bar Mitzvah. My friend gives him a nod, and is then supplied with the necessary prayer-saying equipment—"

"And you sure have a way with words!" Libby interrupted angrily. "I can now write in my diary that today I met a Jewish anti-Semite."

"Whatever turns you on is okay by me, sweetie. So this friend of mine gets provided with a prayer shawl, a yarmulke, and the book, and goes to get his sins off his chest to the Wall—"

Again Libby was incensed. "Did nobody ever tell you it's God people pray to?"

"Sure, sweetie, and I tried it myself – but the way things turned out, He couldn't have been listening."

Sadness briefly entered the man's voice, then the veneer beneath which it was hidden clicked back into place. Nor was it possible for Kate to envisage what someone like Charlene must have been through, she reflected as the tale was resumed and brought to a close.

"But while my friend is having his private moment – or thinks he is – it's puking time again for *me*. A photographer is there taking a picture of it, to sell to him for a souvenir. And if that, together with the rest, doesn't sum up Jerusalem—"

"It sure doesn't for me," said Libby. "Were you never in the Old City on a Jewish Festival? When those who live by the laws of Judaism are out in the streets—"

"The ones who procreate like rabbits, you mean," Charlene cut in.

Libby lost her temper. "Since I happen to believe in their way of life, I'll be one of them if I make aliyah! Though I would live on a religious kibbutz, like where I'm spending some time now, not in the city."

"This poor little girl intends cutting herself off from the world," Charlene said to Kate.

Kate made no attempt to restore the conversation when Libby turned her back on Charlene. Enigmatic though that final remark was, it was clear that the rancour in the air emanated from two opposing and strongly held views about the topic that had arisen time and again since Kate arrived in Israel. It seemed to Kate now that even non-believers like Charlene – had he once been called Charles? – were obsessed by what they didn't believe in. Was Israel a place where in matters concerning religion there was no middle ground?

Kate's interest in her companions' conversation had prohibited her from taking in the scenery, but she now gave her attention to the breathtaking view ahead, where groves of towering cypresses lent majesty to the high, rocky terrain through which they were passing.

"We'll soon reach Jerusalem," Libby told her, "and I meant to tell you that those old military vehicles on that grassy rise we drove by weren't left there because the army is neglectful – they're anything but. What you saw is a memorial to the soldiers lost in the battle for Jerusalem that took place in 1948."

"If there's one thing Israel isn't short of," Charlene said cynically, "and Jerusalem in particular, it's memorials, monuments, and endowment plaques."

"There this person goes again!" Libby exclaimed. "And I guess it's lucky I'm here to counteract the impression of this country you must be getting."

But Kate would see Israel through her own eyes, not through the jaundiced eye of the pathetic creature by her side, nor through that of this tunnel-visioned young girl.

After the driver had set them down in the city, Kate thanked the two for their friendliness toward a gentile stranger.

"But we didn't yet warn you to watch out for your purse in the Bazaar," said Libby.

Charlene gave Kate a big smile that split the heavy layer of make-up masking his blue jowls. "Don't let this be your last trip to Israel."

"We like our gentile visitors to come back," said Libby.

"Cut the 'we' till you've made aliyah, sweetie."

"And I'll hope not to run into you, when I do."

"The lifestyle you'll have, I'd say that's unlikely."

Kate watched them go their separate ways. Charlene teetering in gold court shoes that matched the holdall he was coquettishly swinging and the broad belt hugging a short, black frock around his massive waist. Libby modestly attired in a long-sleeved grey dress.

Though the girl was not yet an Israeli, her decision to make her life here seemed imminent, and how different an Israeli she would be from those who opted for the brash ethos of Tel Aviv, thought Kate. In which Charlene, possibly a drag-queen, not just a transvestite, had found a niche.

What the ex-South African cab driver had told Kate about Dizengoff Circle in the sleeping hours now seemed a good deal more credible than it had then. But one by one her preconceptions of Israeli society were being dispelled. She had expected a larger version of the assortment of Jewish people she had met via the Rosses. In other words, respectable and moderately God-fearing. Well, so much for that! Charlene was, of course, an extreme. But Kate had the impression that in a vastly different way the same could be said of Libby. For the girl, the land that the Bible said God had promised to her people was something holy, and once settled here she would abide by Judaic law and eschew all else.

Kate headed toward the Jewish Quarter, a map clutched in her hand, her brow furrowed in thought, then began traversing the steep steps and alleyways of the Old City, where the sense of history that had until now eluded her took her in its thrall.

Buildings of ancient stone, some with balconies festooned with laundry, lined the narrow route, shutting out the sun. When she reached the Jewish Quarter, some of the heavy doors past which she walked had Hebrew words painted upon them, indicating that they might be synagogues, and instead of the bustling atmosphere Kate had anticipated, an air of peace and quiet pervaded.

As if nobody is in a hurry to get where they're going, she reflected, noting the passers-by, most of whom were men, young and old; those in pairs, or in groups, conversing together, and some thoughtfully plucking their beards as though whatever they were discussing was a major preoccupation. They were, of course, scholars and students of the Torah and the Talmud.

Their aura of an earlier age, the frock coats and the heavy-brimmed black hats, did not seem anachronistic here, as it had when she saw some of their kind on Dizengoff. On the contrary, it was she who seemed out of key. And if she had thought Libby decorously garbed, the several young women she passed, all of whom had at least three children with them, were yet more deserving of that description, their skirts hiding their ankles. And all, for some reason, wearing kerchiefs upon their heads as if they were a uniform.

There was, indeed, something uniform about the women themselves, a serenity that bespoke contentment. Oh well, every woman to her own choice! thought Kate, watching one of them patiently wipe a toddler's nose, and then begin tugging her baby's perambulator backward up the steps Kate was descending on her way to the Western Wall. You wouldn't catch Kate Starling living their kind of life. And why was she calling them women? They didn't look more than a few years older than Kate's daughter, and Emily was not yet fifteen.

When eventually she stood gazing down upon the Wall, beside which was the Gate leading into Temple Mount, Kate found herself emotionally affected as a gentile would not ordinarily have expected to be. Meeting Irina Smolensky had to account for it. It was here at the Wall, where Kate could see both men and women praying, their stature seeming Lilliputian beside the towering stretch of Herodian stone, and the sun beating down upon them, that Irina had wanted her son to be Bar Mitzvah. And so he now would be. Would little Yuli's father by then be in Israel to share Irina's joy? Or, seven years from now, still be awaiting an exit visa to join his family?

Since longer family separations than that were still being perpetuated by the Soviet authorities, Kate did not allow herself to dwell upon it, but sent up her own silent prayer that God would strengthen Mr. Gorbachev's elbow in the matter of human rights.

She gazed for a moment at the gold-crowned Mosque of Omar, visible behind the Wall, on the crest of Temple Mount, where no doubt Muslims were praying to Allah with a fervour equalling that of the elderly Jews swaying back and forth before Judaism's most important shrine. What more graphic illustration could there be of the passion with which both faiths regarded the Holy City? Though it was now in Israeli hands, Kate could not imagine the Arabs ever leaving it at that, and mused briefly upon the conflicts for which religion was responsible. The more so when it spilled over into nationalism, as Iran was currently proving.

Later, Kate visited two shrines of her own religion, the Church of the Holy Sepulchre, and the Garden of Gethsemane whose ancient olive trees were said to have witnessed Christ at prayer, before taking a cab to the Holocaust Museum, where the landscaped grounds and tasteful architecture belied the barbarity within.

Kate had to steel herself to enter, and had noted that some of the people on a bus she had seen unloading its passengers had remained aboard. Nor was she surprised when she heard the guide address the group in German.

Her own tour of the museum caused her gorge to rise, as the evidence of Hitler's "final solution" and its perpetration unreeled for her with gathering force in the stark confines of the exhibition's setting, the inhumanity of the actual perpetrators beyond the comprehension of a normal member of mankind.

She averted her eyes from a photograph of a mass grave heaped with near-skeletons, and had moved on to the next exhibit, the last not gone from her, when she heard a child say, "Why is Grandma crying, Mommy?"

Kate glanced across the room and saw two women and a small girl standing beside a photograph of Belsen that Kate had already seen. Who the hell would bring a young kid to this chamber of horrors!

"Grandma is crying, honey, because that was the camp she was in."

Only a survivor, Kate answered her own question. But why? The mother and child were overtly American, and the granny probably now a U.S. citizen too. Yet the past still haunted her, or she would not have included this macabre family outing in their trip to Israel. How wouldn't it haunt her? But her bringing her grandchild here remained an enigma for Kate.

Though Kate felt like fleeing, the museum was relevant to

the understanding necessary to her assignment and she forced herself to continue her grim appraisal.

She had asked the taxi driver to wait for her and saw him scan her expression when eventually she emerged. But he must be used to seeing people leave that place looking white around the gills.

His own expression was fittingly sombre. But Kate had had no difficulty in establishing that he was a Jew, since he had said when she asked him to take her to the museum that it was a pleasure to meet a gentile who made a point of visiting it, that most came to Jerusalem only to see the Christian shrines.

"Have you been yet to the Bazaar?" he inquired when she got into the car. "If you have not, I would suggest it will be now for you a good place to go."

Kate stopped staring into space. "What you mean is it will cheer me up—"

"And also I can direct you to a café for the good cup of tea."

"Is the café in the Bazaar?"

"But it is not too simple to find."

"If there's a good cup of tea going, I'll find it. The Bazaar will do me fine, thank you." Kate could use not just the tea, but the colourful bustle of life. "You're very kind," she added to the driver.

"That is not how others here have seemed to you, perhaps?"

"I wouldn't say that."

"But many tourists – the diaspora Jews most of all – their opinion of Israelis it is not too good."

"Another cab driver said something like that to me—"

"It is not a secret," he replied with a shrug of his bulky shoulders, "as it is not a secret our opinion of those diaspora Jews. All right, so money they give to Israel, but does that entitle them to pass the judgements like they do? They come here for the vacation and then they go home. What do they know of the everyday life of an Israeli?"

"But tourists are your living, aren't they?" Kate countered.

"That does not mean I have to like the people some of them are."

They had halted at a traffic light and he turned around to give Kate a grin that revealed tobacco-stained teeth, though she had not seen him smoke and there was a *no smoking* notice in the car.

"What I have just said, it does not of course include you."

"How long ago did you stop smoking?" she asked with a laugh.

"What are you, a detective?" he joked, starting the car. "As it so happens, I did so only a month ago."

And your next visit to the dentist isn't yet due, Kate wanted to say.

"But I have since changed my car, and this one, it has not the odour of stale tobacco. So how did you know?"

Since Kate could hardly remark upon his teeth, she replied jocularly, "I come from a family of gipsies and I have a crystal ball."

The driver chuckled. "You are one passenger I shall not forget! Could you also tell me, perhaps, what the future it holds in store for me?"

"I'm afraid my crystal ball only lets me see into the past."

She went to the Bazaar, found it as interesting and colourful as she had anticipated, and eventually located the café which the kindly Israeli had mentioned. Though it was not the English-teashop-in-exile his words had conjured up – Kate had had a nostalgic vision of two maiden ladies from Bath serving buttered scones on dainty china plates – the tea was good, and the Arab café-owner friendly.

She was seated at an outdoor table, pouring herself a second cup, when she saw the Israeli film director walk by on the opposite side of the narrow street, a girl on each arm.

Hey, you Mr. Goldman! Kate felt like yelling, Why do you keep crossing my path? And always with the evidence of your success with females who have less sense than me. Had those with him this time – they were not the pop-singer duo – learned to wiggle their bottoms like that by watching vintage Marilyn Monroe movies? Starlets was what their appearance suggested, and Kate let herself wonder if the film director was on his way to a three-on-the-casting-couch session, before dismissing him from her mind.

Her return journey to Tel Aviv was less interesting, but more aromatic, than the ride to Jerusalem. The sharut was carrying its full load, and Kate, the penultimate passenger to get into the vehicle, was constrained to sit wedged between a couple of swarthy young men whom her nose told her had not bathed in the recent past. The one on her right was, to boot, an advert for what garlic can do to the breath.

Both had on their heads the little caps that Kate had become accustomed to seeing, though more so in Jerusalem than in Tel Aviv. She noticed that theirs were of the knitted variety, which Barbara had mentioned denoted its wearers were of the ultra-orthodox community.

Had they not been wearing the caps, Kate might have thought them Arabs, so dark was their skin. But in Jerusalem, she recalled, she'd seen black men with the caps on their heads – were they perhaps Ethiopian immigrants? – those dramatically rescued by Israel when their survival was threatened.

The sharut driver, who could have passed for a Scandinavian, was conversing in Hebrew with the rabbinical-looking old gentleman beside him, and Kate thinking what a motley population this was, when the man on her left opened a can of beer, gulped some of it, and promptly dozed off. When the can tipped sideways and spilled its contents in Kate's lap, he awoke and instead of apologising, laughed – as the man on the other side of her was doing.

"Are your passengers insured against damage to their clothing?" she exclaimed to the driver, whilst mopping her jeans with a paper tissue.

The reply was a shrug while continuing his conversation

with the old gentleman, whose contribution to the odour-laden atmosphere was the reek of mothballs.

Oh, for some fresh air! thought Kate. And for a sweet-scented bath.

When, eventually, she arrived back at her hotel and saw Goldman beside the desk, chatting to a receptionist, Kate began to feel like a character in one of the glossy movies he no doubt made, in which coincidence was conveniently stretched to the point of incredibility. The next bit of the plot, in such a movie, would be for Goldman to say to Kate whilst she was getting her key, "Haven't I seen you somewhere before?" But this was real life and when Kate left the hotel today she had taken her key with her.

Chapter Three

The following morning, Goldman called her. She had just showered, and answered the telephone wrapped in a towel and dripping water on to the carpet. Why was she not surprised to learn who the caller was? she was asking herself when he made a remark as corny as the one he had not had the opportunity to make last night.

"We really must stop not-meeting like this."

"Is that a line from one of your films?"

"My films don't include lines. I make documentaries and that is why I'm calling you."

"Would you care to expand on that?"

"Most certainly. Over breakfast, if that would suit you."

Kate wanted to reply that it wouldn't, but curiosity impelled her to say, keeping her tone casual, "Since I haven't yet had mine, that wouldn't inconvenience me."

"Shall we make it the Dan Hotel? How would half-an-hour from now do?"

Though the Dan was but a stone's throw from the Yamit, and Kate could easily have managed it, she said, "Forty-five minutes would suit me better."

"I'll be waiting for you in the coffee shop."

The voice matches the man, thought Kate after replacing the receiver. Huskily male wasn't in it! Though her supposition about the sort of films he made had fallen apart, there was no way the rest of how he came over would turn out to be misleading. Kate could recognise a wolf when she saw one.

Nevertheless, the reason he had given for calling her was intriguing. And no less so how he knew her name and where she was staying.

Instead of putting on jeans and a tee-shirt, Kate chose a more feminine outfit, a lime green cotton suit that enhanced her fair colouring. She was stepping into the skirt when she stopped short. Her workaday clothes would do to breakfast with Goldman. Kate wasn't going to make a special effort to look her best for him.

Goldman was seated at a table in the Dan's Patio Café when Kate entered and – wouldn't you know it! – chatting to a young waitress.

He rose and came to meet Kate, displaying more courtesy than she would have expected of him, though the sexist comment he made when they were seated opposite each other was entirely in character.

"How unusual to find a woman who is prompt."

"I'm in Israel to work, Mr Goldman. I don't have time to waste."

"Then let us hope you won't consider what I have to say a waste of your valuable time. Shall we order our breakfast? I myself don't indulge too heavily early in the morning."

Well, it's after the night before, isn't it? Kate privately replied, noting that his face, at close quarters, had a dissipated look which made him none the less attractive.

"Toast and coffee is my usual," she said without bothering to scan the menu.

"But allow me to suggest that here you supplement it with our Israeli grapefruit, which is the best in the world."

Goldman gave the order to the waitress in Hebrew, then sat studying Kate until she was sure the colour must rise to her cheeks.

When, eventually, he said, "Yes, you would do very nicely," Kate was momentarily too taken aback to speak.

She said when she found her voice, "Look – what is all this about?"

"I was thinking how very photogenic you are."

"Then you thought wrong, I never photograph well."

"That can only be attributable to the person behind the camera."

Was he thinking of grooming Kate for stardom? Or amusing himself handing her a line, like the legendary "I can get you into the movies?"

Kate hid her confusion and repeated her question. "Would you mind telling me what all this is about?"

"I'd prefer to wait until our breakfast has been served, then we shan't be interrupted," he replied.

Whilst registering that his excellent English was spoken with an American accent, Kate took in his white silk polo-neck sweater. And that he wore on his wrist a heavy gold identity bracelet. Affluence was part of his aura. But above all, she was aware of his self-assurance. Goldman was a man accustomed to having his own way on all counts.

"While we're waiting for our breakfast to come, you can fill me in on how you knew my name and where to contact me, Mr. Goldman."

"May we drop the formalities?" he answered. "In Israel we don't have time to maintain them, so let's be Dov and Kate."

"If you wish," she said with a stiffness that caused him to smile.

Was it those deep blue eyes in that burnt-brown face that made his appearance so striking?

"I learned what I so far know about you by the same means that you learned who I am," he said. "From the Englishman who was speaking to you and your friends at the café where you and I, fortuitously, both ate lunch that day."

From Mr. Fixit! Why hadn't Kate guessed? Because she'd forgotten his existence – Howard and Barbara were going to laugh their heads off about this.

"You couldn't have learned much from him," she said, "since he's a total stranger to me. And what was fortuitous about it?"

"I'm hoping it will turn out that he's done us both a favour."

A brief hiatus in the conversation followed while their breakfast was served, during which Goldman made amusing

41

remarks in Hebrew to the waitress – why else would she be giggling?

Since two coffee pots were brought, they each poured their own coffee. Goldman watched Kate empty a sachet of sugar into her cup and remarked, "You're not one of those women who has to watch her weight, I see."

"Could we stick with what you invited me here to discuss?"

"You're also a single-minded woman," he observed with another smile.

"One who likes to get down to what we British call brass tacks, too," Kate responded, "so may we, please?"

While they ate their grapefruit, Kate learned that Howard's business acquaintance had made known to Goldman not just her name, but her professional assignment in Israel.

"He said he had suggested that you might like to interview me."

The equivalent of why the Rosses now had double-glazed windows. Mr. Fixit had once again sent the mountain to Mahomet. So much for Kate's thinking her encounter with him couldn't acquire a sting in the tail! But unlike the Rosses, Kate wasn't going to fall for it.

"I can only tell you what I told him, though it seems he wasn't listening," she said, "that interviewing celebrities isn't part of my brief." If Goldman thought that buying Kate breakfast would get him some free publicity in her paper, he wouldn't be getting his money's worth.

Goldman's next words cut short her satisfaction.

"Since journalists are experts at asking loaded questions, I never give interviews."

"Does that mean you have something to hide?"

"Who hasn't? And the question you just asked proves me right about journalists. Okay, so we now know where we stand. You're not interested in interviewing me and I'd say no if you were. But I do have a proposition to put to you."

Kate gave her attention to buttering some toast, so he

42

would not see her wary expression. "I'm listening. Do go on."

"When mention was made of the nature of your assignment—"

"Look – I didn't discuss it with him," Kate interrupted. "And what he gleaned was from my friends, after I was introduced to him. Not from me."

"Little though that may have been, Kate," said Goldman, "it was sufficient for him to tell me your brief is 'Israel, Forty Years On'."

This was the first time he had called her Kate, and he had done so with the familiarity of people who knew each other, which he and she certainly did not. But he was the sort for whom familiarity doubtless came easily, which it didn't for Kate.

"Shall we get down to whatever this meeting is about?" she said, noticing that business breakfasts seemed not uncommon in Israel.

A large table in a corner beside some decorative greenery was occupied by men, only the youngest of whom was casually dressed, files beside their plates, and a girl eating while she took notes. Other tête-à-tête meetings, like her own with Goldman, were taking place, too. And the common language between Israeli businessmen and the foreigners with whom they dealt was evidently English. Mention of Antwerp and diamonds had twice drifted Kate's way.

"I was enjoying lingering over coffee with a beautiful woman," said Goldman.

Kate took that from where it came.

"But let's get down to our discussion by all means. After which I'm hopeful that you and I will do a deal. Your assignment, you see, coincides with the subject of my next film."

Coincidence again. "If you're worried about my articles clashing with your documentary—"

Kate was left under no illusion on that score.

"Dov Goldman has no need to fear competition."

"Thank you for telling me."

"I find it amusing that you consider yourself competition for me."

Kate's sarcasm had gone over his head. And she hadn't been implying any such thing. But she wouldn't bother saying so to this egomaniac. Whatever his proposition was, it could go to hell and him with it.

"Nor, as you must be aware," he went on while surveying her with those arresting eyes, "are you likely to be the only foreign journalist sent here to damn my country with faint praise at this time."

"That's what I was about to say, though I wouldn't have described my assignment the way you did," Kate replied.

"Naturally you wouldn't. But you're not an Israeli. May I have your permission to smoke?"

"I'm surprised you bothered asking for it, but you may have it nevertheless."

He took a pack of Gauloises from his pocket and said as he lit one, "I seem to have made the wrong impression on you."

"What impression were you trying to make?" she answered noting that his brand of cigarettes went with his macho image.

Again she was treated to a long glance, but this time she held his gaze.

"Dov Goldman doesn't try to impress," he informed her. "He is what he is and others may take it or leave it. Now that we have that clear, shall we proceed?"

Kate was tempted to thank him for breakfast and leave, but said instead, "Proceed from my being no competition for you?"

"From the point we'd reached when I asked if you'd mind my smoking."

"Me coming to damn Israel with faint praise, you mean? But I'm not that kind of journalist."

"That," he replied, "you still have to prove. And let me tell you, before you assume otherwise, that I didn't invite you for breakfast to ask you to be kind to my country. Since the day the state was born it's been under the international microscope and we are well accustomed to criticism from all sides. That said, I can put my proposition to you—"

He stubbed out his cigarette, took a tube of mints from his pocket and popped one into his mouth.

"Right after breakfast?" Kate was unable to stem the comment.

"Mints are my other addiction. Would you care for one?"

"No thank you."

"Okay. So let us begin with the obvious," he said crunching the mint between strong white teeth that implied he paid more visits to the dentist than the kindly cab driver did.

"Your subject and mine are the same," he went on, "but I am an insider and you are on the outside looking in. I am in a position to transform your bird's-eye view to one with insights unavailable to a foreign reporter—"

"I'm not a reporter, I'm a feature writer," Kate interrupted, "it's people and their everyday lives I'm here to write about."

"And what I'm offering you is the opportunity to tag along with my film unit. My plans for the project are now complete and shortly we'll begin our travels."

Though there was something insulting about being invited to "tag along", Kate would be crazy to turn down such an offer, which would not only smooth her path, but allow her entrée to situations beyond her ken. There was just one snag – "What's in it for you?" she asked.

"If I replied that you're a very decorative dish, that wouldn't surprise you, I'm sure," he answered, "and I would be lying if I pretended it had played no part in the matter."

"But I'm still waiting for the real reply to my question."

Before supplying it, he lit another cigarette. "A Dov Goldman documentary about his country is a highly sale-able product, Kate. Since programming is planned well ahead, the film I haven't yet made has already been sold in

45

the international TV marketplace, including, of course, the United States and Britain, for transmission this time next year – on the eve of Israel's fortieth anniversary celebrations.

"I am in the happy position of owning the independent production company which finances my work," he revealed, "and enabled, therefore, to make decisions without a money-man breathing down my neck, and all the rest of what goes on in that respect for a freelance director hired to make a film."

He glanced toward the big table that Kate had noticed, where a heated debate now appeared to be taking place.

"Those people are involved in making a cops-and-robbers movie, and that poor guy they're getting at, the one without the tie, is hired to direct it. I heard his casting ideas for the leading lady differ from those of the executive producer. And the look on his face takes me back to the days before I had my own company."

Kate switched her gaze from the young director, whose hounded expression denoted an urgent desire to escape, and returned Goldman to his still incomplete proposition. "If we don't stick to the point, we shall be here all morning—"

"Which I wouldn't mind in the least, since you're my companion and I'm hoping you'll say yes. I'd been toying with an idea, Kate, and the Englishman telling me about you clinched it. How would you like to feature in my film?"

Such was Kate's surprise, she almost said, Who, me?

"You now know why I said you would do nicely," Goldman went on. "And look – why don't we vacate this table for those people queuing by the entrance? I have a suite here, where it would be more comfortable to continue our meeting."

Since Kate would not have put it past him to try to bed her to cement the deal she hadn't yet made, she replied, "I prefer my business meetings to be conducted more formally, thank you."

He lit another cigarette from the stub about to singe his fingers, and if there was one thing Kate couldn't stand it was a chain smoker. Added to everything else she couldn't stand about this man, and his confidence was top of the list. Dov Goldman would get the shock of his life if a woman turned him down, be it a business matter or one more intimate, she was thinking when he replied, "As you wish, Kate," and gave her one of his too attractive smiles.

"If you're offering me a job as an extra, I'm a member of the National Union of Journalists, not of Equity," she told him tartly.

"Now what did I do to deserve that?"

Kate left him in ignorance.

"To continue, Kate, it had occurred to me to include in my film the reactions of an outsider standing alongside me during the making of it," he said, "and of my conversations with that person on location."

"I wouldn't call that an original treatment."

"If you see originality as important to this project, you're in the wrong end of the writing trade. You should be writing fiction."

Kate had said what she had to take him down a peg, and had now herself received a verbal rap on the knuckles. "What I do see," she retorted, "is that you want to set me up as an outside opinion, to balance your insider film."

"And what would be wrong with that?"

"Nothing. If you weren't the one doing the editing."

"How did you know I do my own editing?"

Why were men invariably amazed when a woman made an astute observation? Like the cab driver who'd stopped smoking – no, that wasn't a fair example. But Kate's reply to Goldman wouldn't be a joke about having a crystal ball. Did he think she was born yesterday? That she didn't know a film could be slanted, changed out of recognition, by what happened afterwards in the cutting room?

A pause followed, isolating them in a pool of silence that heightened the bustle around them. Kate could hear the clink of crockery punctuating the medley of conversation, and the heated debate at the big table was still going strong. The atmosphere at her own table was that of sparring

47

partners each awaiting the other's next move. What was Goldman thinking? His expression told her only that he was reassessing her. But she had left him in no doubt that she had him well weighed up. And how differently he'd have handled this meeting if his quarry weren't female!

Quarry, Kate? Isn't that a little melodramatic? Nevertheless, it was the word that had sprung to her mind – perhaps from an instinct that there were depths to Goldman irrelevant to his magnetism for women. An inner ruthlessness that belied his smooth exterior. Side by side with this thought was remembrance of how their paths had kept crossing, as if a determined fate had propelled Kate toward this moment – now her imagination really was getting the better of her! Mr. Fixit, not fate, was responsible for where she now found herself.

Though strictly speaking that was so, there remained something uncanny about the element of coincidence that had preceded Goldman's eventually calling her. And why me? Her commonsense entered the argument. There were any number of freelance professionals, British and American, whom he could have engaged for his purpose. It didn't have to be a journalist who happened to be handily covering the same subject as his film. But he'd said that hearing what Kate's assignment was had clinched the idea—

Kate's reasoning veered back and forth, but did nothing to rid her of the feeling that there was something not quite right about any of this. Nor did she consider herself so devastatingly attractive that he would go to such lengths to add her to his conquests.

He then cut into her conjecture with a remark that caused her to put down her coffee cup.

"You ought not to have gone to the Holocaust Museum alone."

Kate eyed him speechlessly.

"It's a chilling experience, but since we hadn't yet met, I didn't think it suitable to offer you the company of myself and the German friend I had taken there."

48

If Kate had not been so affected by the insertion of yet another coincidence into the string of them already dogging her, she might have replied sarcastically that he had had a busy afternoon, given his appearance later, with two girls, in the street where she was sitting drinking tea. Instead she remained silent, part of her mind marvelling that friendship with a German was possible for a Jew.

Since the design of the horrific exhibition was such that those viewing it were not at all times within each other's sight, there was no mystery about Kate's not having noticed Goldman; and perfectly possible that he had walked by while she was looking at one of the glass-cased photographs and documents.

Though Goldman could not have known who Kate was when he saw her on the beach, and the square in Herzlya was where many people made for to get a snack lunch, the occasions on which their paths had subsequently crossed seemed too numerous to attribute to mere chance.

Was Kate letting herself believe that he'd tailed her to Jerusalem? From her hotel to where she'd got into the sharut, and on from there? That it wasn't by chance that he was beside the reception desk when she arrived back last night?

Since his appearances had been overt, and he'd just made a point of letting her know he had seen her where she hadn't seen *him*, what was it all for? A softening-up process, so he could finally call her and employ the corny opening gambit he had? "We really must stop not-meeting like this."

A shudder of recollection rippled through Kate – which the term "soften up" would always evoke in her. What but that was the false amenability ladled out to her by the KGB when she poked her nose into the Smolensky case? And when the softening-up hadn't worked, it was off with the velvet glove and the iron hand snatching little Yuli Smolensky from under Kate's protective wing.

But this was Israel, not the Soviet Union. And why was it necessary for Goldman, a distinguished film director, to do what Kate's too-fertile imagination was telling her he might have, before putting his proposition to her?

Kate's reason asserted itself. Then instinct again took over. Israel was a country prickling with undercurrents. An article in the *Jerusalem Post* had made reference to an under*ground* – though she recalled its being in the past tense.

It was, too, a country whose militant settlers had put themselves on land they considered theirs according to God's law, where the Arabs who had lived there before the 1967 war, and still did, thought the Jews had no right to be.

In the short time she had been here, Kate had gleaned in conversation with English-speaking citizens that there were some Israelis who viewed withdrawal from the occupied territories as the road to peace, and others who saw it as rendering their country the more vulnerable to attack.

Given the petrol bombs currently being flung at Israeli vehicles in the West Bank and Gaza, Kate would be risking her neck by going there. But it had to be done, and her mother had said she wouldn't sleep a wink, on that account, till Kate returned home.

Incidents of that kind were from time to time reported in British papers. But what did reportage tell you of the deep-seated human emotions that nurtured Arab-Jewish animosity? Though land was at the heart of the matter, the protagonists to whom it meant so much were flesh and blood, with all that implied, Kate thought as the silence at the table lengthened and Goldman went on chain smoking.

Someone as well-informed as Goldman could put Kate in the picture about the real strength of Israel's "Peace Now Movement" and perhaps introduce her to some of its activists. When she'd mentioned it to the cab driver who ferried her from the sharut to her hotel, last night, his wrath had descended upon her head; which meant there was strong feeling against it. "Peace at any price movement it should be called!" he had irately said, after which he had told her he had lost a brother in the 1967 war which, though another had followed in 1973, seemed to be the one etched upon Israeli memory. And Kate reflected now that giving back the territories occupied in that war might, to some, seem an insult to those who fell in the battle.

But how had her mind wandered from where she was at with Goldman, to this? From an instinct that neither he nor his proposition were quite what they seemed? The thoughts that had progressed from there had to be Kate's trying to rationalise her feeling that Israel was a country where anything was possible. And what did she think Goldman was? A Secret Service man in the guise of a film director?

A possibility so over the top that Kate wanted to giggle, which would also have relieved the strain of sitting opposite him for at least five minutes with neither saying a word.

The silence was then broken by Goldman's bursting out laughing, when the gawky young Israeli he had said was to direct a cops-and-robbers movie shouted, "Lo! Lo! Lo!" to his companions and abruptly departed, spectacles askew and hair awry.

"I've made exits of that kind myself, Kate, but I don't remember subjecting myself to torture-by-money-man for as long as he managed to endure it. 'Lo' means no, by the way—"

Kate made a mental note of that useful Hebrew word.

"But I'm hoping you don't intend saying to me what he just said to them."

They were back where they were before Kate stopped him short. A woman not unaware of her own sex appeal engaged in a not unpleasant sparring match with a man who used his to manoeuvre gullible females. But he now knew that Kate Starling was no pushover when it came to exerting her grey matter. And, should the circumstances perchance arise, would discover that the same applied on more personal ground.

"If I gave you my word that none of your comments would be cut from the film, would you say yes, Kate?"

"I might."

"Whether or not to make that concession required some thought—"

"That's quite all right, I had some thinking of my own to do."

"Then let's shake on it."

"Not so fast!"

His smoothness was such that his keeping his word was questionable. On the positive side, however, think what travelling with his film unit would do for Kate's assignment. But the sixth sense telling her there was more to this than met the eye was still niggling away.

"I can't give you a split-second decision," she said. "I need some more time."

Though Kate spent the rest of the day writing her impressions so far, Dov Goldman and his proposition had remained in the forefront of her mind.

She had settled herself at the balcony table, her notebook beside her typewriter, the intrusive street sounds drifting upward impinging upon her concentration, and by early evening, her work completed, was still undecided.

Leaving the man himself out of it, featuring in a documentary would be good experience should she eventually switch to TV and have to appear on camera. She allowed herself a vision of Kate Starling presenting the one-o'clock news and came face to face with her own ambitiousness. You want to be one of the few women journalists up there with the men, don't you? And why not, if you have what it takes?

Briefly, the thought that the changes she had wrought to her life had put her, for the first time, fully in command of it, overwhelmed her. When she married Alun, she was an eighteen-year-old trainee reporter, and still living under her parents' roof. Motherhood had quickly followed, and bang, like a pricked balloon, went Kate's hopes of the career now open to her. She'd taken it philosophically – or fooled herself that she had – until her cathartic experiences in Moscow triggered off the situation that had culminated in Kate's finally putting herself first.

She gazed at the gently swaying leaves of the palm trees lining the promenade, beyond them the sea seeming molten gold in the last rays of sunlight as the day drew to an end, the remains of the fruit juice she was sipping gone tepid, and her thoughts far away.

Did her kids think Kate's pursuing a career that could include lengthy absences meant she loved them any the less? A question to which there was no answer followed: How could a woman devote herself to her children as unstintingly as Kate had for so many years, loving them to bits, and at the same time nurturing an unadmitted resentment that their presence in her life had cut short what she might otherwise have done with it?

You can't be the only woman who has asked herself that, Kate – nor was it just Emily and Jason who held you back. Alun was an easy-going husband, but show me the wife who doesn't defer to marriage itself.

She glanced down at the ancient portable typewriter on which she had rattled off articles for a local paper, with one eye on whatever she'd got cooking for the family supper and the other on the clock, and ran her fingers affectionately over the keys. Though she could now afford to replace it with an up-to-date machine, and would when she found time to, she would never part with this one.

But there was no room for sentiment in the professional life of a woman forging ahead. Kate returned her mind to the decision that still had to be made and went to make herself some tea, thankful that she had opted for an Aparthotel whose accommodation included a miniature kitchen, though she had so far made little use of it.

While she waited for the water to boil, her thoughts again began veering back and forth. Why was she still hesitating about accepting Goldman's offer? Featuring in a documentary to be networked worldwide was an opportunity most journalists would grab. The trouble was that the man and

53

the offer went together. During filming Kate would be glued to Goldman's side, and given the antipathy he aroused in her . . . There was also that inner voice saying, "Don't do it," to which logic could not be applied. Call it a premonition.

Since when were you prey to premonitions, Kate? Since all those coincidences that might not have been coincidences. What but that, and his finally calling her, had led Kate to think Goldman might not be just the philandering middle-aged film director he seemed?

Among the intangibles, too, was Kate's feeling that the man-woman contest she was all too aware of at the breakfast table had only just begun and could lead to trouble of a personal kind. Only if you let it, Kate.

Meanwhile, as the kettle reached boiling point, Kate reached her decision. If a premonition was sufficient to make her look a gift horse in the mouth, where would she ever get, in a profession where gift horses were thin on the ground? She forgave herself the double cliché!

She almost went there and then to call Goldman, but decided that it would do him good to be kept waiting for her answer, and did not make the call until late that night.

A woman answered the telephone in his suite, which did not surprise Kate. She made her tone businesslike. "Would you please tell Mr. Goldman that Mrs. Starling wishes to speak with him?"

"Dov is fast asleep."

The phone had barely rung before it was answered, and the woman's stilted English was softened by the sweet cadence of her voice, enhancing Kate's vision of a silken-skinned arm stretching to pick up the receiver, lest the ringing disturb the slumbers of the man with whom she was in bed. Was it the brunette who had joined him on the beach?

"To whom am I speaking?"

"That is of no importance. If you wish for me to take a message, I will oblige."

"Please tell Mr. Goldman to call me first thing tomorrow morning. I have plans to be out for the rest of the day."

Kate wasn't going to give Goldman her answer via one of his easy lays! But why had she added the downright fib she had? she asked herself after ringing off. That damned man-woman thing was already inserting itself where it had no right to be – Kate playing hard to get, and not for business reasons. So much for her own objection to sex and sexism entering into everything.

She went out to the balcony and saw that Tel Aviv was not allowing the Sabbath Eve to deter it from springing to life as it always did at this hour.

Rock music was thumping its way upward to Kate's ears from a café on the promenade. The car park between the Dan and the Yamit was fast filling up, and arriving revellers, whom Kate could see were mostly young people, seemed to be thronging toward the entrance to a disco situated beneath her hotel.

Drifting her way, too, were the carefree sounds of youth, the voices and the laughter. She watched a couple leave the car park with their arms around each other, the girl's head resting upon the boy's shoulder, her flimsy white dress caught by the sea breeze, she gazing up at him, and he down at her, as they walked. They looked too young to be a *married* couple, but if perchance they were, Kate sent them a silent wish: Long may the romance last for you.

With a broken marriage behind her, Kate was under no illusion that the youthful rapture she had just observed could come again to someone of her own age. There were women who thought you could, in that respect, shed the years; that love could work that magic. But if Kate ever again fell in love, she wasn't expecting it to be like that. Nor, right now, was she prepared to set herself up for what love did to a woman whatever her age. Put herself emotionally at the mercy of a man.

If Kate were required to cite an example of that final thought, she need look no further than her friend Audrey, a strong character if ever there were one, but currently in pieces because the man for whom she had left her husband had begun playing around.

Kate left the balcony and went into the bedroom. Time for a solitary career woman to call it a night! But would she sleep? Though it was long past midnight, her mood was suddenly as if she had taken one of the pills known as "uppers". Why go to bed when the whole of Tel Aviv appears to be out on the town?

A few minutes later she was on her way to join the late-night crowd, her red leather jacket around her shoulders to keep out the chill she had felt on the balcony.

On reaching the promenade, it was again difficult to believe that this was Israel on the Sabbath Eve. But, as the transvestite had made plain, Tel Aviv wasn't representative of Israel. And those for whom Judaic law was a way of life probably viewed Tel Aviv as their forefathers had viewed Sodom.

Watching a youth accost a passing man and engage him in conversation accounted for Kate's supposition. She was conscious, too, of a sense of incongruity. How could there be a city like this in a country where religious observance held such sway that public transport stopped running on the Sabbath?

The glances Kate was receiving from men, as she strolled past the open air cafés, confirmed the wisdom of her deciding against making her way to Dizengoff Circle to observe first hand what went on there late at night.

A journalist she might be, but a lone female she still was. And one whose preconceptions that a Jewish state equated with a respectable society had, by now, been dashed to the ground. So much so that when she herself was accosted, and by *two* men, she thought it time to get off the streets and entered the next café she reached without pausing to note if it was an ice-cream parlour, or the source of the burger aroma mingling with the sea breeze.

It turned out to be a pizza house, and Kate reached for the

menu, hunger pangs reminding her that she had eaten nothing since breakfast. Food had slipped her mind, which given her preoccupation wasn't surprising.

Finding that ham was among the assortment of toppings on offer was another shock. Kate knew that not all Jews kept to kosher food but ham in the Jewish state? How much more brazen could defiance of the religious laws get! She thought it unlikely that a Jerusalem pizza place would offer her favourite topping, and felt guilty ordering it though there was no need for her to.

The handsome blonde waiter standing with pencil poised over pad beside her said, with a smile, "You would also like coffee? Espresso, or cappuccino?"

Since the Israeli version of the latter was so lavish with cream it was more like a dessert than a beverage, Kate ordered a large espresso. "And I wouldn't mind having it immediately. I need warming up."

Like others seated around the red-gingham-clothed tables, she had chosen to sit indoors, and thought that the few who were sitting outside must be hardier than she.

The waiter returned with a steaming cup of coffee in less time than it would have taken Kate to make herself a mug of Nescafé, and she watched him go to stand beside a youth as fair-haired and upright in stance as himself.

"Are those two boys brothers?" she asked the waitress who came to put a carafe of water on the table.

"No, they are the cousins. The one who has taken your order, him I like the best."

The girl poured some water into a glass for Kate, whilst adding, "He is the one who me I am dating."

"He seems a nice boy," Kate said conversationally.

"But my parents if they knew I am dating him, they would not like it. And I am soon to leave Tel Aviv to do my army training."

While Kate was trying to fit those two bits of information together, she asked if the military service Israeli girls did included learning how to use a rifle.

"Of course, but for only the self-defence." The girl gave Kate a smile that dimpled her olive cheeks. "Please do not to return to your own country believing that in Israel the army sends women into battle. You would like for me to bring for you another cup of coffee?"

"No thank you, I'm enjoying talking to you. Have your boyfriend and his cousin done their army training yet?"

"They are German boys."

Kate was left to absorb her second big surprise within the space of a few minutes. German boys working in Israel seemed no less incongruous than ham on the menu. And the girl's reason for keeping from her parents that she was dating the handsome youth was now crystal clear. Kate could well imagine their reaction. What was the Holocaust Museum but a permanent reminder to Israelis, on their own soil, of the barbarity that ensured six million Jews did not live to see the Jewish state born.

That girl must have had quite a struggle with herself, Kate surmised.

"Please to be careful," the boy said when he put the pizza before her, "the plate is exceedingly hot."

Kate gave him a friendly smile. "Thanks for warning me. And I've just been hearing where you're from."

He stood, hands behind his back, watching her cut a chunk of pizza and advised her to allow it to cool on her fork.

Did this lad think she had never eaten pizza before? No, he was just being solicitous, which went with his well-bred demeanour. "Are you a student, at home?" she inquired.

"Of the languages. I have also spent some weeks in your country."

"Then you're here to practise speaking Hebrew?"

"That is not a language in my curriculum, and that is not why I am here."

When Kate asked him if many young Germans came to work in Israel, his reply was cryptic.

"More than you would perhaps expect."

With that, he excused himself and returned to stand with

his cousin beside the counter, on which an array of fruits and cheeses was temptingly displayed.

Kate got on with her meal, pondering upon what the boy had left unsaid. Was coming to work in Israel a signal of goodwill from the young intellectuals of the new Germany? Their way of saying that the crimes of a previous generation would never be repeated? Since neo-Nazism was said to be more than a mere flicker from the ashes in their country, as in others, if Kate's supposition was correct it was a hopeful sign.

The girl returned to speak to Kate.

"Hans, he told me that when he visited Yad Vashem he afterwards threw up in the men's room."

This left Kate in no doubt that Yad Vashem was the Hebrew name for the museum.

"You know perhaps that this is the solemn weekend for Israel?"

"Everyone seems to be out enjoying themselves—"

"But it will not be that way tomorrow night," the girl replied gravely, "on the eve of Holocaust Day."

Holocaust Day, in addition to the museum, Kate registered; signifying the importance Israel placed upon its people never forgetting that chapter of Jewish history.

She then learned from the girl that Jewish communities in the diaspora honoured that day, and that its purpose was remembrance of the dead.

"From sunset tomorrow, everything will close down, until sunset on Sunday," the girl went on, "the cafés included. And at eight o'clock on Sunday morning, if you are walking in the street you will see all the vehicles halt, and those riding in them get out to stand for the minutes of silence. You will hear the siren that sounds at that time everywhere in Israel. My grandmother, she says it makes her go cold. Also that I am her special grandchild – I am named Esther, for her sister who has died in the camp."

Kate said sincerely, "It's been a pleasure to meet you, Esther."

"And for me to meet you."

"Your grandmother's a survivor, then?"

Esther nodded. "And each year she goes to the memorial ceremony in the grounds of Yad Vashem, to say a prayer while the candles are lit there for all who perished. You may watch the ceremony on TV if you wish, which I and my family always do."

If ever there was a nation bound together by past horrors, this is it, thought Kate. No, not just Israelis, but Jews everywhere. Suddenly, Kate stopped seeing Irina Smolensky's plight in Moscow, representative of the oppression of Soviet Jewry, in isolation, and saw it for what it was: just one more chapter in the harrowing history of an ancient people.

Kate recalled the threesome she had noticed at the museum, and her own censoriousness about a child being taken there. But who am I to pass judgement? she thought now. What did Kate know about the feelings and motivations of a survivor of the camps?

There was now only one other occupied table in the pizza house, and Esther had gone to have a word with the elderly man seated there.

"If there is nothing else you would like, I shall ask Hans to make out for you your check?" she said when she returned.

"Are you waiting for me and that old gentleman to leave, so you can close up?" Kate said with a laugh.

Esther shook her head and glanced at the man, who was drinking wine, his tatty-looking pinstripe jacket hanging on a chair, and a bulging, plastic carrier bag beside him on the floor.

"Old Maxie," Esther told Kate, "he is here every night and remains even after we have closed the door and we are clearing up. It is then that he begins telling us of how he grew up in Vienna and how wealthy was his family— but we think that perhaps now he does not have the family, or the home—"

To Kate, old Maxie looked like the male version of the "bag ladies" who aroused her pity when she saw them, here or there, in London. As with some of them, there was about him, despite his surface appearance, the remnants of refinement. How did he get from the beginnings he possibly had to this? Was he a survivor, too? But who wasn't, of something or other? thought Kate. And there were those who picked themselves up and began again, and old Maxie's kind who gave up the fight.

"Maxie, he was a violinist, but the Nazis, they broke his fingers," said Esther.

And bang went his living and his future. Kate could not imagine herself surviving something like that. Esther went to ask Hans for Kate's bill, and Kate glanced at her wristwatch. Two a.m.! This hadn't turned out to be the cheering little outing on which she had impulsively set forth, given the sombre quality of all she had learned while eating her supper. But the few days Kate had been in Israel were sufficient for her to have likened her assignment to unfurling a colourful tapestry, into which shades of a more sombre hue were threaded.

While she was paying Hans, she remarked to him that Esther was a lovely girl. "She told me that you're going out together."

"But my parents would not approve. Before I left Frankfurt, my father instructed me I must not become involved with an Israeli girl."

So it's a two-way thing with the parents' generation, thought Kate, before Hans hastened to explain, "That is not because they are Israeli, but because they are not, like me, Christian."

Kate was still musing upon that when she left the pizza house. If and when Jew and German eventually forgot the past, for a boy and a girl like those Kate had just encountered, religious differences would remain in the way.

She was asking herself what her own reaction would be to

61

Emily or Jason wanting to marry someone Jewish, while turning up her collar against the sea wind, lengthening her stride and aware of her own elongated shadow on a sparsely populated pavement lit, at intervals, by the globes atop lampposts that gave the promenade a sophisticated resort appearance.

Her thoughts progressed to Jason possibly falling in love with Barbara's little girl, when they grew up. Despite her close friendship with the Rosses, Kate envisaged their objections to the match, though they were not overly observant Jews. It struck Kate then that, for Jews, "marrying out" went a good deal deeper than just breaking Judaic law; that it was for them perhaps like a crack in the cement that bonded them together as a people.

Meanwhile, Kate laughed at herself, Jason and little Rebecca Ross were still at the age when, each time they met, he made fun of the brace on her teeth and she pulled his hair. You and your over-fertile imagination, Kate!

A moment later, she stopped in her tracks. Was seeing Goldman enter a café, yards from where she stood, imagination?

No – and it was one coincidence too many. So much for Kate's casting instinct aside and making the decision she finally had. She watched him emerge and enter the next café. As though he was searching for somebody. And who else but me? Time for a showdown! thought Kate, no longer immobilised.

She was one pace short of the café entrance, when Goldman strode out and they came face to face.

He was the first to speak. "How nice to see you, Kate."

As if they had found themselves guests at the same tea party! This, however, was the middle of the night – and after Kate's having been told on the phone by his probable bedmate that he was fast asleep—

"What are you doing here?" she demanded.

He took her arm, and short of wresting it away from him, she had no option but to let him walk her past the outdoor tables, whose lowered parasols were receiving a whipping from the wind.

"And if you tell me you got up at this hour because you felt hungry, and were going around inspecting menus to find what you fancied, I'm not going to believe you," Kate added tersely.

"I was looking for you, and why wouldn't I say so?"

Brass tacks at last! "Would you mind also saying why? And how you knew where I'd be, Mr. Goldman?"

"I thought we'd agreed to drop the formality."

"Unless I get a credible explanation for this, you may consider the formality restored," said Kate. "And there is no necessity for you to steer me along," she added, aware of the pressure of his fingers on her arm. If he weren't so attractive, he'd be easier to deal with!

"No necessity, but a politeness I learned from my father," he replied without removing his grasp, "who was raised in Vienna when ladies from my parents' background expected such courtesies from gentlemen."

"There was an old man from Vienna in the place I was just in."

"That would have to have been the pizza house. Old Maxie is one of the local characters. But why he chooses to sit there, instead of in one of the cafés other elderly Viennese frequent, is hard to understand."

"Hasn't it occurred to you that being in their midst – given how he's ended up – might be too painful for him?"

"How very perceptive you are, Kate."

"But not perceptive enough to know why you came looking for me, or the rest of what I'm waiting for you to tell me, Mr. Goldman." If he thought he'd succeeded in diverting her from the questions she'd asked, he had better think again.

"My parents, however," he continued to digress, "never became part of the café society Viennese like those I just mentioned took with them to wherever persecution propelled them – though neither could have envisaged their

63

metamorphosis into the kibbutzniks they eventually became."

Was there anyone in Israel who didn't have a story to tell, thought Kate.

"But that's just one of the jokes life plays on people," he went on. "My parents got out of Europe before the final whistle blew, when Israel was still Palestine, and the state no more than a dream. A dream with which my mother and father were at one time not imbued—"

"I thought Jews everywhere were imbued with it," Kate interrupted. "And why are we going this long way round to my hotel? We ought to have taken the short cut—"

"But you didn't notice that we didn't."

Damn the man! And what his remark implied.

"If I'd returned you directly to the Yamit, there'd have been no time for us to talk, Kate. You would have left me standing in the lobby and headed straight for the lift to your room," he said with a laugh.

"How did you guess?"

"It is how women behave, give or take the details."

Kate was getting madder by the minute. "May I remind you I'm still waiting for the explanation I asked for?" she said haughtily.

"Which you'll receive when I've corrected that wrong impression you got that Jews everywhere were imbued with the Zionist dream. Germany and Austria were notable exceptions in that respect, and assimilation well under way when Hitler made it graphically clear that a Jew is always a Jew."

He fumbled in his pocket for a cigarette, and Kate was obliged to stand shivering while his lighter fought the wind, before he again took her arm and they moved on.

"That's what it took to turn my mother and father into Zionists, Kate. Instead of opting for England, or the States, which in the mid-thirties most early refugees did, they came here with a group of young couples and founded the kibbutz where I was born in a tent."

From such humble beginnings spring great men, Kate wanted to say snidely, but the feeling with which he was telling this story – and she could not have failed to see the moral of it – stilled her tongue.

"My father told me he'd carried my mother up a rocky hillside," he went on. "Her labour pains began while she was working beside him clearing away the boulders and stones. She's outlived him by several years, and is now eking out her remaining ones sitting on the verandah of the house they built together.

"On the Golan Heights – with a view you have to see, Kate – and when I go visit her, and find her sitting exactly where she was when I last kissed her goodbye, I wonder if she still thinks what she and Father devoted their lives to was worth the struggle."

"What a dreadful thing for an Israeli to say! Nor can I understand your saying it," Kate opined. "My friends from London told me that the kibbutzim were the foundation stone of the Jewish state."

"I was referring to the structure that's been built on it. And now let me explain my unexpected presence at your side. You called me about my proposition, I presume?"

But Kate was by no means certain that she would now give him the same answer she would have then. "Who was it that I spoke to, by the way?"

"Aviva is my personal assistant. She was with me, briefly, that day on the beach in Herzlya."

Kate's assessment of the brunette's function was correct, though it probably was not her *sole* function, given the bedroom scene Kate's phone conversation with her had conjured up.

"I'd fallen asleep in an armchair," Goldman promptly dispelled it, "and when I do that, Aviva knows better than to waken me. Cat-naps are the best sleep I get. When I awoke and she gave me your message, I called you immediately."

His lengthy roundabout route had led them to the far end

of Hayarkon Street, and he now turned Kate around to head back toward their hotels.

This wasn't a route, he's been taking me for a stroll, Kate thought. "My message was for you to call me early next morning," she said.

"Which, by then, it was, if earlier than you had meant. You'll find that Dov Goldman doesn't pay too much attention to the clock. Okay, so I was told by the desk that you were out, and the rest you know."

"Not quite."

"Did I leave something out?"

"Yes. Why the urgency?"

"You'll find that I'm impatient, too," he said as if a long relationship lay ahead of them.

"And that's the reason?"

"Look — I don't have time to sit drumming my fingers while someone makes up their mind whether or not to accept an offer I've made them."

Nor, it seemed, was he accustomed to having to do so — and especially not if the person concerned was female.

Kate halted outside the Dan and said, "You're home, Mr. Goldman, and I don't have far to go, so I'll bid you goodnight now."

"Without giving me your answer?"

"Call me around midday."

"According to Aviva, you're going to be out."

"But I'm sure that you, of all men, must know it's a woman's prerogative to change her mind."

With that, Kate went on her way, aware of Goldman watching her receding back. When she reached the Yamit, and turned to look, he was still there.

A sleepless night followed for Kate. What there was left of it, she thought, tossing and turning. Despite Goldman's valid, if eccentric, explanation, she was back with her indecision. There was also the remembrance of his strong fingers gripping her arm.

At seven a.m. she rose and made herself a cup of the

British panacea for all ills and found herself yearning for home while she sipped it, remembering being assailed by homesickness in Moscow, and seeing herself again on her first night there. In a room with yellow curtains, and counterpanes to match on the twin beds, wearing the blue dressing-gown she had on now, and the same pink velvet mules on her feet.

The two beds had that night increased Kate's loneliness. She hadn't known then that a little Russian boy was shortly to occupy one of them. Or that the trip would culminate with Kate and the man who had shared it together in *his* bed.

The sense of setting forth into the unknown that had preceded Kate's Moscow experience was with her now. It hadn't included premonitions – Kate wasn't given to them – but would she have let herself in for all that had happened if she'd known it was going to? Brushing shoulders with the KGB included?

Nobody in their right mind would. But without that experience, Kate would still be letting apathy pass for contentment, instead of grasping whatever life offered her.

Talking of offers, you'd better stop behaving like that man thinks all women behave, she told herself, and remember you're a professional. But the effect Goldman had upon her made that easier said than done. That amused smile of his, and she left to divine his thoughts. The power and the magnetism she was unable to deny. The hidden depths she sensed in him. What was she doing? Taking an inventory? No. Trying to analyse her own feelings, and what they added up to was a mixture of attraction and antipathy, laced with distrust.

Nevertheless, Kate's decision to accept Goldman's offer would stand. Its usefulness to her assignment must come first. When the film unit left Tel Aviv, she would leave with them.

Part Two

CHAPTER ONE

The hostility between Kate and Aviva was immediate and
thinly disguised. But it was there before we met, crackling
when we spoke on the phone, Kate reflected as the unit set
forth on its travels.

Aviva was driving Goldman's Volvo, and Kate seated
beside him in the back. A minibus carrying the crew and the
equipment followed behind.

"How long do you expect the filming to take, Mr.
Goldman?" Kate inquired.

"Too long for you not to drop the formality right now,
Kate. Since I'm the money-man, how long we take is open
ended."

"And it would overrun the budget I have set, if I did not
keep my eye on things," Aviva chipped in.

"Aviva isn't just my PA, she's all things rolled into one,"
Goldman declared with one of his smiles.

I bet! thought Kate. "How useful for you," she said.

"Just so long as she remembers who's boss."

Goldman returned his attention to the notes he was
studying when Kate distracted him, the clipboard to which
they were attached balanced on his knee, and the Gauloise
he was, as usual, smoking clamped between his lips,
apparently unaware that each time an item of conversation
was exhausted, a strained silence followed.

They were heading toward Nazareth, and Aviva was none
too pleased that Goldman had acceded to Kate's request to
include visiting Irina Smolensky in the day's itinerary.

Though, by chance, the absorption centre in which Irina
was living was one of the locations Goldman had planned to

71

film, the shoot had been arranged for next week, and the rearranging and subsequent rescheduling had made work for Aviva.

Since that kind of thing was part of Aviva's job, Kate would not have expected the fuss she made, which had ranged from complaints about the cost of the necessary phone calls to a final tirade about hotel bookings having to be changed for the unit's overnight stops.

Kate had quickly noted that the Israeli woman was nothing if not inflexible and sometimes behaved toward the crew as if she were their drill sergeant, but had no doubt that this particular bit of inflexibility was due to Goldman's accommodating Kate.

"Sheket, Aviva!" Goldman shouted, when she suddenly resumed her carping. A stream of Hebrew followed, and Kate would later learn that the first word he had uttered was not the angry oath she had supposed, but that it meant, when used in that context, "be quiet".

Kate thought it time to set a rule of behaviour. "Since everyone in the unit speaks English, including both of you, I'd appreciate the courtesy of my language being spoken in my presence."

"Shall I send out a memo to the crew, Dov?" Aviva said sarcastically.

"You wouldn't have to send out too many," was Kate's cool response. "I'd expected the unit to have more people in it than there are," she said, addressing Goldman. "Are they freelances, as is usual in my country?"

"Technically, yes," he replied, "but all but the assistant cameraman have worked with me on my previous projects."

"You realise, of course, that Kate is interviewing you?" Aviva butted in, and received another barked, "Sheket!" from her boss.

How could Aviva put up with the way he spoke to her? Kate certainly wouldn't, and Aviva's being in love with him – which she plainly was – had to account for her remaining in his employ. Briefly, Kate was sorry for her.

Then another onset of carping followed. "If you knew, Dov, what trouble I had to get us hotel rooms for tonight — "

"I don't want to hear about it," he cut her short, "and nor does Kate."

"But I appreciate the trouble Aviva has gone to for my sake."

Kate was left under no illusion on that score. "Whatever Dov asks me to do, I do."

"In that case I'll withdraw my gratitude." And this journey must seem to Dov Goldman like hell on wheels, thought Kate – but serve him right! "Do the absorption centres vary much?" she asked him.

"The whole question of absorption is in some ways a minefield, Kate."

"Would you mind elaborating on that?"

"Don't let her pick your brains, Dov — "

Kate managed to control her rising anger. "Picking brains, Aviva – as you choose to put it – is part of my work. And if Mr. Goldman isn't prepared to let me pick his, the deal he and I made is off."

"Any helpful information I can give you, you're welcome to, Kate," Goldman said. "As for my remark about absorption, to put it briefly, the government doesn't do enough to help immigrants who have nobody but officials to turn to."

Kate recalled Barbara's saying something similar.

"A roof over your head and a pittance to live on until you find work – which many don't – sums it up," said Goldman, "and that has to be one reason for some immigrants returning whence they came, or trying their luck elsewhere."

"Could the government afford to do more for them?"

"One of the mines in the minefield," he replied cryptically, "is that America is said to be subsidising ex-refuseniks here, but what that cash gets used for—?"

Goldman glanced through the window at a cluster of small, stone houses perched on the verdant terrain through which the car was travelling. "That, by the way, is an Arab village," he digressed before going on to say pensively, "There is one canvas seen by the tourists who come here, Kate, and another they don't see."

"I wouldn't say that applies only to Israel—"

"But because we are Jews, and after only four decades of statehood still considered to be on probation . . ." Goldman left the rest unsaid, and added, after a pause, "There is also the matter of the financial support we receive from Jewish communities worldwide."

"Are you saying that makes Israelis feel beholden?"

"I've yet to meet one who does. What I'm saying is quite the opposite, Kate. That financial generosity, welcome though it is, has drawbacks for the recipients in our case. Too many who don't live here feel entitled to a say in our internal policies."

"And there are times when he who pays the piper calls the tune?"

"There's that, too."

While Kate was still fanning away smoke from his last cigarette, Goldman lit another, popped a mint into his mouth, and told her they were approaching the point where they would cross the River Jordan.

Which was also a checkpoint. Kate noted some soldiers searching a vehicle, its Arab occupants standing by.

The crossing was made via a narrow bridge. Was this really the Jordan? thought Kate, gazing down at the muddy water. There must surely be more scenic stretches, she was conjecturing when they reached the opposite bank, and Goldman said to her, "I expected you to inquire why our car wasn't searched. You're slipping, Kate!"

"Or it could be I'm not given to asking obvious questions! How could your government not take precautions to protect its citizens? Am I right in assuming that the vehicle we saw being searched probably had a West Bank number plate?"

Goldman made another of his cryptic comments. "There is also the other side of the coin."

"Which includes some of Israel's religious extremists

74

going on the rampage in the West Bank and Gaza," said Aviva.

Kate put two and two together and made five. "Are you by any chance active in the Peace Now movement?"

"Laudable though their activities are, no," Goldman replied.

A pause followed which Kate would later pinpoint as the first time she felt as if a verbal shutter had been momentarily lowered. Then Goldman began dispensing information about Nazareth, and the moment passed.

Apart from a sarcastic interjection that Kate was using Goldman as a travel guide, Aviva remained silent unless she was required to supply, at the film director's request, an answer to one of Kate's questions. By the time they reached their destination, Kate was marvelling at the Israeli woman's wealth of knowledge.

As they entered the city where Jesus had spent his childhood, Kate could not but be stirred – non-churchgoer though she was – and imagined Him walking hand-in-hand with Mary in these winding, cobbled streets, unaware of what lay in store for Him.

Goldman then told her that Nazareth's population was mainly Christian Arab, which was like learning that Jesus had received posthumous freedom of the city in which he grew up.

"The Jewish community here was almost wiped out, by the Romans," Goldman added, "which makes Upper Nazareth yet another testament to our amazing ability to survive."

Kate glanced through the window to where he was pointing, cricking her neck in the process, and saw what looked like a sizeable town on the heights above the old city.

"It's one of Israel's immigrant-townships," said Goldman, "but I'll have to ask my human encyclopaedia to tell us when it was founded."

"I believe in the late fifties," Aviva supplied, "and would you please stop calling me that, Dov."

"I'd consider it a well-deserved compliment, if I were you," said Kate.

"But you are not me, and I am not the big-headed person. Would you like me to park by the Church of the Annunciation, Dov, so you may escort Kate inside and continue to be her tour guide?"

"That does it!" he exclaimed. "From here on, Aviva, you'll drive the bus and Yosef will drive me."

"Since that isn't your usual arrangement," said Kate, "why don't I travel with the crew?"

Goldman's response was, "I don't care which, just so long as I don't ride with the two of you again."

And the same went for Kate's being cooped up with him and his human encyclopaedia. Not only was Aviva's behaviour toward Kate hard to take, Goldman's bracketing them together in his final remark was unfair; and as if he had thrown up his hands and said, "Women!"

The schedule allowed for a lunch break before filming at the absorption centre, and Kate found herself seated between two of the crew, beneath the shabby awning shading the rough wood tables outside what could not be called a restaurant.

A far cry from the pavement cafés of Tel Aviv, she reflected, struck again by the sharp contrasts that characterised not just Israel, but her people.

While her companions studied the menu, Kate eyed the place – little more than a hole in the wall, and open to marauding flies – where she could see the food being prepared. A none-too-salubrious-looking Arab woman was rolling little balls of whatever, flattening them with her hands and dropping them into the frying pan on what looked like a stone-age stove. On an outdoor counter was an array of sticky cakes, which doubtless made the flies feel spoiled for choice.

Aviva, she saw, was nonchalantly eating black olives and hummus, from the dishes already on the table. And no doubt feeling pleased that Goldman hadn't elected to sit beside Kate.

When the Arab owner came to take their order, Kate took one look at his filthy apron and quailed. Chaim the cameraman, seated opposite her, who hailed from North London, smiled at her expression.

"If you're going to let ambience put you off your food, Kate, you'll be missing a lot of meals on this trip. The kebabs at this place are too good to miss, believe me. And charcoal broiling is also sterilisation," he added with the throaty chuckle Kate would come to associate with this fatherly man.

Since hunger pangs were making themselves felt, she took Chaim's advice and ordered a kebab.

Dishes of felafel, and a basket of hot pitta bread, were brought immediately to the table.

"The felafel is just pounded chick peas made into rissoles," Chaim reassured Kate.

And from their size and shape, they had to be what the woman was rolling and flattening in her hands. But Kate began helping the others make short work of them, dipping them and some pitta bread into the hummus, as Chaim instructed. The food tasted divine and the heck with the consequences!

While they waited for the kebabs, plans for the afternoon's filming at the absorption centre were discussed, and Kate kept out of it, stemming her excitement at the prospect of seeing Irina and Yuli soon, and privately assessing the young man sitting next to Chaim.

Did Yosef have any duties other than driving the minibus? He had struck Kate as being the only quiet one in this otherwise voluble group of people, and his studious appearance, enhanced by horn-rimmed glasses, made him seem an unlikely candidate for his job.

She switched her gaze briefly to Chaim, whose being a Londoner had seemed as surprising as finding someone with a South African accent driving a Tel Aviv cab. Kate had still not adjusted to the high proportion of immigrants in Israel's population, and found it hard to think of Chaim, and the two ex-Americans who completed the crew, as Israelis. She had expected them all to be Sabras, like Goldman and Aviva, but only Yosef was Israeli born.

A lull in the conversation allowed Kate to ask Chaim's assistant cameraman how long he had lived in Israel.

"I made aliyah when I was eighteen, so I guess it's going on six years."

Shmuel's freckles and snub nose gave him an impish appearance, and Kate had thought him still in his teens. "You're from New England, aren't you?"

"Brookline, to be precise."

"A friend of mine who lives in Boston mentioned he sometimes drives out to the Brookline shopping mall," Kate recalled.

"Him and all the other Bostonians," said Shmuel, "and oh how that takes me back——"

As his accent had reminded Kate of Calvin Fenner's distinctive drawl.

"Care to guess where I hail from, Kate?" said the sound recordist, his smile enlivening his somewhat saturnine countenance.

Avrom, like Chaim, was middle-aged and grey-haired, but the resemblance ended there. Kate could envisage a friendship with the plump and bearded cameraman, who exuded geniality. But there was about the lanky American an air of disenchantment – or was it cynicism? – that precluded, or so it seemed to Kate, her getting to know him on a personal level. Indeed, his asking her to guess where he hailed from had felt like being put to the test. And she really must stop thinking of him as American! And remember that a Jew who emigrates to Israel is automatically and immediately granted citizenship.

"I'm not an expert on American accents, Avrom," she replied with a laugh. "But yours is certainly very different from Shmuel's."

"And for your information, he comes from the windy city," said Shmuel, "in other words, Chicago."

Kate decided it was time she began using some of their terminology. "When did you make aliyah, Avrom?"

"Long enough ago to know Israel is the only place a Jew can be himself."

"With that I agree," said Chaim.

"But you guys had better take care," Aviva chipped in from the other end of the table, "or your comments could feature in Kate's articles."

"The one I just made she's welcome to quote," said Avrom, "which isn't to say I think Israel is perfect."

"Tell me the country that is," Kate replied. "But I have to say that Israel strikes me as a place where nearly everyone you encounter has an axe to grind. The cab driver who took me to Herzlya, the morning after I arrived, was sounding off about religious fanatics not letting him live his own life. And I read in the *Post* that there's some sort of underground movement here – or did the government stamp it out?"

The fleeting pause that followed reminded Kate of the one in the car. With something added. It was as if those seated with her at the table had closed ranks.

Then Goldman lit a cigarette and laughed.

"Did I say something funny?" Kate asked.

"You must excuse us if we find your bewilderment amusing, Kate."

A cue for the *others* to laugh – or so it seemed to Kate. As if they were following Goldman's lead. But she had sensed immediately that the respect the crew accorded him was over and above the norm; and that each, in their own way, had a personal relationship with him – which, in Shmuel's case, included an element of adulation.

Come off it! she said to herself. Goldman is at the top of the tree in their world. But Kate's instinct that there was more to it than that remained. Nor, any longer, was it instinct alone. That closing of ranks had definitely happened, and it had happened after Kate mentioned an underground movement.

"I am not in the least bewildered," she replied.

79

"Then forgive me for thinking you were. Our many-faceted society is not easy for a foreigner to fathom."

"But fathoming happens to be part of my trade." And let him make what he would of that.

The kebabs were brought to the table and the conversation turned to matters more mundane. Though Yosef remained as withdrawn as usual, while Goldman chatted with Aviva, Chaim and the two ex-Americans regaled Kate with remembrances of their pre-aliyah life, no doubt evoked by Kate's asking Avrom and Shmuel how long they had lived in Israel.

"Isn't Chicago where the Mafia used to hang out, Avrom?" Kate said while helping herself to more rice.

"But what did respectable Jewish families know from the Mafia?" he replied with a shrug. "And I haven't been back to my birthplace since before the '67 war."

That milestone in the Israeli memory had surfaced yet again, and it struck Kate as odd that nobody ever mentioned the war more recent in Israel's history.

It would be some time before it seeped through to her that the humiliating outcome of the 1973 war had rendered it something Israelis preferred to forget; and that many viewed it in retrospect as an exercise embarked upon for the wrong reasons.

Kate had still to discover, too, that the milestone aspect of the 1967 war was not just a means by which Israelis marked this or that event in their personal lives, as Avrom just had. On a national level, it was the event which had led Israel to assume an occupier role repugnant to most of its citizens.

Meanwhile, Kate was enjoying her meal and the company, the atmosphere at the table now such that she again told her instinct where to go. When she breakfasted with Goldman, he'd said she should be writing fiction, and he could be right! If every time there's a pause in the conversation, I let my imagination run riot—

"But I guess there's no country that doesn't have a Mafia of one sort or another," Avrom went on.

80

"Including Israel?"

"Call them thugs, and the answer is yes."

"But that isn't the meaning associated with the Mafia, is it?" Kate countered. "Organised crime, and all that — "

"There's such a thing as organised thuggery," said Chaim.

"And the organisers and their hoods," said Shmuel, "aren't always the kind a nice English lady like you would expect, Kate."

Kate ate a sliver of the green pepper that had come with her kebab. "Are you by any chance referring to religious fanatics throwing stones at passing vehicles, on the Sabbath? The cab driver I mentioned told me that—"

Chaim wiped some flakes of rice from his beard and put down the napkin. "If that was the sum total of their interference in other people's lives, we'd learn to live with it, Kate."

"You might, but I would not," said Yosef, with an intensity of which Kate would not have thought him capable.

"What those zealots are doing to Israel!" he exclaimed. "And since Kate is a foreign journalist, I would like for her to know it and she has my permission to quote me."

Goldman then brought the lunch break to an end, though the others had barely finished eating. "Today, we don't get time for dessert. Let's get the show back on the road."

He had risen from his chair and was gone from the table before Kate had time to put down her fork. Though the others seemed not to mind his abrupt departure, Kate was unaccustomed to such rudeness.

Aviva had gone immediately to pay the bill, and Kate could see Goldman tapping his foot impatiently, casting restless glances at the passing traffic, while she and the crew made their way to the street corner on which he had positioned himself.

Though there was no question about why Aviva put up with Goldman's treatment, the crew weren't in love with him. How could Chaim and Avrom, between whom Kate was walking, bring themselves to pander to Goldman's moods? To get up and go the minute he beckoned?

While they lengthened their stride to keep up with Goldman, who was ahead of them with Aviva – and Aviva almost running – Chaim divined Kate's thoughts, and tried to placate her. "This is just Dov's way, Kate. Patience isn't one of his virtues."

"Does he have any?" she snapped.

Shmuel, behind them with Yosef, overheard. "Dov is a unique person, Kate."

And if that wasn't adulation . . . The weather had remained unseasonably hot for the time of year, and Kate could feel the sun beating down upon her head. She hadn't even had time to put on her sunglasses, and after this hasty trek to where the vehicles were parked, she would look how she felt – a sticky mess – when she visited Irina.

"What time are we due at the absorption centre?" she asked.

"Three o'clock," said Avrom.

"Then what is this rushing for? It isn't two, yet. And I'd like to go somewhere to wash and tidy myself up."

"Dov isn't going to like that," said Chaim.

"Too bad!"

When eventually they reached the parking lot, further delay ensued. Both vehicles had had their tyres slashed.

Instead of shouting with rage, as Kate surely would if the Volvo were hers – and Goldman also owned the minibus – his reaction was deathly silence. As for the others, all they did was exchange glances.

"Is this the sort of thing Arabs might have done?" Kate inquired.

"I," said Yosef grimly, "can think of people equally suspect."

Goldman then delivered some sharply spoken sentences to Yosef in their own language. During which Kate had the feeling that the others were carefully avoiding looking at her. And after which Yosef strode from the car park.

"I've sent Yosef to find a couple of cabs to take us and the equipment to the absorption centre," Goldman told Kate, "we can't hang around waiting for tyres to be changed, he can organise all that when we've left."

"Thanks for the translation," she replied. But what had the part of it he'd left out concerned? Yosef's expression had been similar to Jason's when Kate ticked him off and he knew he deserved it.

"I see no reason for me to hang around *now*," she said, "so, if you don't mind, I'll find somewhere to wash and brush up and make my own way to visit my friend."

"I haven't heard the expression 'wash and brush up' since I left England," said Chaim, "where I seem to remember it being written outside some of the public lavatories."

Kate didn't pause to tell him she hadn't seen it written anywhere – she had picked up the expression from her father – but went nonchalantly on her way. And how pleasurable it was to leave Goldman standing there.

Kate's visit to Irina was not as she had imagined it being, and the same could be said of the absorption centre.

Perhaps because the term had a clinical ring, she had expected an establishment run on institutional lines, and a consequent atmosphere of desolation.

There was nothing of the latter in the scene that met her eye when she entered a foyer dwarfed by the number of people aimlessly milling around, and Kate's first thought was that when the film unit arrived they would have trouble finding space for the equipment. Her second was that everyone looked as people did on a rainy day in a holiday hotel. As if they didn't know what to do with themselves or their kids – of which there was no shortage.

Kate resigned herself to a long wait at the reception desk on her right, where a queue had formed. There was another beside the phone near the entrance. And the motley of cultures from which those constrained to live together under this roof sprang was bewildering.

83

Kate could hear Russian being spoken on the phone – and so loudly, it had to be a bad line. An Ethiopian family, parents and three young children, stood patiently in the queue for the desk, and Kate noted again, as she had when she saw some Ethiopians in Jerusalem, the delicacy and refinement of their features.

Directly ahead of Kate, awaiting their turn and volubly resenting it, were a couple of youngish Australians, and Kate an unintentional eavesdropper when they lowered their voices.

"If I'd known how long it'd take us to get jobs, an' that we'd have to stop in a place like this till we do — " the woman said.

"Turn off the record, will you, Shirl? The answer, like I keep tellin' you, is a kibbutz."

"'N I keep tellin' you I'm a townie. Like yourself, Merv."

Kate wanted to ask them how long they had lived at the centre, but the expression on Shirl's fleshy face prohibited her from doing so, and she envisaged this couple cooped up, day in, day out, in the limited accommodation allocated to them, prisoners of the circumstances in which they now found themselves.

If Barbara and Howard made aliyah, they wouldn't be without money, or their own home, and Howard could probably set up in business. But for people like Shirl and Merv, and their counterparts from whichever country, whether idealism, or oppression elsewhere, had propelled them to Israel, the immediate future seemed bleak. And why were all these people queuing to speak to the girl at the desk? If a pipe in your kitchen sprung a leak, or one of your kids broke a window playing ball, was this what you had to do?

Kate quailed at the thought of what it must be like to live in one of these centres. The matter of absorption was a minefield, Goldman had said, and Kate now found herself pondering if one of them might be the psychological welfare of those who had expected more of Israel than she was able to provide.

A poignantly familiar childish voice cut into her thoughts. "Kate!"

It was followed by an excited stream of Russian, and she turned and saw Irina Smolensky standing with Yuli beside her, and a baby in her arms.

Then Irina burst into tears and Kate stepped from the queue to embrace her. It was the first time she had seen Irina weep, and why was she doing so in Israel, when her spirits had never flagged in Moscow?

That the tears weren't those known to flow at emotional reunions was clear to Kate, since Irina wasn't just weeping, she was sobbing, and when Kate linked her arm and walked her away from the queue, Yuli happily holding Kate's hand, Irina still seemed unable to speak.

"Let's go where we can be private," said Kate. The last thing she wanted was for Goldman to arrive right now and manipulate Kate's visiting Irina into his documentary – which she had bluntly refused to allow.

There was no privacy in the lift that bore them upward to where Irina and her children lived, and Irina managed to control her tears and nod politely to the Ethiopian family Kate had noticed, with whom they shared the ride.

It occurred to Kate, then, that until they had learned to speak their new, common language, communicating with each other was an additional difficulty for the assorted emigrés living in these centres. Though Irina spoke English, it was unlikely that the Ethiopians did.

Kate noticed that the petite, black woman was pregnant – as Irina was when Kate last saw her. Shortly after Irina's arrest, when Kate had contrived to visit her, and had feared for the child now in her arms; as later she had feared for little Yuli's future when he was taken from Kate and placed in a Soviet Children's Home, where he would be raised to forget his Jewish origin.

As they walked along the corridor to Irina's quarters, Irina said, as if she had read Kate's thoughts, "God, He has been good to me."

But not quite good enough, thought Kate, since Irina's husband was still being refused permission to leave Russia.

"And I am ever thankful to my friends in the West who have Him helped," Irina added. "When you came, Kate, with Barbara and Howard, to my humble home in Moscow, I was overcome by the presence of those who cared. It made me feel the not forgotten person. And I wished it that I had a better meal to offer to you."

Kate did not tell her that they had already eaten dinner at their hotel, and recalled the simple repast Irina had put before them. Some coarse bread, and a salad of potatoes, carrots, and onions, in a delicious yoghurt dressing.

When they entered the small apartment, Yuli still holding Kate's hand, Kate thought it remarkable that the little boy had not forgotten her, given the traumas he had afterwards suffered. The brutal separation from Kate and Calvin, with whom he had briefly felt secure, and that coming so soon after his seeing first his father, then his mother, forcibly removed from his home by the KGB.

But Yuli was now looking up at her and saying delightedly, "Kate! Kate! Kate! Cal! Cal! Cal!"

Another poignant reminder. When Kate and Calvin took him under their wing, the child's experiences had rendered him the next best thing to dumb, as if his tongue was petrified along with the rest of him. Then little by little he had begun speaking, and Kate could remember her own and Calvin's joy when he had finally said their names. And gone on doing so – with the same repetitiveness with which he had said them now.

For Yuli, Cal and I are a single entity, thought Kate, and that's how he's always going to think of us.

Irina handed the baby, whose colouring was as dark as Yuli's was fair, to Kate, and went into the tiny kitchen that led off the basically furnished living room, to make some tea.

It's as though we had seen each other yesterday, Kate registered; and not in the least as if Irina and I had met only twice before today.

Kate sat down on a narrow divan – or was it a camp bed? – the gurgling infant on her lap, and Yuli beside her, reflecting upon how harrowing circumstances could provide a short cut to close friendship. When the chips were down, there was no time for the preliminaries and the social niceties.

Her eye was roving the room, taking in the second divan, against the opposite wall, the two folding chairs and the small laminated table; the poster with a lakeside scene, and Tiberias printed on it; the far from new-looking pram which was probably also where the baby slept at night, and Irina and Yuli on the divans.

Basic this most certainly was – and scrupulously clean and tidy, as Irina had kept her home in Moscow – but to an ex-refusenik, this represented sanctuary. Irina's situation couldn't be equated with that of the disgruntled Australians in the queue by the desk. Yet Kate sensed in the unhappiness Irina had not managed to hide from her something over and above a natural distress about the prolonged separation from her husband.

Kate could see Irina in the kitchen, now listlessly taking some biscuits from a packet and putting them on to a plate.

"I haven't told you yet how beautiful your baby is," Kate said.

"And it is her father who she looks like." Irina brought the tea and biscuits to the table. "We have given it to her a name from the Bible, Kate. And my little Rachel, she has put on the weight much, since the month she has been in Israel."

"Are you breast-feeding her?"

"She is already ten months old, and Yuli I fed only till he was seven months – already he had the sharp tooth! For Rachel there was not the mother's milk – but how else could I expect it?"

"What you went through," said Kate, "was enough to dry any mother's milk up. I see you brought that red feather with you to Israel," she added, with a smile.

They had gone to sit at the table, and Irina was feeding orange juice to the baby, the feather to which Kate had referred serving as an ornament, and again standing in an empty bottle, as it had in Irina's flat in Moscow.

"The feather, it was on a hat my poor mother, she was throwing away, when I was a child. I asked to have it, and have it kept ever since," Irina said simply.

Kate thought of all her own childhood mementoes. The china shepherdess her parents had given her on her tenth birthday. The dressing-table set from Gran, on her fourteenth, and so on and so forth. But life had stripped Irina of mementoes, if not of memories, and it was no wonder that she treasured that dilapidated-looking feather.

Meanwhile Yuli had gone to the kitchen to get himself some more milk, allowing Kate to ask Irina how he was faring. "He's going to be tall when he grows up," Kate remarked.

"Like his father. It is only the fair colouring that Yuli has from me."

"And I have to say you both look a lot better than when I met you—"

"Of the body, Kate, better of course I feel. Here, Yuli and me, we are eating the real meals – though for me to manage upon the money I receive, it is not easy."

"Have you found other Russians at the centre to chat to?" Kate inquired.

"Sure," Irina replied, adding with a wryly reminiscent smile, "since all here like me are Jews, and this is not the Soviet Union, my neighbours they are not going to snub me."

Irina put down the feeding bottle, and transferred the baby to a suitable position for patting its back to help it burp. "But here, Kate, the people they are each much concerned with their private problems — "

"If you want to talk about yours, I'm listening," said Kate.

"I have spoken of it to Barbara, when she came with Howard, and she has promised me to do what she can. Jerusalem, Kate, is where I expected it I would live. It did not it occur to me that there, there would be no place for me and my children. That the Israeli government would put it me so far from what Israel it means to me."

Kate had never before heard Irina sound bitter. Not just bitter, resentful, Kate registered when Irina added, "And the isolation I feel in my heart Kate, though at the centre I am among many people, I cannot it describe to you. Why did God let them do this to me?"

This was, too, the first time Kate had heard Irina express reservations about God's mercy. How had she got through her darkest hours in Moscow without doing so, and be doubting God now?

Since Kate's own faith had never equalled Irina's, it was a question she could not answer. But Irina's referring to isolation had reminded her of something she had not yet taken out of her shoulder bag.

"Do you remember what I said I'd bring you if you got to Israel, Irina? And you said, 'Not if. When.'" Such had Irina's certainty been, though the conversation had taken place when Kate visited her during her incarceration.

"It was after I tried to comfort you with a quotation," Kate reminded her.

But Irina needed no reminding. "You told it to me that no man he is an island. And what you are thinking of me now, telling to you that I am isolated in my heart! Of myself I should be it ashamed, Kate."

"I don't agree." Kate took the volume of Donne's poetry from her bag and said while handing it to Irina, "To tell you the truth, I found the strength you displayed in Moscow, though I admired it, almost inhuman. But now you're behaving like an ordinary human being again. If Jerusalem was where I'd dreamed of being and they stuck me miles and miles away, I'd be complaining to whoever from morning till night."

"But it would do you no good," Irina replied. "There are many in this centre who have it tried. Also many men who cannot find it the work while they are living here, high on

89

this hill and away from everything. The Ethiopian man you have seen in the elevator, he is one of them. It is not to be where is the Western Wall that he and others wish it to leave here, but to find the employment. That family, they have lived in this place, I am told, for two years."

"How is it decided which centre new immigrants are housed in?" Kate asked, as Irina resumed feeding the baby orange juice.

"We are put in which one there is space for us, Kate. When I arrived, there was not space for me in a Jerusalem centre, like I have said, and so it must remain."

What a "Catch-Twenty-Two" situation, thought Kate, recalling the exchange between the Australian couple. Shirl had said they would have to stay put until they found work; but they had been housed where jobs were apparently in short supply.

Irina rose to set her baby daughter in the pram, her figure girlish in a blue cotton frock, and a lock of corn-coloured hair visible beneath the white kerchief tied around her head.

"I am thinking, also, Kate, how my husband will not to accept how it is for him when he joins us here."

Again there was no "if" about it for Irina, though the number of Soviet Jews being granted exit visas was still strictly limited. Kate had not met Lev Smolensky, but while in Moscow had learned enough about him to agree with Irina.

"I see you haven't let your hair grow again," Kate remarked.

"And I have told you for why, on the day you promised to me the poems book you have so kindly remembered."

Irina's shoulder-length hair had been shorn by the KGB, and she had viewed it as God's punishment for her defying a religious custom.

"I am a married woman and should not have let vanity stop me from barbering my own head and afterwards keeping it covered."

To Kate, it seemed a bizarre custom, and she couldn't

envisage Barbara Ross submitting to it. But it had to be why all the young wives she'd seen in Jerusalem's Jewish Quarter had kerchiefs on their heads.

Yuli had returned to the table some minutes ago, but seemed content to sip his milk and gaze at Kate. She would have liked to stretch out a hand and ruffle his hair – but he was wearing one of those little caps.

Nor had she obeyed her impulse to hug him when he appeared at her side downstairs. Yuli was back with his mum, and by no stretch of the imagination the waif she and Calvin had taken into bed for a cuddle, the morning after the one-night stand to which this child's plight had finally led them.

"When I told it to Yuli that you were coming, Kate – since then he has not stopped the saying of your name and of your American friend. I have kept telling to him this afternoon to be patient and Kate she would soon knock upon our door – and it was Yuli who tells me that Kate she does not know it our door number and will have to wait to inquire it at the desk. It was then that we come downstairs."

"Your son is a bright lad, but I knew that in Moscow," Kate replied.

What he was thinking right now was anyone's guess. But two things were certain: Yuli knew something Kate intended keeping secret – that one-night stand was it – and he was happy to see her again.

The baby had begun giving vocal evidence of her wish to be picked up, and Yuli went to help his mother rock the pram.

A heart-stirring picture for Kate and how she would remember them. A family still incomplete, in a place nobody would want to call home on the heights overlooking the old city of Nazareth.

CHAPTER TWO

Kate's deduction that there could be more to the film unit than its surface appearance was lent no further credence during the next couple of days, which passed by in an atmosphere of professionals at work.

The crew could not have been more proficient, nor Aviva more businesslike in coping with her many tasks. Chaim's jovial good nature did not falter, whatever the circumstances. And there were no more outbursts from Yosef, who when filming was taking place seemed content to tinker with the engine of the minibus, or sit reading wherever he found a patch of shade.

Nevertheless, Kate's unease would not go away. And there remained the enigma of Goldman himself.

By Thursday of that first week, the stark contrasts within Israeli society were plain to Kate, and it seemed to her a country polarised not just by political and religious differences, but one in which part of the population was living in the twentieth century and the rest in a bygone age.

Though she was aware that for the ultra-orthodox Jews to whom the latter applied it was how they wished to live, could the same be said of the inhabitants of those squalid hovels? As the minibus trundled through an Arab village, en route to the next location, Kate asked, "Are the people who live here Israeli citizens?"

"Certainly," Yosef replied, and added in the polite manner in which he always addressed her, "My apologies for the condition of this road bumping you up and down, Kate."

Avrom, who was seated in the back with Chaim and Shmuel, saw Kate take off her sunglasses and wipe the sweat from the bridge of her nose. "Why you want to travel with us guys and the equipment, when you could ride in an air-conditioned car, beats me, Kate!"

"You're good company," she answered. And it was wiser to let the hostility between herself and Aviva remain no more evident than necessary. Did Goldman think himself the cause of it? Well, wasn't he?

But Kate would not allow herself to dwell upon that. "Thanks for making the detour to show me the village," she said to Yosef as they rejoined the highway. Aviva wouldn't have done so unless Goldman had ordered her to. "Will Dov mind if we get to Tiberias a bit later than he does?" Stupid question!

Chaim fiddled with his bushy beard. "That depends, Kate, on what mood he's in."

"He's moody as well as bossy, is he?"

"It goes with the territory," said Shmuel.

Kate said, "His artistic temperament, you mean?"

"And that isn't all," said Avrom.

One of the moments to which Kate was becoming accustomed followed. When something hovered fleetingly in the air and was gone before she had time to wonder why gooseflesh was raised on her arms.

As always, one of her companions changed the subject.

"So what did you think of the Arab village, Kate?" Chaim inquired.

"I was sorry for those who live there. Do they have running water?"

"In that village, probably not," Yosef replied, "but in others they do."

"I must say the people looked very friendly, especially the children," Kate remarked, recalling two small, dark-skinned boys who had waved as the minibus passed by.

"But wait till we hit the West Bank," said Avrom, "where fear, as well as poverty, figures in the scenario."

"Would you care to expand on that?"

"It's a good thing Aviva didn't hear you say that!" Chaim joked.

"That beautiful broad sure has her knife into Kate," said Avrom.

How could the men not have noticed? "That might be because she's used to being the only female on the team," Kate said.

"No, Kate," said Yosef. "Aviva she is not that type of woman. It is her affection for Dov."

"Which anyone would have to be blind not to see," Kate answered. Nor was it just affection. Passion was there, too.

"Dov and Aviva go a long way back," Avrom told her. "She was born and raised on the same kibbutz he was and, I guess, hero-worshipped him along with the rest of the junior kibbutzniks. Aviva is now thirty – and so would Dov's daughter have been, if she and her mom hadn't been wiped out in a guerrilla attack."

"I didn't realise that Dov had ever been married."

"Well," said Chaim, "now you know he's a man with a deep sorrow in his past. Aviva, too, would have died that day if she'd been fit to go to school, instead of in the kibbutz sick bay with a fever. It was the school they blew up. Dov's wife was the teacher. Can you imagine the aftermath of that, Kate? A kibbutz without children, except for a few tiny tots?"

Kate glanced through the window at the towering cliffs of Mount Arbel and said after a silence, "The same happened to a Welsh village, some years ago, and I went cold when I read about it in the papers, like I did just now. A mountain of coal slack capsized on to the village school and buried all the children alive."

"But tragedies like that aren't built-in hazards of every-day life in Britain, Kate. Here, give or take the details, and the greater or lesser degree, something as casual as riding on a bus can be taking your life in your hands, and everyone knows it."

Chaim had echoed Kate's thought when she watched some young people laughing and talking as they boarded a bus.

"Visitors to Israel often complain that Israelis are prickly people," Chaim went on, "but they don't pause to consider why."

Kate told him that she had already had the reason explained to her by a taxi driver. "And I'm beginning to understand why, myself."

Yosef then launched into a criticism of Chaim's defensiveness. "No born-Israeli would find it necessary. Why must we apologise for how we behave in our own country?" he capped it.

Chaim's response was, "Kate will now go home thinking all Sabras are as arrogant as you."

"If we are, perhaps we have reason to be."

"And one reason," said Chaim, "is you weren't raised, like those of us who weren't born here, feeling you had to apologise for this, that, or the other because you're a Jew. Or watching out for your behaviour, lest it reflect on every Jew in the country."

"Was that why you never robbed a bank, Chaim?" Shmuel ribbed him.

"It would certainly have made me think twice about it. I still remember the consternation that rippled through the British Jewish community when there was that scandal about Rachman making a fortune by letting slum property, in the sixties."

"And some epitaph for him to have in a country that had allowed Jews to settle there!" said Shmuel. "If I'd been a Britisher, I wouldn't have been able to hold up my head in school."

"And from what I am now hearing," said Yosef, "I am thankful that my parents did not inflict upon me the necessity ever to be ashamed of what I am."

Kate then sat through several minutes of the three ex-diaspora Jews letting the Sabra have it. "Shame doesn't enter into it!" and "Split loyalties are beyond your ken!" were among the heated statements hurled at Yosef, providing Kate with a new aspect of her friends the Rosses, as British as herself, but dogged by an insecurity that sprang from their Wandering Jew roots.

It occurred to Kate now that though the birth of Israel had finally cut short the painful wanderings responsible for the legend, for Jews who chose to remain where they were born and bred, whose previous generations had been sharply reminded that they were different, there was a price to pay for the choice they had made. They were never going to stop feeling different.

The verbal onslaught upon Yosef was still going on. How could he just go on driving as if he were deaf to it? Kate would long ago have pulled up at the roadside and told those doing the shouting to get out, and it was she who finally brought it to an end, for which it was necessary for her to yell louder than the voices issuing from behind her.

"Would you three mind shutting up!"

"Sorry, Kate," Chaim said sheepishly.

"I'd have thought Israelis had enough enmity to contend with from the Arabs," she lectured them, "without the sort of in-fighting I just had to listen to."

"Since I did not say one word in retaliation, you cannot include me," said Yosef.

"That's what got me madder and madder," said Shmuel, combing his sandy mane which fury had somehow disarrayed. "And my final word on the subject is, Dov excepted, Israel would be a great place to live if it weren't for the Sabras!"

"May I quote you on that?"

"Oh my God – I forgot you're a journalist—"

"*You* might have, but I did not," said Yosef. "And see, now, what the three of you have done to damage Israel? It will appear in foreign newspapers that the 'olim' from Britain and America hate the Sabras."

"I wouldn't put it that strongly," Kate interceded,

enjoying herself. Since they'd taken her tongue-in-cheek remark seriously, she'd get her own back on them for subjecting her to what they just had. "What does 'olim' mean? I'm a stickler for accuracy in my writing."

"It's the word for an immigrant," Chaim supplied, and Avrom asked why he was aiding and abetting her.

"From here on," he said to Kate, "all we're going to talk about in your presence is the weather!"

"An excellent idea," said Yosef.

Then Kate burst out laughing. "I was having you on, you nuts—"

"But compared with other things," said Chaim, "what you heard just now was no big deal. And if you thought it implied disunity, forget it. My wife's a Sabra, and we've managed to live together despite what I can't get her to understand. Our marriage is too strong to be seriously damaged by trivial differences. And the same goes for Israel. I don't know how better to put it to you, Kate. It's when the differences are the opposite of trivial that — "

"Okay, Chaim, you've made the point," Avrom cut him short, and Kate saw that Yosef's hands had suddenly tightened on the steering wheel.

The silence that followed reminded Kate of the unnatural hush when the tyres were found slashed, and she recalled that nobody other than herself had bothered looking at any of the other vehicles in the car park, to check if they had received like treatment. Almost as if the film unit, Goldman included, knew that their vehicles had been singled out. And so they had. Kate hadn't paused then to wonder why. But there were too many unanswered "whys", she thought now. Another was why had Avrom cut Chaim short?

Over-reacting again, Kate? Chaim had made the point, and he is inclined to ramble on.

"If I live to retire, Tiberias is where I'd like to end my days," Avrom restored the conversation. "The only thing I miss about Chicago is the lake. Our house was close to the shore and the family used to picnic on Sundays."

Chaim said, "He should see the English lakes, eh, Kate? One of my boyhood memories is of a day trip to Windermere, with my school."

"And one of mine," said Yosef, "is of Tiberias before the developers moved in."

They had been travelling through lush countryside, Kate feasting her eyes upon the Sea of Galilee – the biblical name by which Lake Tiberias was known – and were now in a stream of traffic crawling along the lakeside road.

Ahead, the trappings of a modern resort were visible: gleaming white buildings, and a marina complex. When they reached it, Kate noted the "designer label" appearance of the outfits some of those thronging the promenade were wearing.

"Is this where wealthy Israelis take their breaks?" she asked.

"Well, some of the hotels are sure expensive," Avrom replied. "But the people you're noticing are probably American tourists, Kate."

"And long may they continue to come," said Yosef. "Our economy needs them."

"Is that why Dov is including Tiberias in his film?"

Yosef replied tersely, "Dov is not making a travelogue to advertise Israeli resorts. That, he leaves to those who do not have his many talents. It is advisable, Kate, that you do not underestimate Dov Goldman."

"Lighten up, will you, Yosef?"

Again it was Avrom who had interceded. As if, thought Kate, in Goldman's absence the lanky sound recordist saw himself as being in command. But in command of what? This wasn't a work situation.

They had almost reached the hotel where the unit would stay overnight, and Kate saw Goldman emerge from the forecourt with Aviva, glance at his watch, and begin pacing.

Yosef too had seen them and said, "I am now wishing I had not made the detour."

"Blame it on the traffic," Kate replied lightly.

"I do not lie to Dov."

"Then you can blame it on me."

"It was I who succumbed to your persuasion."

"If that's what you call acceding to my casual request – and I'd have understood if you'd said there wasn't time – fine! But the traffic was responsible for most of the delay, wasn't it?"

"Nevertheless, to say to Dov what you suggested is not the whole truth."

Kate lost patience. "Why are you making this ridiculous fuss, Yosef?"

No reply was forthcoming. And whatever it was that Kate was imagining – or not imagining – was in the air again. Why had none of the others said to Yosef what she finally had? Another "why" to add to the rest. Nor was their still being stuck in the traffic helping to calm Kate.

Instead, she sat edgily gazing through the windscreen at the man whose powerful influence over his cohorts was present even when he himself was not. Cohorts, Kate? Well, it was certainly a word that jelled with her irrational suspicion.

She slotted it into her mental filing cabinet and noted that Goldman had stopped pacing and was now standing with Aviva beneath a tree, the two of them talking animatedly. Aviva had changed into a clingy summer frock and was looking up at Goldman, her satiny black hair falling carelessly over one eye – Kate hadn't seen her wear it in a chignon since that day on the beach – and was fingering his arm, while they spoke.

"You could be in luck, Yosef – Dov doesn't seem in a bad mood, to me," Kate said with a smile belying the feelings that intimate picture stirred in her. Added to them was the thought of alighting from the minibus looking a sweaty mess in her workaday tee-shirt and crumpled jeans.

Was Kate thinking of entering into competition with the human encyclopaedia? Aviva's bright mind and lively personality would, under other circumstances, have made her a welcome companion. But you and Aviva are never going to be friends. For one thing, she sees you as competition. And for another?

The minibus crept forward and finally turned into the hotel forecourt, where Yosef found some shade in which to park. Though Goldman could not have failed to see the bus arrive, he made no attempt to come to greet them, but went on talking to Aviva, who gave them a casual wave.

Kate unstuck herself from the plastic seat and testily refused Yosef's offer to help her jump down from the vehicle's high step. While doing so she missed her footing, wrenched her ankle, and yelped; which seemed like poetic justice for she knew not what.

"You ought to've let Yosef give you a hand," Goldman called to her.

Kate's response was to muster her dignity, adjust her shoulder bag, and head for the hotel entrance. Before she reached it, Goldman called to her again.

"We don't carry walking sticks with the equipment, Kate, but we do have some support bandages and Aviva is an excellent nurse."

Was there nothing at which Aviva didn't excel? "I am perfectly all right, thank you."

"Then why are you hobbling?"

Had a walking stick been handy, and Goldman too, Kate would surely have used it on his head! As for those treacherous thoughts she had let herself have – they could get back where they belonged. Which wasn't in Kate Starling's mind. Right now, there wasn't room for *any* man in Kate's life – and least of all for a man like Dov Goldman.

Later, while the unit was filming at the marina, Kate's increasing dislike for Goldman could not detract from her judgement that he was indeed a gifted director.

Had he been dealing with actors, no doubt his manner would have been as autocratic as it was with the crew. But with ordinary mortals – How had he got that family party to go on eating ice-cream and chatter away as if they didn't know they were being filmed?

Kate had watched him pull up a chair to their table and help himself to a spoonful of the mountainous sundae the small boy seated beside him was rapidly consuming.

"Come and join us, Kate!"

Her cue to enter the action. Could she get there without limping? Soaking her ankle in cold water hadn't relieved the pain, and the purplish swelling that had quickly risen must by now be twice the size it was an hour ago.

Kate put a smile on her face and tried dragging her foot.

"Give this lady your chair, Damien," the child's buxom mother instructed him, and added, when he looked none too pleased, "The kids today aren't like when I was one."

Meanwhile the scowl Kate was receiving from Damien reminded her of his evil namesake in *The Omen*. She watched him retreat with the remnants of his ice-cream and sat down in the chair he had reluctantly vacated, keeping the conversational ball rolling as, when those being interviewed were British or American, Goldman had asked her to do.

"I have two myself, so you don't have to tell me," she commiserated with Damien's mum. "You're from the North of England, aren't you?" she rattled on, noting Goldman's surprised reaction to hearing that she had children. Which equated with her own on learning he was once a family man.

"Mrs. Marks is visiting her Israeli family," Goldman usefully supplied, "and they've kindly invited me to film their happy reunion."

"Who is going to say no to Dov Goldman?" said the prosperous-looking gentleman seated opposite Kate.

Apparently nobody but me, she thought.

"Stanley and Madge are my brother and sister-in-law," Mrs. Marks told her. "But which Jewish family in England and the States doesn't have Israeli relatives nowadays?"

"Too many," her brother replied.

"That's right, you tell her," said his wife.

Goldman flashed Kate a glance implying that this might be some of the film footage that would not end up on the cutting-room floor – which meant it could also be worth including in Kate's articles.

Since on film you didn't ask people if they'd mind expanding on that – Kate was learning fast – she said humorously, "Tell her what?"

"The same thing my sister-in-law eggs my brother on about, whenever I come here on holiday," said Mrs. Marks, before that lady could get a word in. "Luckily, though, I can afford to stay in a hotel and don't have to accept the hospitality she never offers me."

Double-Dutch though those final words were, the enmity between Stanley's wife and his sister was evidently something neither bothered to hide. But the point at issue was still unclear to Kate.

It was Stanley who explained, and with a cutting remark. "The State of Israel wasn't founded just so diaspora Jews could come here on holiday."

He paused to dab his flabby lips with a paper napkin, before saying to his sister, "And if more of you don't come and settle here, we could end up in the same position as South Africa. I'm not one of those who thinks we should chuck out all our Arabs," he added, to Kate and Goldman. "You can't repatriate people to where they don't come from – and the ones I've got working for me are good lads. But the rate they multiply, we'll be overrun before we know it."

"And for that you'd like me to move here with my only child?" said Mrs. Marks. "So my Damien would end up cannon fodder?"

Cannon fodder in the eighties? But its modern equivalent was what Mrs. Marks meant, and Kate sympathised with her. "Wouldn't you say your sister's feelings on that score are how most mothers would feel?" she said to Stanley.

His reply was, "Including Israeli mothers, but they don't have any choice, do they?"

"Your sons were born after you and Madge settled here, or you two might not have made the choice you did," Mrs. Marks countered sharply.

But this is more than just a carping session between an Israeli man and his British sister, Kate registered. What Goldman was getting on film right now, and Kate for her articles, were attitudes illustrating Israel's major need, and of the deaf ear being turned by the source of supply, for whatever personal reasons.

Mrs. Marks then proceeded to enlarge upon hers. "My Damien was a gift from God when I thought He wasn't going to bless me with a child. I was over forty when Damien was born," she said to Kate, before adding on a note of near-hysteria, gazing wildly around her, "Where has Damien gone to? I don't see him anywhere. If he's fallen into the lake, I'll never forgive you for bringing us to Tiberias for the day, Stanley!"

"How's that for gratitude?" said her sister-in-law.

Such was her anxiety, Mrs. Marks let it pass. "Why don't you go and look for your nephew, Stanley! You speak Hebrew, and I'm a stranger here — "

She was heaving herself out of her chair when the little monster appeared from inside the café and came to stick out his tongue at his uncle.

"You now have the answer to your question," Stanley told her.

Mrs. Marks clasped Damien thankfully to her bosom. Kate would have walloped his behind, and felt that Stanley was itching to do so.

The sister-in-law had meanwhile folded her arms and pursed her lips. "Did you ever think, Stanley, that we would hear a Jewish person call themself a stranger in Israel? Well, we have now, and it doesn't surprise me that it came from your Beatrice's mouth."

These people had plainly forgotten that they were being filmed and their conversation recorded, thought Kate – and that had to be due to Goldman's special gift. He was now giving Mrs. Marks a sympathetic look, and had a listening expression on his face.

When she spoke, it was to him. "It's because I'm now a widow that Stanley and Madge think they can get me to do what wouldn't be right. Would you bring your son to live in Israel?" she appealed to Kate.

A picture of her chubby lad making himself a peanut-butter sandwich in the kitchen flitted before Kate's eyes, and another of Jason and Emily picking blackberries in a peaceful English lane. If they were Israeli, the army would claim Jason five years from now, and Emily even sooner, to train them for the ever-present possibility of war.

Kate reflected that it wasn't surprising that the brash exterior she had noted had cloaked the inner fears of Israel's younger generation. Like those kids she'd seen boarding the bus in Tel Aviv, their demeanour self-confident to the point of arrogance, and their loud voices splitting the air.

Kate's children were lucky they weren't Israelis. "I certainly wouldn't, Mrs. Marks."

She was then subjected to the watery-blue gaze of the sister-in-law. And to a query and comment whose bluntness reminded her of her late grandmother, who like these people had come from the North of England and hadn't believed in shilly-shallying.

"Are you Jewish? You don't look it."

Kate was thankful to be able to say no – or she too might incur the wrath of this middle-aged couple whose indeterminate appearance belied the fire within.

Stanley and Madge were the sort you would pass in the street without noticing them, their drab clothing a testament to what grey could do to a sallow complexion. Indeed, the diamond ring on Stanley's little finger, from which Kate had assessed him as prosperous, seemed incongruously flashy on such a man. Madge's sole illustration of affluence was not jewellery – she wore only a wedding ring – but her also-grey lizard skin shoes and handbag.

Betwixt them, Mrs. Marks, now toying with the several

chains around her fleshy neck, looked, in her brilliant blue trouser suit, as a kingfisher might flanked by a pair of sparrows – though her shape was that of a pouter pigeon.

The sparrows gave the pouter pigeon a peck – via Kate.

"This lady's not being Jewish accounts for the answer she gave Beatrice, doesn't it, Stanley?" said Madge.

"My sister," he replied, "is looking for people to side with her."

"But that won't wash, will it, Stanley?"

Not one peck, but several – Kate was sorry for Mrs. Marks.

"You haven't the emotional ties with the Jewish state that make people come to settle here," Stanley said to Kate. "People like Madge and me, that is."

He glanced at his sister, who avoided his eye. "Others buy off their consciences – and without their conscience money where would Israel be? I'm the first to admit it. But money can't buy what we're crying out for."

Kate told him that he was not the first Israeli who had said that to her, and received a let-down glance from Mrs. Marks.

"Whose side are you on?"

Since an outside observer had no right to be judgemental – and Kate had better bear that in mind – she remained silent.

But could even the judgement of Solomon have resolved this one? she thought, recalling from her Sunday-school days the Old Testament king's wisdom in deciding which of two women was the true mother of a child: She would let the other woman take him, rather than have him die.

In Solomon's time, though, the Children of Israel had not yet dispersed to make their lives in host countries from which, after struggling for integration, most would not choose to return when the dream of the land of milk and honey being theirs eventually materialised. Nor was the point at issue around this table the sole reason.

From what Kate had so far learned and observed, the realisation of the dream did not live up to that biblical description by any stretch of the imagination. How could it?

105

Israel was a twentieth-century state, and Tel Aviv a monument to the defiance of those citizens who wished it to be one; to take its place in the modern world. But there were some who saw progress as the sinful path to the destruction of Judaism. How would the internal tug-o'-war, of which Kate first became aware when she travelled to Jerusalem with the devout girl and the transvestite, end? If the ultra-orthodox won, Kate couldn't envisage Howard and Barbara, when the time came, retiring to Israel as his parents had. Their lives being dictated by anachronistic rules and regulations very definitely wouldn't be for them.

While Kate's thoughts had progressed from the wisdom of Solomon to the internal divisiveness she could not, by now, have failed to discern, Goldman had entered the conversation and was listening to Madge and Stanley grumble about the cooking smells that went with having Sephardi next-door-neighbours.

"Sephardis are from places like Iran and Iraq," Goldman told Kate, "whose ethnic culture is quite different from that of the Ashkenazim, which includes our friends here and me."

"Would Ethiopians, like we met at the absorption centre, be in the former category?" Kate inquired.

It was Madge who replied, though Kate had addressed Goldman. "Certainly not. They're coal black."

Goldman inserted a sly question. "Does that mean you wouldn't be pleased if your son married one of them?"

"My sons are already married, so I don't have that problem."

Racism in Israel? thought Kate. But people's having themselves been on the receiving end of it was no guarantee that they were incapable of racist attitudes toward others. Wasn't there, in fact, an eminent black clergyman preaching anti-Semitism to his own community in the States, right now?

While Kate became aware of her swollen ankle beginning to throb painfully, and that the wind suddenly ruffling the lake was chilling her bare arms, Goldman gave her her cue that he now had all the film footage he required from this interview.

"Thanks for letting us sit in on your family reunion, folks," he said, playfully tweaking one of the *enfant terrible*'s golden curls.

"It was interesting for me to meet you," Kate said, dreading the moment when she would have to get up and walk.

"I just hope you didn't get the idea that *I* have no emotional tie with Israel," said Mrs. Marks.

"On the contrary." And Kate would not for anything swap places with those who had.

When they had departed the table, Kate again dragging her foot, she exclaimed to Goldman, "Some family reunion! And have you noticed how horrid children often look like little angels?"

"A better question," he replied, "is why is an intelligent woman behaving like a fool? You can hardly walk, Kate."

"I am absolutely fine."

Her ankle chose that moment to prove otherwise. If Goldman hadn't caught her arm she might have taken a tumble.

"The reason it gave way is you can't bear to put your foot down for the pain," he said swooping her into his arms, "and you ought to've taken this afternoon off, like I told you to."

"Please don't make a scene, Mr. Goldman!"

"Back with the formality, are we?"

"Put me down!"

Instead, he carried her through the crowd that had gathered to watch the filming, now goggling as if watching a sequence entitled "You Tarzan, Me Jane" – and how wouldn't they? thought Kate, as Goldman deposited her in the director's chair on which was emblazoned his name.

"Get the first aid box," he instructed Aviva, whose narrow-eyed expression left Kate in no doubt of her feelings.

As if I deliberately sprained my ankle to get Goldman's solicitous attention! No, even a woman as possessive as she is toward Goldman wouldn't think that, Kate. But it certainly nearly killed her to see you being carried in his arms.

And, embarrassment aside, what did being in his arms do to *you*? All that brute strength, the scent of cologne and tobacco, and the heat of him burning into you – she cut short the torrid thoughts of which she wouldn't have believed herself capable and gave Goldman an angry glance.

He interpreted it as pain. "Maybe we should get you to a hospital and have that ankle X-rayed, Kate."

The crew were hovering by with equal attentiveness. "Could be we have a stretcher case here," said Avrom.

"You'll have a straitjacket case if this nonsensical fuss continues!" Kate flashed. "I am not used to being babied."

"But aren't you carrying British stoicism a little far?" said Chaim. "If you'd worn a support bandage, you might not be suffering as you are now."

And on more counts than one.

Goldman then repeated his opinion that she ought not to have worked this afternoon.

"Are you saying my presence at that table wasn't useful?"

"On the contrary, Kate. The way the interview went confirmed how right I was to ask you to join up with me."

Even when he paid a compliment he managed to display his ego!

Aviva flounced toward them carrying the first aid box and dumped it beside Goldman, who was kneeling by Kate.

"You will find what you require in neat and tidy order. But please do not ask me, Dov, to bandage the ankle. It was refused at the time when it would have most helped. Why should I do it now?"

With that, Aviva marched off to sit in the minibus. The crowd, thought Kate, must now be thinking they were watching a rehearsal for a searing drama – and Kate wouldn't add to that impression by kicking Goldman in the teeth with her good foot, though she was having to grit her own teeth, such was her chagrin while he deftly dealt with her ankle.

When the deed was done, she mustered the politeness to thank him, took over the job of rolling down the leg of her jeans, and rose from the chair.

"See how the bandage takes the strain?" he said.

And had Kate had one with her, she would have made use of it hours ago. The ridiculousness she'd displayed was as unlike her as those torrid thoughts.

"But you may as well sit down again," the cause of both went on, "until the equipment is loaded and we're ready to leave."

"I'm fine standing, thanks."

Chaim shook his head, tugged his beard, and sighed. "What can we do with her? She's a product of where I used to live."

Kate was grateful for that myth. Goldman, however, was regarding her amusedly through the smoke he had just exhaled – though he was unlikely to have figured out that she wouldn't for a moment longer than necessary occupy a chair with his name printed on it.

Kate was eating the light supper she had ordered from room service, when Aviva paid her a visit.

"The men are concerned that you did not join us for the evening meal, Kate. The baked fish we have had in the restaurant was delicious."

Kate forked up some chicken salad. "I'm enjoying this, thank you."

Aviva settled herself more comfortably in the armchair where she had seated herself without being invited to sit down, crossed her shapely legs, and straightened the skirt of her coral silk dress.

And here's me in my last year's dressing-gown! thought Kate. But few women could compete with Aviva in the glamour stakes. Not even those for whom their appearance was their life's work, which couldn't be said of the human encyclopaedia.

Aviva's gaze roved to Kate's ankle. "Dov, he thinks that

you have remained in your room this evening because you are suffering. But me, I think you are sulking."

"I'd appreciate it," said Kate, "if you didn't apply your own tendencies to me."

"I am sorry for how I behaved about the bandaging, Kate. But was that any different from how you behaved earlier?"

When Kate made no reply, Aviva went on, "But how else can it be? When two women want the same man?"

"I beg your pardon?"

"Why are you pretending with me, Kate? I am not pretending with you. And I have yet to meet the woman who would not fall for Dov. This is not for me a new situation. But when whoever she is has gone from the scene, I am still there."

"After helping her on her way, no doubt," said Kate, "but you've got it wrong about me."

Aviva gave her a mocking look and remarked upon how pretty her slippers were, as if they were having a cosy chat. What sort of chat *were* they having? One in which one woman was warning the other off.

"It is Dov who helps them on their way, not me," Aviva said, "when he has tired of them."

"After which you welcome him back with open arms?" Kate drank some water to help swallow her distaste.

"I am the woman Dov needs."

"But, from what you've been saying, he doesn't seem to know it."

"One day he will," Aviva declared confidently.

"You could be old and grey by then."

"I am prepared to wait."

"And I have to say I pity you," Kate voiced the opinion she had already privately held.

Aviva sprang up from the chair, her dark eyes like sparking coals in the perfect oval of a face which in repose was that of a madonna.

"The time may come when you will pity yourself, Kate! It is not just because I have the deep feeling for Dov that I have

110

said to you these things. It is, too, in *your* interest that I beg of you to be careful."

"Did you make that little speech to all the competitors you mentioned, Aviva?" Kate got a mental picture of a procession of assorted females getting into Goldman's Volvo and alighting on the opposite side.

"It was not necessary for me to do so."

"Then why did you make it to me?"

"You are not eating your supper, Kate," Aviva stalled, and said after a pause, "The others, they were sexy—"

"Thanks for the insult."

"But that was all," Aviva completed the sentence. "Also, at the time when such past involvements have occurred, for Dov to be distracted was of less importance."

"Why?"

"I would like some of that mineral water you are drinking, if I may — "

"Get yourself a clean glass from the bathroom."

"The glass you are using is not going to poison me."

Nor were you suddenly attacked by thirst, Kate silently replied. The mineral water was a diversion that went with so much else that Kate was still trying to tell herself she was imagining. Like that string of coincidences not really being coincidences. The special respect for Goldman. And the unnatural reaction to the slashed tyres. Why they were slashed, and by whom, was just one of the many whys and wherefores.

Kate had no sooner succeeded in pushing all that to the back of her mind, when something returned it to the forefront. Along came another moment like this one, when she got the impression that one or another of her companions had said more than they'd intended saying, and something intangible then hovered in the air.

Aviva, eyeing Kate surreptitiously over the glass from which she was sipping mineral water she didn't want, was probably regretting that jealousy had led her to shoot off her mouth and arouse Kate's curiosity.

It was then that all the whys and wherefores crystallised for Kate into just one question: What were they keeping from her?

Aviva put down the glass and rose. "I must allow you to finish your supper and get some rest, Kate."

"That would be very kind of you."

"But I advise you to consider carefully what I have said."

"Any particular bit of it?" Kate said more flippantly than she felt.

"Believe me, what we have been discussing is not the joke, Kate. You know, of course, that the unit's stopover, this weekend, will be at Dov's house in Haifa. I myself shall not be there—"

So that was it. Aviva wanted no monkey business in her absence – and doubtless thought Kate the easy lay she wasn't. Though her tone when she mentioned the weekend was casual, she couldn't fool Kate.

"And nor will Yosef," Aviva went on, "who, like me, always goes home for Yom Hazichoron."

"And what might that be?"

"It is Israel's day of remembrance for all our soldiers fallen in battle. There are few families here who do not have a grave, or more than one, to visit, and this coming Sunday those who have will make the pilgrimages. My mother and I shall go together to where my brother is buried. And Yosef, who is the only one left of the three sons his parents had, will take them to the cemetery where the two they have lost lie. Yosef was their youngest, and they are now quite old."

Kate could not but be affected by Aviva's moment of sadness. But the cause of it, and on so large a scale, was the price of Israel's survival to enter, a few days hence, her fortieth year.

"But the Arab people too have suffered the terrible bereavement," Aviva said, "and on Yom Hazichoron I am weeping for their dead also."

"Do many Israelis feel that way?"

"How could they not? And the number who are speaking their minds about that and other matters is increasing."

Kate replied, "I haven't noticed Israelis hesitating to speak their minds. And why shouldn't they? Israel isn't a dictatorship."

"It could, however, so easily become one. And now I shall say to you goodnight, Kate."

Aviva was gone before Kate had time to take in her parting remark – or its possible significance to Kate's mounting suspicion.

The following morning, Aviva could not have been more friendly when Kate joined her at the hotel's elaborate breakfast buffet.

"It was not my intention last night to upset you, Kate."

"You didn't."

"How is your ankle?"

"It could be better."

"Over the weekend, you will be able to sit with your foot raised upon the leather hassock Dov has in his living room."

"How exciting," said Kate, while trying to fish a boiled egg out of a steaming container piled high with them.

Aviva got one for each of them, using a pair of tongs, and Kate said that if she had done that she would have broken the eggs.

"They are hardboiled, Kate."

"Hot hardboiled eggs? Would you mind putting mine back?"

Aviva glanced over to where Goldman and the crew were breakfasting at a window table. "One of the men will eat it – though not Chaim, who has retained from his birthplace some of the foibles I have noted in you. Like the putting of vinegar upon the fish and chips. I have also seen Chaim make of the chips a sandwich!"

Kate, whose eye was roving the buffet in search of something a Britisher would consider breakfast food – and that didn't include red peppers, or pickled herring – told

Aviva that where she came from chip butties were reckoned to be a tasty snack, adding, "But they're bad for the figure. I wouldn't advise you to get addicted to them, Aviva."

"You, of course, do not have that problem, as I have noticed, Kate. But I shall attribute the remark you just made to what I have told to you last night. And you must make that allowance for me also. As I said then, how else can it be between us?"

"You are welcome to Dov Goldman," Kate informed her. "Now may we please leave it at that?"

Kate was moving away, a glass of juice in one hand, a plate in the other, when Aviva grabbed her arm and pulled her back, after which they stood together staring down at the croissant now on the floor.

Aviva retrieved it and stood with it in her hand. "I am sorry, Kate."

"Are you also sorry for almost jerking my arm out of its socket! And for making my being with the unit more difficult than it need be?"

"What I am the most sorry about, Kate, is the way this must seem to you — "

"Obsessive, you mean!"

"That I am prepared to agree. But it is not all. Do you know the story of Samson and Delilah?"

Was Kate going mad? Or had Aviva already reached that state? The Israeli woman had lowered her voice to a whisper – and conspiratorial was suddenly how this felt, accounting for the prickling at the back of Kate's neck.

Kate tried to make sense of what Aviva had said. "Are you telling me that Dov Goldman needs protecting from himself?"

"I can say no more and have already said too much."

"But allow *me* to tell *you* that the Wolf and Red Riding Hood is a better analogy for Goldman vis-à-vis women than the one you chose."

Kate plonked another croissant on to her plate and departed. Her arrival at the table terminated the Hebrew conversation in which the men were engaged.

114

After joining in the general inquiries about the current state of her ankle, Goldman gave his attention to his morning paper and Chaim gave his to Kate's plate.

"All that time to put together such a tiny breakfast?" he said disapprovingly.

"Chaim has to have someone to nag when he isn't with his wife," Shmuel said with a grin.

"Someone to take care of, you mean," Kate defended Chaim, "and I appreciate his trying to take care of *me*."

"Is that a crack at the rest of us?" Avrom inquired.

"No. It certainly isn't."

Kate could not complain that the crew didn't do their best to make her feel welcome among them. Why then did that outsider-feeling keep bugging her? "Why" again! But as people, these blokes were a decent lot. Yosef, however, seemed not to enjoy mixing with the rest of the unit, retiring to his room immediately after the evening meal, instead of repairing to the bar, or the lounge, with his colleagues. Though it was early days for Kate to presume that his habit, it had confirmed her immediate feeling that Yosef was a loner by nature.

It struck Kate now that none of the members of the unit were naturally compatible. Chaim's joviality and Avrom's cynical air did not make for closeness between them. The same went for Shmuel's outgoing personality and Yosef's withdrawn demeanour. How to account, then, for the extra dimension binding them together that Kate had detected? Over and above the unity of a group of people brought together by their work. Or was Kate imagining that, too?

Aviva sat down beside her. "I had trouble deciding what to eat this morning," she explained her late appearance at the table.

Adding dissembling to her other talents, thought Kate, but she could hardly have said she'd needed time to pull herself together after a set-to with Kate about Goldman.

"Women!" the director glanced up from his paper to exclaim.

"And almost nothing is what the two of them have ended up with on their plates," said Chaim.

Kate noticed that Aviva had put back the hardboiled eggs – but they had certainly ruined each other's appetite. Kate was having trouble swallowing down half of her croissant.

"Yosef and I don't want to set off too late is why I am finally having just some bread and herring," Aviva answered.

But dissembling probably came easily to her, since the whole damn lot of them are dissembling to *me*, thought Kate. Or are they?

It wasn't just her throbbing ankle, or Aviva's rabid jealousy, that had kept Kate awake until the small hours, but a whirl of possibilities, some of them frightening – and no doubt evoked by Aviva's parting remark that Israel could easily become a dictatorship.

Possibilities hard to relate to a nice lad like Shmuel, who still had about him the aura of the American high-school boy he once was. Hard to relate, too, to fatherly Chaim, born and bred in England. Was it that easy to discard the conditioning of a conventional past and step into a subversive role?

Kate's assessment of Avrom was that he would find it less difficult than the two upon whom she had just reflected. There was about him a hint of the ruthlessness she had sensed in Goldman – nor would it surprise her to learn, if her suspicions were correct, that Avrom was Goldman's lieutenant.

Was Kate Starling really having breakfast with a bunch of activists up to heaven knew what? Far-fetched though the notion seemed, it lent to Aviva's citing the fable of Samson and Delilah a significance that had escaped Kate until now. If ever there were a story of a strong leader's downfall via a woman, Samson and Delilah was it.

But one thing *didn't* jell with Kate's suspicions. Would the leader of a subversive group bring a stranger into their midst?

Goldman glanced at her over the top of his paper and the

116

back of her neck prickled for the second time that morning. A smile would not have accompanied his glance if he were able to divine Kate's thoughts.

Briefly, she considered getting the hell out of a situation that had begun giving her the creeps. Professionalism stemmed the urge. Nor was Kate the sort who ran from *any* situation.

She drank some coffee and calmed down, listening with half an ear to Avrom and Chaim discuss filming the crowds who flocked to Dizengoff on the Eve of Independence Day.

"On Sunday night, Avrom and I could find our equipment being joyously wrecked," Chaim said to her.

"How can people go out and celebrate, after spending the day visiting cemeteries?" Kate voiced the feeling that she most certainly could not.

Goldman entered the conversation. "The rejoicing is a symbolic gesture many find hard to make."

"Where does the symbolism come in?"

"It isn't by chance that the day of mourning our fallen immediately precedes Independence Day, Kate. The two are linked. Those who lie in our military cemeteries gave their lives for a cause Jews have died for down the ages. The survival of our race. What but that does the State of Israel stand for?"

"But I wouldn't say symbolism is in anyone's mind after they've had a few, or otherwise got into the party mood, and are making merry on the streets!" Chaim put in with a chuckle. "Remember the last time you and I shot Eve of Independence Day footage together, Avrom?"

"*Advance* footage, for a feature film that never got made," Avrom recalled. "But that's the movie industry, in which an entire project can capsize overnight for some trivial reason!"

"Literally overnight, with that project," Chaim reminded him. "But I shouldn't think its producer would agree that returning unexpectedly from a trip, and finding his wife in bed with the director, was trivial."

117

"An occupational hazard I've put behind me," said Goldman with a smile.

"And for which you would no longer have time," said Aviva, returning Kate's mind to the Samson and Delilah theme and its possible implications. As the fleeting pause that followed was typical of other such moments when one of the company said something of significance to all but Kate.

She put a smile on her face and said lightly to Goldman, "I'm getting the impression that being your own money-man is a lot less fun than when you weren't."

"If fun were of paramount importance to me," he replied, "I would accept the offers I get from Hollywood. A director of my talent could make for himself a fabulous life there."

Ego rearing its head again, thought Kate. "I don't doubt it," she said, conscious of Aviva's stony profile beside her – as if this casual chit-chat between Kate and Goldman was a trailer for a forthcoming between-the-sheets scene in which Kate, alias Delilah, would take scissors from her nightie pocket and cut off her lover's hair. Where the analogy fell down was that Goldman, alias Samson, was balding to say the least and, by that stage of the proceedings, the nightie would be long gone.

Kate stopped envisaging sex with Goldman and continued leading him on verbally. "I admire the choice you made."

Though this was true, it had nearly choked her to say it, nor would she have if getting closer to Goldman wasn't essential to the task she had set herself. Kate had finally accepted that she had imagined nothing and there would be no more veering back and forth.

Imagining one or two strained silences was possible, but not a whole series of them. And you didn't have to be a detective to deduce that the reaction to the slashed tyres implied a significance known to all but Kate. As for the coincidences preceding Goldman's calling her, well, even her unimaginative dad would agree that they were cause for scepticism.

There was, too, one piece of possibly tangible evidence, though of what she had not yet allowed herself to conjecture. A big metal trunk that travelled with the equipment, its contents weighty enough to prevent it from rattling around, like the rest of the stuff did as the minibus sped along. Kate had never seen it opened and had noted that it was padlocked, deepening the mystery by which she felt herself surrounded. As the implications of Aviva's equating Goldman with Samson, in the context she had, lent an overall credence to the picture Kate was bit by bit putting together.

"That's the first compliment you've ever paid me," Goldman replied to her grudging remark.

As though his path was paved with them, which it probably was, and Kate would swallow her scruples and ladle out more, if necessary.

That cunning must be matched with cunning was a lesson she had learned from the KGB – though theirs had surpassed hers – and from now on it was how she would play her hand. The people with whom she was breakfasting at a table overlooking the Sea of Galilee were not what they seemed, and Kate's presence among them had to be for some nefarious purpose that could add an unforeseen dimension to her assignment.

PART THREE

Chapter One

Since Goldman was no less shrewd than Kate, her change of tactics did not go unquestioned.

Why had her pointed coolness suddenly been replaced by the flatteries he received from lesser women? It had taken no longer than the ride from Tiberias to Haifa for Dov to perceive the difference in Kate, and their arrival at his home had clinched it.

"This is the sort of place I'd expect a man of your taste to live in," she had said.

Okay, he ruminated, so she's right about my good taste, but yesterday she wouldn't have given me the satisfaction of having her say it.

Meanwhile, she was upstairs taking a bath – after admiring her host's choice of tiles, and shutting the door in his face. Dov hadn't expected an invitation to soap her back, but would she, before she turned tack, have shut the door so gently?

"Something's going on with Kate and I don't like it," he crystallised his thoughts to his companions on the terrace.

Chaim exchanged a glance with Shmuel, and Avrom put down his glass of lager.

"And how you three reacted to what I said indicates how edgy we're all getting," Dov told them.

"The more so for the lady's presence, if I may say so," Avrom replied, "and on more counts than the main one. I'm surprised that Aviva didn't welch on her Yom Hatzuur date with her mom, to stay glued to your side. This isn't the first time I've seen that broad in the throes of jealousy, but this episode, at this time, could prove pernicious."

Dov put out his cigarette in the outsize ceramic ashtray that lived on his terrace table, and lit another. "You may safely leave the handling of Aviva to me. And don't let me hear you call her a broad again."

"A mere figure of speech, Dov."

"And one that implies disrespect for someone I care about."

"But not enough to make her your wife," said Chaim.

"What is this!" Dov flashed. "Home truths night? Would you care to join in, Shmuel?"

"I wouldn't dare."

"Come on. I invite you to."

Dov got up from his wicker chair and went to lean against the gnarled tree whose branches shaded the terrace by day. "If Yosef were here, no doubt he too would have something to contribute to this topic. Which of you would like to speak next?" he said challengingly.

Avrom drank some of his lager before saying, "Why don't I be the spokesman and put what we think in a nutshell?" He glanced at the others. "Okay, guys?" They nodded. "The general consensus, Dov, is that the ongoing situation with you and Aviva is getting in the way of what we should all have our minds on."

Dov hid his shock that meetings to discuss him had been held behind his back. "And how would the rest of you suggest that be remedied? By voting Aviva out of the group, perhaps?"

Avrom replied, "Can you envisage the woman-spurned repercussions, if we did and you backed us up? Bearing in mind that the woman concerned is in a position to blow what we're hoping to achieve?"

Avrom was treated to a glance that caused him to quail. "If you really believe what you've just implied, you don't know Aviva."

"Since we don't intend putting it to the test, and the status quo must therefore continue, there'd be less undercurrents, Dov, if Aviva were less unhappy and insecure."

Dov was pacing beneath the tree and stopped short. "Let me get this clear. Is the rest of the group requiring me to marry Aviva for the sake of the cause? If so, the answer is I wouldn't do that to her and the cause doesn't need me to."

Dov went to the drinks trolley to add a shot of Scotch to the liquor the melting ice cubes in his glass had diluted. Did the others construe his doing so as a sign that his nerves required bolstering? . . . though it was something they'd seen him do many times before?

He returned to lean against the tree, the sense of isolation he occasionally experienced suddenly as cold as the glass his hands were cradling, listening to the night sounds beyond the thick bushes closing in the garden that had long been for him a haven.

But a stone's throw away was the dark bulk of Mount Carmel, at which he was pensively gazing, the majesty of the mountain's summit blending with an inky sky in which the moon had not yet risen, and the lights on the winding road rising from far below casting a ghostly glow.

Inner loneliness – what else but that was this feeling of isolation? – is the price a leader pays for the allegiance of those who follow him, Dov reflected in the silence that now hung heavy between him and the men he had carefully selected, as he had the absent Yosef, to spearhead the fight for Israel's salvation.

Were they now, when the burgeoning movement had begun swelling, questioning Dov Goldman's singlemindedness? His strength to set into action what might finally be necessary?

Though the revelation that they had met secretly to discuss him had felt like a knife in Dov's side, he would not allow the wound to fester. But that didn't exclude being watchful for further signs of erosion. Nor did it rid Dov of the certainty that should the knife ever stab him in the back, Avrom would be the perpetrator.

Kate's appearance on the path leading from the house to

the terrace caused the men to emerge from their private thoughts, and English to be spoken – though Shmuel's verbal reaction to seeing her was of his own vernacular.

"Wow! You look a million dollars in that get-up, Kate!"

"It didn't cost anything like that much," she said with a laugh.

She had paused beneath a trellis arch to finger the honeysuckle entwining it, and had briefly remained there. But it was no wonder that the men had looked surprised. This was the first time they'd seen her wearing a dress.

"Is there a Hebrew word for 'wow', Shmuel?" she asked going to join them at the table.

"Not that I know of, Kate."

"Like the Jewish word 'chutzpah'," said Avrom, "there are some Americanisms that express what no other language can. And you're sure looking stunning tonight, Kate."

"A real English rose," Chaim embellished the compliment.

"Allow me to echo that," said Dov.

"And my thanks to you all for saying so. Would one of you like to get me a gin and tonic?"

The three at the table nearly fell over each other to oblige, and Kate got the feeling that she had suddenly stopped being for them "one of the boys" – and all it had taken was putting on a flimsy frock and some extra eye make-up and lipstick! Whatever her purpose in their skulduggery, it didn't preclude their falling for feminine wiles.

"That's if Dov has some gin and tonic," she added.

"I shall personally mix it for you," he said as Avrom, first to reach the trolley, was about to do so.

While Avrom offered potato crisps, and Shmuel placed before her a dish of olives, Kate exchanged a smile with Dov – for whom she had never been one of the boys. Kate was treading dangerous ground in more respects than one. Would tonight be when he made his first pass at her?

Dov's thoughts at that moment would have confirmed for Kate that possibility. The glimpse he'd got of her in a bikini,

126

that day on Herzlya beach, hadn't prepared him for the effect those elegant legs had on him, for the provocative sway of her hips when she wore high heels, he was reflecting while mixing her drink.

"I don't see the support bandage," he said prosaically when he brought the glass to her, "and ought you to be wearing those shoes?"

"My ankle isn't painful now, Dov. But I promise to be good and wear the support and my flat sandals when I'll be spending time on my feet," she answered, giving him a smile.

A *playful* smile, he noted, and accompanying an amenability at odds with the woman she had until today seemed to be. Correction. The woman he was sure she really was. Whose fragile English rose appearance tonight belies the strong character that singles her out from the women you've encountered and discarded in the past. Some of whom could not be called weaklings, but were no match for Dov Goldman. It would have to be one who was whom he would hesitate to send on her way, lest he never again met another like her.

Meanwhile, it was Kate Starling, now sipping a drink with those who saw Aviva as the greater danger of the two, whose behaviour was giving Dov cause to rethink the wisdom of inviting an outsider to feature in the documentary, serving unwittingly an additional purpose.

While Chaim dipped into his fund of Jewish jokes, and Avrom and Shmuel, who had heard them all before, obliged by joining in Kate's laughter, Dov's mind returned to Herzlya's golden sands, when the brief relaxation he was allowing himself was cut short by Aviva's arriving with a cable from New York.

Dov recalled Aviva's saying, while he was scanning the message, that the American journalist's falling sick when they needed him was a bad omen for the group, and his own laughing this off. Dov's concern, at that moment, had been the lack of time not just to find a replacement, but to check out the new guy when he found one. That hadn't been a problem with his first choice, who'd been based in Israel at the time Dov engaged him.

Dov glanced at Kate. The replacement, as luck had it, wasn't a him, it was a her. What's all this with luck? he asked himself sharply. That isn't something you believe in. But the way things were shaping up – and because of Kate Starling – it was hard to disregard what Aviva had said about a bad omen. Easier said than done to laugh it off now, when the least that could be said was that since Kate joined them some kind of rot had set in. Or had it been there before and Dov just hadn't known it?

If this was a conversation with Aviva, instead of Dov ruminating, she would by now have said that Kate had put the evil eye on them. Aviva had never shaken off the superstitions passed down to her generation of Sabra women by their diaspora-born grandmothers. Superstitions rooted in the forebodings of a ghetto past, where oppression and poverty had fostered a primitive folklore.

Dov could remember the woman, now dead, who was once his mother-in-law, spitting three times when someone remarked upon how healthy his baby daughter looked, lest sickness consequently befall the child. And his own mother, whose Viennese background set her, in her own mind, above those of peasant stock, had doubtless done the superstitious spitting mentally. She had not demurred when his young wife tied a red ribbon around the baby's arm to ward off evil, and had not stayed to witness the quarrel that followed when Dov removed the amulet.

Dov allowed his mind to move painfully forward from that long-ago quarrel to the day, ten years later, when he had run from the kibbutz orchard to the school, his ears still deafened by the explosion of what he had known had to be hand grenades.

Though he had let himself hope that God had spared his wife and child, the havoc that met his eye said otherwise. Long before the small bodies and that of their teacher were brought from beneath the rubble, two Arabs lay crumpled in the barley field, cut down by bullets as they fled.

A matter of little importance to Dov, as he'd knelt weeping beside his dear ones, like broken dolls upon the grass. He could still recall the sun blazing down on his head, and noticing that Rivka had that day let Shoshannah wear for school the silver chain they'd given her for her last birthday. Bits of the chain were entangled in the child's singed hair, and the "mazel"-pendant had attached itself to some coagulated blood on her neck.

Much good that lucky charm, commonly worn as jewellery, had done his little girl, was Dov's first coherent thought. Then he became aware, amid the sounds of mourning all around him, of parents comforting each other, and from that day on had carried within himself a lonely ache harder to bear by far than the isolation upon which he had earlier reflected.

The affection he received from Aviva was the nearest he came to assuaging it. Nor had the transient affairs he had experienced over the years fulfilled, even while they lasted, Dov's real need.

Sex had been low on the list of what Rivka was to him. And would the others believe that his relationship with Aviva was not what they assumed it to be?

Maybe for some men it was possible for a woman to be to them lover and daughter rolled into one, but not for Dov. His seeing Aviva as a surrogate daughter was responsible for her inserting herself into his life. Why had he put it that way? As if her doing so was deliberate. But in retrospect, deliberate was how it seemed, and Dov could not know Aviva as well as he did without knowing she was capable of being calculating.

After her army service, she had not returned to live on the kibbutz. Her father had died in the interim, and nothing could have been more natural than Dov's taking her under his wing when she enrolled for a business course in Tel Aviv, where he was then based. Before he knew it, she was spending more weekends at his place than in the flat she shared with some other girls.

The rest, including his firing an inefficient secretary and Aviva's stepping into that role, was history. Little by little she had taken him over and he had amusedly let it happen. On all fronts but one. When he got back from a party one night, and found her in his bed, he was as shocked as if she were truly his daughter, and had retreated without a word.

Aviva had not tried those tactics again in the five years that had since passed. But sometimes, if work put them beneath the same roof, she came to his room for a late-night chat and Dov hadn't the heart to say he was tired and turf her out.

Kate prodded Dov back to the here and now. "You're being a very neglectful host!"

Playful again, Dov registered, going to sit at the table.

Chaim resumed the conversation to which Dov had not been listening. "But Avrom is a bit of a misogynist, Kate, as you may have gathered."

"Any particular reason, Avrom?"

"Two, actually. And I'm still paying alimony to one of them."

"Who broke up the marriage, you or her?" Kate inquired.

"I guess I have to accept responsibility for that."

"Is she capable of supporting herself?"

"That klutz couldn't hold down a job if she tried," Avrom said with a snort. "And if this is one of your sly peeps into Israeli life, Kate, I have to tell you that Irma has never set foot in Israel. It was to escape from her I made aliyah, and the only good thing she did for me. The cheques she is still receiving twenty-five years later are the cost of my freedom, and a monthly lesson I still hadn't learned when I made my *second* big mistake."

Kate said after a pause, "Since I'm well able to support myself, and it was I who ended my marriage, I told my ex I wanted nothing from him for myself, only for the children.

And it could be that that's helped Alun and me to stay on amicable terms."

Avrom swigged some of his lager and set down the glass emphatically. "You bet your life it's helped. I mean what guy is going to stay friendly with a female who's taking a chunk of his earnings after giving him the boot? But I guess you're one on your own, Kate."

And the more dangerous for that, thought Dov, given how easily she had engineered Avrom's respect. What was she up to? Vision of loveliness though she looked tonight, the terrace lamps rendering her hair a cobwebby gold, gazing from one to the other of us with those innocent grey eyes, a professional snooper was what she remained; no different from any other journalist who had smelled a dynamite story.

The guys now hanging on Kate Starling's every word thought Aviva capable of blowing the gaff. But Dov's hunch was they'd put their money on the wrong filly.

It crossed his mind – regretfully – to fabricate a reason to rid the group of her presence. But she wasn't the kind, if she *had* sniffed something out, to leave it at that. Instead, she'd begin delving, asking questions in Jerusalem, or wherever, until those capable of effective action began pondering why a British journalist was so interested in Dov Goldman. The signs were already there that at a lower level obstacles were being put in Dov's way – the slashed tyres could be just the beginning.

Sending her packing was out. And the catch-as-catch-can contest there could be between Dov and Kate from here on a stimulating prospect. Dov didn't for a minute doubt his ability to outwit her. Meanwhile, he was enjoying surveying the soft curve of her breasts beneath the filmy bodice that invited speculation about how she would look in the raw.

Dov doubted that there was a guy present, including the archetypal staid married man, Chaim, who didn't wish himself alone with Kate Starling in this romantic, garden setting. At Shmuel's age and stage, she could without too much effort have the lad eating out of her hand. Avrom was another matter, but from how he was now looking at her—

If she were just a sexy dish, Dov's amusement at the turn things had taken tonight, with her and the guys, would not be tinged with apprehension. But her visible assets plus her intelligence and the warmth she was now putting out were a disarming combination. She could finish up being resident confidante to the crew.

All of whom had their bleak moments, Dov reflected, when a slip of the tongue might easily be made. He had better put out the strong warning he was about to issue when the matter of himself and Aviva intervened.

In the meantime, let them enjoy her company, though Dov had no doubt which of her male companions Kate would choose to be alone with. He and she had wanted each other from the moment their eyes met across the coffee shop table, and something would have to be done about it.

Later, when they had just sat down at the kitchen table to eat the pasta and meatballs Kate had cooked, the telephone rang and Dov went to his study to answer it.

"I'm surprised you don't have an extension in your kitchen," Kate remarked when he returned. "But that could be because kitchens don't figure in your life."

Dov stood beside the dresser on which an assortment of mugs were hanging, fingered one of them absently and said, without replying to Kate, "Get me a whisky, would you, Shmuel?"

"What's the matter, Dov?"

"Just do as I asked. And bring the bottle to the table. I might not be the only one who needs it."

While Shmuel did as he was bid the silence was electric. Kate could hear a tap dripping at the sink, and saw that Dov's hands were trembling as he lit a cigarette.

"That was Yosef on the phone," he said after gulping the liquor. "As you know, I let Aviva take my car, so she could chauffeur her mother to the cemetery on Sunday. She was to drop Yosef near to where his folks live—"

"And?" Avrom said when Dov paused.

Dov licked his lips, which despite the drink suddenly felt parched, and forced himself to go on speaking. "They didn't get too far on their journey. The brakes failed while the car was travelling downhill toward the main highway—"

"Spare us the details," Chaim cut in, "they would have had to be gory. But we know Yosef is alive, or he couldn't have called you. How about Aviva?"

"They were both taken to hospital. Yosef got away with some cuts and bruises, and was given a sedative to deal with the shock. They left him to sleep it off. And have just told him Aviva has undergone surgery, but wouldn't let him see her."

Dov fixed his gaze on a food mixer on the work counter, last used when Aviva was here and decided to bake him a cake. "They said to Yosef that it's touch and go for her."

Troublesome though she was, Aviva was love and loyalty personified, and the man at whom her love was directed when she eventually stopped misdirecting it at Dov would have himself a fine wife. Add to that: *if Aviva recovers.*

Kate cut into Dov's thoughts. "I seem to've lost my appetite and I'm sure that goes for everyone. But instead of your all reaching for the whisky bottle, why don't I make a pot of tea? In England, we say there's nothing like it," she said rising to fill the kettle. "Remember, Chaim?"

The cameraman managed to nod, but not to smile.

"Where do you keep the teapot, Dov? Perhaps you wouldn't mind getting it for me. Shmuel can fetch some mugs to the table." Kate put the kettle on the hob to boil and opened one of the wall cupboards. "That seems to be a packet of teabags on the top shelf. Will you get it for me, please, Chaim?"

"No task for me?" Avrom quipped.

"Yes, you can bring the milk from the fridge."

He said while doing so, "You're a tower of strength, Kate."

Dov had to agree. Kate's matter-of-fact manner and her stirring them all from their shocked immobility was helping those who knew what she didn't. The implications of the car crash. And there was no doubt who the target was. Whoever had monkeyed with the brakes could not have known that today Dov Goldman would be travelling in the minibus.

Dov drank some of the tea Kate poured for him, but the hot liquid did nothing for his inner chill. Action had swiftly followed the warning that the slashed tyres patently was, indicating that there were those who would stop at nothing to quell the rising crescendo they feared and had learned the name of the man orchestrating it.

Chapter Two

Kate found herself, that weekend, with some solitude she had not anticipated.

She had risen on Saturday morning to find all but Shmuel gone from the house, and he with instructions from Dov to take her to Tel Aviv, where accommodation at the Yamit had again been reserved for her.

They had made the journey by hired car, not, she had noted, a meter cab, the driver an Arab with whom Shmuel passed much of the time conversing in Hebrew.

As to the whereabouts of the others, the information Kate elicited from Shmuel was sparse: they had gone to the hospital in which Aviva still lay hovering between life and death, and would afterwards have some business to attend to.

Kate spent much of the day drafting the introductory article for her assignment. Well, trying to! She ripped yet another sheet of paper from the typewriter and consigned it to the waste bin she had fetched to the balcony, where she was again working.

As you've been consigned to the lesser matters Dov Goldman hasn't time for today, Kate, she thought gazing restively at the necklace of lights tracing the promenade route to Jaffa, of which the rooms she was this time occupying afforded a splendid view.

She had not ventured out lest the telephone ring, and it was now early evening. If Dov was too busy to call her himself, why hadn't one of the others kept contact with her?

Had she known which hospital Aviva was in, Kate would have telephoned to inquire about her condition. Despite their several confrontations, each had in her own way respected the other and, as Kate had reflected, might have become friends were it not for the man who stood between them.

Now, whatever came or went, Aviva was gone from the scenario she had equated with Samson and Delilah, in which she had doubtless cast herself as the faithful handmaiden trying to avert impending disaster.

Since Kate intended finding out, by fair means or foul, exactly what Dov Goldman was up to, the analogy she had initially thought far-fetched was seeming increasingly less so.

What would she do if her findings necessitated passing them on to the Israeli authorities? First things first, Kate. Meanwhile, her deduction that the unit was a cover for a subversive group, and Goldman its leader, was further confirmed by his and the crew's reaction to learning the car brakes had failed.

Though horror at the tragic result was to be expected, Kate had rarely seen people so *shaken* as Dov and the other men were last night. Distress on Aviva's behalf had seemed to be the least of it. Put together with the slashed tyres, how it looked to Kate was that Aviva was a casualty of something other than a road accident, and that Dov Goldman knew *he'd* had an accidental escape.

Why was Kate letting herself fear for the safety of a man up to no good, whom she disliked intensely?

She slammed the cover on the typewriter and clicked it shut. The end of a futile writing session. And the eve of another day of mourning in the country she had not even begun to fathom. Her sole certitude was that religious differences were setting Jew against Jew, which, given that Israel was the triumphant culmination of the long struggle to preserve Judaism, didn't make sense to an objective observer.

The door buzzer prodded Kate from her musing and a second buzz implied urgency. When she opened the door a trio of gloomy faces heralded the news she was about to receive.

"Aviva didn't make it, Kate," said Avrom.

"And I guess we could use some of your nice cups of tea," Shmuel added.

"In other words, Kate, may we come in?" said Chaim.

While they trooped past her, Kate controlled the urge to ask where Dov was. She watched Chaim and Shmuel put themselves side by side on the sofa, and Avrom sit down in the armchair. Though she hadn't invited them to do so, it was as if they felt at home with her. But a subtle change in Kate's relationship with them had somehow come about last night – and once again it was difficult to relate them to the possibly dangerous activists she had deduced them to be.

Chaim supplied the answer to the question she hadn't asked.

"Dov felt like being alone, Kate. He's grief-stricken."

"Well, he's known Aviva all her life, hasn't he?" Kate replied. And his knowing it could have been him now lying dead must be adding a sharp edge to his grief – how wouldn't it? Nor was it easy for Kate to contain her own sense of outrage. That vibrant personality snuffed out, and the beautiful woman Aviva was, mutilated in the pursuance of a cause.

Kate went to the kitchen section of the living area to make the tea, and thought, while she busied herself with the preparations, that which of the possible causes in this turbulent society the group represented was anyone's guess. But until she found out, she had no way of determining who had taken such desperate measures to stop Goldman short.

"Needless to say, Kate, we're pretty cut up ourselves," Avrom said.

Then why don't you stop whatever you're doing? she wanted to confront them. Instead, she dropped some teabags into the pot and replied, while pouring the boiling water into it, "I haven't yet voiced my own sadness about what you came to tell me."

Avrom then came to get the milk out of the fridge for her, and she was assailed by déjà vu. But what was her making tea for these blokes, and the atmosphere now emanating from them, but that bit of last night repeating itself?

Before she had time to put the tea things on the tray, Shmuel was there doing it for her, and Chaim looking in a cupboard for the sugar, which she had forgotten.

That bit of last night repeating itself, with an added element. Kate was getting the feeling that there was something these three wanted from her.

When they were all back in the sitting area before the window, Kate on the sofa between Chaim and Shmuel, Avrom cleared his throat and gave her a smile.

"The tea is sure welcome, Kate," he said after sipping some, "but the reason we dropped by, instead of calling you, is we're worried about Dov."

"When we left his suite, after he told us to go away, he was sitting with his head in his hands," Shmuel revealed.

"We didn't like the look of it," said Chaim.

Kate stopped herself from saying, Why come to me? "What do you mean, you didn't like the look of it? Under the circumstances it's perfectly understandable."

Circumstances you lot think I've accepted as the tragic result of a mechanic's negligence, when the car was last serviced. As anyone not in the position to deduce otherwise would assume. My could-be *dicey* position, thought Kate, recalling the padlocked metal trunk carried with the film equipment, which she had never seen opened. While its contents might be legitimate, it might equally well be a cache of small arms.

A speculation Kate would perhaps, before last night, have dismissed as over the top. But not any more.

"The point is," Avrom said to her, "that devastated though he may be, Dov still has a film to make."

Other unfinished business, too. And his cohorts seemed dismayed by what they doubtless viewed as a sign of weakness.

"The sooner he gets back on the ball the better," Avrom went on, "and since you're professionally involved along with the rest of us, we'd like to enlist your aid."

"If you're asking me to intrude upon his privacy, I wouldn't think of it," she replied. "And he'd probably send me away, as he did you."

"What's the betting he won't?" said Avrom. "And we think you're the one who could pull him out of it. You're a helluva nice lady, Kate."

Questionable though their motives were, Kate divined that Avrom had added the last bit sincerely. But that wasn't why she agreed to do as they asked. Who knows what a man might let slip when his mood is grey and his guard down?

Nor need Kate have any scruples, given that man's having had none when deceiving *her*. She paused only to freshen herself with a shower and put on the lime green two-piece outfit she had eschewed in favour of a tee-shirt and jeans for her first meeting with Dov Goldman.

The contest of wits-laced-with-sex begun then was still going on, though Kate couldn't have envisaged the turn it would take, she thought as she walked the short distance to the Dan, an Aran sweater around her shoulders, her hair flying in the wind.

She ran a comb through it before crossing the hotel foyer to the lifts, and a few moments later was alone with Dov Goldman for the first time.

"How thoughtful of you to come, Kate."

"It wasn't my idea, Dov." The heck with *unnecessary* dissembling. "The crew thought you could use some company."

"And told you I didn't want theirs, which I guess I made too plain."

"If the same goes for mine, I'll understand—"

"Yes, I'm sure you would, Kate. Now come and sit down, instead of standing there on that sprained ankle." He ushered her into the spacious lounge. "Is it getting better?"

139

"Yes thanks, but my little mishap has been minimised by later events, wouldn't you say?"

Dov watched her seat herself on the sofa, with the natural grace he had noted, as he had the proud way she held her head. This was a direct woman if ever he'd met one. The disconcertingly playful creature of last night – *before* the call from Yosef – was back in the box of tricks.

Was there a box of tricks? Time would tell. Dov sat down beside her and stubbed out his cigarette in an overflowing ashtray.

"Can I fix you a drink, Kate?"

"I didn't come for you to have to play host, Dov. If you're having one, I'll join you."

"Have you eaten tonight?"

"No, as a matter of fact. And if you haven't either, why don't we get some sandwiches sent up? As my grandmother used to say, it's easier to face up to whatever you have to on a full stomach."

Dov called room service, and said after replacing the receiver, "What I have to face up to, Kate, is life without Aviva."

Kate continued to speak her mind. "I hadn't realised she meant quite that much to you, though I'd heard from the others that you'd known her since she was a child. But what you just said – well, it was how a man might speak if he lost his beloved. That wasn't my impression of how things were with you and Aviva."

Dov got up to gaze through the picture window.

"How things were with me and Aviva was, sadly, different for each of us," he said without turning. "What I'm saying is we loved each other, but how she loved me wasn't how I loved her."

"If that means what I think it does, you had the advantage then, didn't you?" Kate replied.

Dov turned to look at her. "But I'd like you to believe I didn't make use of that unhappy situation."

"Unhappy for Aviva, you mean?"

140

"Unhappy for me, too."

Why did Dov feel the need to set things straight with Kate Starling? Whose serious gaze was now meeting his, as if she was deciding whether to believe him or not. He hadn't, since Rivka died, cared a damn for how any woman but his mother viewed his behaviour. But with this one—

"Last night on the terrace, your eyes looked grey, but tonight they look green," he remarked irrelevantly.

"My ex-husband used to say they changed colour according to my mood."

"I shall bear that in mind."

Kate tried to drag her gaze from his, but it was as if a magnet held it fast, and she felt the colour rise to her cheeks.

The arrival of their supper was a welcome interruption. Saved by the buzzer, if not by the bell! From him? Or from herself?

Whichever, the polite young man now depositing a tray that looked like a miniature banquet on the coffee table would soon be gone.

She watched Dov take out his wallet and hand the waiter a tip so extravagant, if any other bloke had done it she'd have thought him out to impress her. But wasn't everything about Dov Goldman larger than life?

Kate tried to envisage him working on a kibbutz, as he once had, and found it impossible. Equally so to visualise him as a young man. Instead, he seemed to her set in time exactly as he now was, with neither past nor future attached to him.

Dov saw Kate shiver. "If you're feeling cold, I can turn on the heating — "

"I'll be fine when I've eaten."

"Then help yourself to food, while I pour us some wine. I can recommend the chopped liver."

Kate tried some and found it delicious. "I didn't know what I was missing till my friend Barbara introduced me to Jewish cuisine," she remarked. "And nor did my kids – Barbara sometimes invites us for the Sabbath Eve supper, and she's given me several recipes. Including one for that marvellous carrot stew—"

"Which we call tsimmes. Did she also give you the one for cholent? It has butter beans in it."

Why were Kate Starling and Dov Goldman sitting here discussing recipes? But it was safer ground than they had begun treading before the food arrived. "No, but I'll ask her for it," she replied. "Not that it's me who does the cooking."

"With your roving career, and two children, I imagine you have a housekeeper—"

Kate smiled. "A very good one – she's my mum. But the furthest my career had taken me until this assignment was Northern Ireland. Which, in some respects, is a parallel situation to what I'm observing here — "

A memory then returned to Kate of herself and her grandmother watching TV in Gran's cosy sitting room, Easter greeting cards propped up on the mantelpiece, and Kate eating a chocolate egg. Pictures of the Royal Family at Windsor, outside the church, were on the screen, and Gran passing approving comments about the Queen Mother's hat. A minute later, they were looking at a man Kate hadn't known then was the Reverend Ian Paisley, leading a march escorted by police, and she could remember Gran, who'd always talked to children as if they were adults, saying, "We've just seen the two faces of religion, Kate, one after the other."

At the time, Kate hadn't known what Gran meant, nor been able to make sense of what she had said when the news was over and she turned down the sound during the commercial break.

All these years later, though the exact words eluded Kate, their import had gained strength, she reflected, sipping some wine. What with things going from bad to worse in Northern Ireland, Iran leading the way for Muslim fundamentalists to run amok, and ultra-orthodox political parties wielding the balance of power they had achieved in Israel.

"Your eyes are now grey again," Dov observed.

"I'm told they usually are when I'm being thoughtful."

Dov topped up their wine glasses and returned the bottle to the ice bucket. "I shall bear that in mind, too. Would you like to share the thoughts you've just been having?"

"I was recalling a long ago evening."

"That isn't very flattering to *me*."

His ego again! But such was the atmosphere between them right now, Kate found it amusing, not offensive.

"Who was the fortunate man?"

"My life wasn't yet complicated by men. I was only about twelve, and spending a weekend up north, with my Gran, whom I'm never going to stop missing now she's gone. But things she used to say often come back to me." Kate gave him the gist of her grandmother's final remark, that Easter Sunday night. "One of which was that godliness could be useful for grinding axes on."

"The same lady you quoted just now, about facing up to things better on a full stomach? She was right on both counts." Dov ate some more of the chicken breast on his plate, and smiled. "But let's not turn this into an evening of serious discussion, Kate."

He handed her the wine glass she had just put down, and picked up his own. "Instead, would you please join me in toasting the person Aviva was?"

Kate raised her glass to the woman she would always think of as a flame suddenly snuffed out, and had the feeling that the gesture Dov had asked her to share was for him like closing the door on whatever his relationship with Aviva had been. If what he had said earlier was meant to imply the absence of bed, how could that have been possible for two such overtly sexual people?

One of whom was no saint! thought Kate, while Dov was again topping up their wine glasses. When he'd said, "Let's not turn this into an evening of serious discussion," Kate had almost replied, "What sort of evening do you have in mind?" – as if she didn't know.

"If you wouldn't mind raising your glass a second time, we'll now drink to you and me," he said.

"To our business arrangement, you mean?"

Was she playing with him again? No. Fending him off. "Business couldn't be further from my mind right now, Kate."

Since Kate had let herself forget that she was here for a purpose unrelated to the effect Dov had on her, she knew the feeling.

A moment later, that thought had gone from her head and her glass from her hand. "What are you doing — "

His kiss silenced her protest and rendered her putty in his skilful hands.

Kate's one-night stand with Calvin Fenner, in Moscow, had the distinction of being her sole marital infidelity, and mind might have prevailed over matter in less emotive circumstances. There was now no husband to be unfaithful to. Was she going to become a sleeper-around, like some of the other divorcees she knew? Certainly not.

Then why was she letting this man, still as shrouded in mystery as he'd been from the beginning, and no more likeable, do the things he was doing to her? Her panties had just joined the rest of her clothes on the floor, and she could hear herself moaning while he explored the portion of her he had just exposed.

He, however, was still fully dressed – which served to heighten the eroticism·of his seemingly using her as and how he wished for his own pleasure. How could she be enjoying his kind of love-making? If it could be called that, she thought, seated naked on the sofa while he stood between her legs lighting a cigarette.

Why wasn't she telling him she wasn't his kind of woman? Because apparently she was, but hadn't known it.

"Would you prefer us to go to the bedroom?" he asked.

"What's wrong with here?" she said wantonly.

Kate's last coherent thought when eventually he undressed and stood before her was that his erection matched his ego.

Later, while they finished the bottle of wine together, he wearing the monogrammed silk dressing-gown that went with his image, and Kate a hotel bathrobe, she reflected with a private smile that the condom he had produced at the crucial moment must have been custom-made for a penis his size. Nor was Kate offended at his using one. Anyone who had sex with someone they'd recently met, without taking that precaution, was thumbing their nose at Aids. But in this case, Kate would've been the one taking the risk.

"Your eyes are now grey again. What are you being thoughtful about, when you should be relaxed?"

"Permissiveness, actually," Kate replied, "since one thought leads to another. You see, I don't make a habit of doing what I did tonight."

"And you're conjecturing about my probable past?"

"You could hardly be the man you just proved yourself to be if you hadn't one."

"May I take that as a compliment?"

"You may take it as a simple statement of fact." Kate rested her head on his shoulder and looked up at him. "If you're fishing for compliments, though, I'd call you a master of the art." Kate paused. "Unfortunately, however, for me something was missing."

"If you'll tell me what, I'll include it the next time," he said with a smile.

"And what you just said illustrated what I mean. You know all there is to know about turning a woman on and satisfying her – and how wouldn't you, given all the practice you must have had? But having the right switches flicked – to put it crudely – isn't my idea of a man making love to me."

"And you're sure giving it to me straight."

"What I'm actually saying, Dov, is you'd win first prize for technique, but you'd be bottom of the class in the tenderness stakes."

Strain had now entered the atmosphere, and Kate thought it time to make her exit. What purpose had this evening served? Instead of Kate using it as she had intended,

Dov Goldman had with her acquiescence used *her*, and suddenly she was unable to meet his gaze.

Having to gather up the garments he had stripped off her – still in a heap beside the sofa – made matters no easier. "If you don't mind, I'll dress in the bathroom," she said stiffly.

"Why would I mind? My lady visitors often do."

It was with that crack – though it was probably true – ringing in her ears that Kate left Dov alone with his thoughts and regretting that he had made it.

If he hadn't known before that he'd gone overboard for Kate Starling, he sure knew it now.

She did not take too long to reappear fully clad.

"I'll dress and walk you to your hotel, Kate."

"That isn't necessary," she replied, "since I doubt that anything worse could befall me on the way there than I experienced here."

Was she inferring he'd raped her? No, just hitting back at him for trying to humiliate her. "Call me when you get there."

"I shall do no such thing."

She was gone in a trice and without saying goodnight, leaving Dov to visualise her striding alone through the dark. When had a woman last aroused protectiveness in him? Not since he lost Rivka.

But a man who now felt he was living on borrowed time ought not to be falling in love.

CHAPTER THREE

Yom Hatzuur was a day when again Kate found herself alone in Tel Aviv. Not only was it set aside for ceremonies in military cemeteries and family visits to soldiers' graves, today Aviva would be buried and Kate had not presumed to accompany the men to the funeral.

Instead, Kate tried again to collate her notes and was working on the balcony when the siren commanding silence throughout the land sounded its mournful wail.

Even an outsider could not but be affected by the hush that followed the sudden halting of traffic and by its significance. Kate's hands lay stilled on the typewriter keys, and from her bird's-eye view she saw people alight from their vehicles on the seafront road and stand with their heads bowed.

An exact repetition of *last* Sunday, when the victims of the holocaust were remembered, and no less thought-provoking for Kate. Again it was as if the whole of Israel was united in remembrance. Well, except for Israel's Arab citizens, for whom it must surely be a reminder of the incongruity of their own situation. Another such reminder was that though some elected to serve in the Israeli army, they were not equipped with rifles.

But Kate was coming to see Israel as a country in which incongruities and paradoxes abounded. There was in the attitude of some of its citizens too, something that smacked of the colonialism of the one-time British Empire; a built-in superiority to the Arabs who worked for them, as evinced by Mrs. Marks's brother, who had declared during the interview in Tiberias that his Arabs were good lads. Yet side by side with his kind of Israeli, and their Westernised strivings and achievements, were the kibbutzim, representative of a quite different system of society; and the enclaves in which the Bible was the law.

How was it possible for any government to hold together such diverse threads? Kate reflected as the siren signifying that the solemn minutes of unity were over pierced the air. A nation couldn't thrive succoured by remembrances of its past alone. What about its present and its future?

Kate returned her attention to her work, and arrived late at the meeting Dov had called to tell her would be held in his suite that afternoon. She had kept her side of the brief conversation brisk and businesslike, which could hardly have surprised him.

Her entrance served to rouse the men from the subdued aftermath of seeing Aviva laid to rest, and Kate made no reference to where they had been that morning.

Though they were drinking coffee, a pot of tea awaited her.

"It'll be stewed by now, Kate," said Chaim, "shall we order you a fresh pot?"

"This will be fine, thank you."

"Then shall we get down to business?" said Dov.

Was he remembering the very different scene enacted in this room last night? No. Dov Goldman, to whom it must have been not uncommon, would shrug it off more easily than Kate could.

While he issued instructions for that evening's filming on Dizengoff, Kate averted her eyes to a potted palm – beside which her crumpled garments had lain – and it occurred to her that another layer of subterfuge had entered the action: What she and Dov knew, but the crew didn't. Nor would she wish them to know that she'd joined the ranks of Dov Goldman's conquests.

Briefly, while she sat in their midst sipping tea, Kate felt herself caught in a web in which danger lurked like a menacing spider. The string of "coincidences" culminating in her entrapment. The road accident that wasn't an accident, intended for Dov, that had instead put paid to Aviva. The crew's embroiling Kate on a human level masking their real motive, that had led to her intimate entanglement with Dov. And a treacherous emotion she didn't want to recognise was love had rooted in her heart.

Nor was it impossible that Dov Goldman set out to get you where he wants you for more reasons than the bodily satisfaction you afforded him last night. What better way was there to gain a woman's loyalty than via her heart-strings? Aviva was a graphic example, Kate thought, surveying the man at the core of it all, who with his balding head bent over his notes, and a pencil stuck behind his ear, nobody would cast in the role of The Great Lover.

Get your professional cap back on your head, Kate! The reason you haven't cut and run is your assignment – and the extra dimension it's acquired includes finding out the real role for which Dov Goldman has cast *you*.

This lot thought they had Kate fooled and she would let them go on thinking so. Somehow she would manage to discover what they were up to, and by the time Dov Goldman realised he hadn't been dealing with a naive English rose, but a crafty British journalist, Kate would be long gone with her story, she was thinking when he cleared his throat to command attention.

"Okay, folks. Here's how I see it from here on. Shmuel will take over Aviva's duties, and Yosef, who'll be back with us on Tuesday, will fetch and carry for Chaim."

Shmuel's baby face displayed his hurt reaction. "I'm an assistant cameraman, not an odd-job guy, Dov — "

"Don't you have union rules about who does what?" Kate inquired.

"All we need right now is union interference!" Chaim exclaimed.

"But there isn't going to be any, is there?" Dov said smoothly. "Perhaps I should explain to Kate that this unit is a handpicked team, and that the reason I whittle down my crew to the basic necessity is less people means less trouble. In a larger unit, Avrom would have an assistant sound recordist, and Chaim wouldn't be doing his own lighting — "

"I wasn't thinking of reporting you to the union," she cut in, raising a laugh.

As for all that eyewash about why the crew was small! Well, they weren't just a film crew, were they? But what were they planning?

"By the way, what sort of equipment do you store in that big metal trunk?" she asked casually.

"It's where Chaim and I keep our odds and ends," Avrom answered.

"The reason it's padlocked," said Chaim, "is the minibus could get broken into."

"And I've certainly felt sorry for the two of you, having to haul the trunk into our stopover hotels."

"It goes with the territory," said Avrom.

I bet, thought Kate.

"Okay," Dov declared, "so the unit's a team, like I said, and one unlikely to disintegrate in an emergency situation with a project not yet completed."

If that wasn't double entendre – one meaning for Kate and the other for the crew – Kate was a Dutchman's auntie. Avrom, now carefully examining his fingernails, and Chaim, fiddling with his beard, must be privately whewing with relief that their leader was back on the ball. And yet another layer of subterfuge was Dov's not knowing, as Kate did, the extent of their anxiety about him.

One sort of web this most definitely was, was a web of all-round deceit, Kate thought, while noting that Shmuel still looked none too happy, and as if he were trying to bring himself to say something.

When eventually he did, his tone was respectful. "Would you mind telling me, Dov, why Yosef can't fill in for Aviva? Why put him in the job I'm trained for and he isn't, since I'm no more qualified to be a PA than he is."

"I'd have thought engaging a temp from an agency the obvious solution," Kate said.

"But I suggest you leave me to decide what's best for my project," Dov replied, "which doesn't mean I don't appreciate your trying to be helpful."

Or that he'd hesitated to put Kate in her place; reminding her of his peremptory treatment of Aviva, whose unswerving devotion to him had finally led to her death.

Meanwhile he had returned his attention to Shmuel and was bathing him with a smile. "You're my choice for this special responsibility, Shmuel, and if I didn't think you could handle it, I wouldn't be giving it to you."

"I won't let you down, Dov."

"There's no need to tell me that."

Kate reflected that the Dov Goldman charm worked upon whomever he exerted it, be they male or female. He was a man whom it seemed nobody – Kate included – could say no to. But from now on she'd be the exception that proved the rule.

As for the one-time American high-school boy seated opposite her – on the sofa where she'd learned the real meaning of the word "erotic" – his face had lit as if he'd won a fortune on the football pools. And suddenly it was no longer hard for Kate to understand how ordinary blokes like Chaim and the two from the States had been recruited for whatever Dov Goldman's cause was. Though it was doubtless a cause which they too espoused, as many people felt strongly about this or that, few would lend themselves to subversion on that account.

Yosef, the sole intellectual among them, would, with the intensity he had little by little revealed, have required no persuasion. And the others had fallen prey to Dov Goldman's charisma, Kate summed up her thoughts.

"Since Aviva kept an immaculate filing system," he was now telling Shmuel, "you'll have it as a guide about scheduling, etcetera, and how far ahead she'd gone with hotel reservations. It'll be a simple matter for you to take over where she left off."

Dov glanced at Kate. "Callous though it perhaps seems to you, holding this meeting immediately after Aviva's funeral is what our attitude has to be."

"You seem to have forgotten I'm a professional myself." And why wouldn't he, after stripping her down to a sex-symbol?

"Aviva will be missed, but we can't bring her back," he continued his pep-talk, "nor would she want her death to account for a project she helped plan, and believed in, going adrift."

Again he was referring not just to the film. But when did the group engage in their underground activities? Given that apart from yesterday and today, Kate had worked, eaten, and spent the evenings with them, it would have to be when she was sound asleep.

Her several attempts to learn, via general conversation, if they were leftists or the opposite had been carefully diverted. But how they came over was as people of the middle ground, Dov included. Moderates, like Kate herself. But moderates didn't employ extreme methods, nor find it necessary to go underground. If the blokes had worn those little caps on their heads – which none of them did – Kate would have deduced the group to be religious fanatics. Since that was out too, what else in the Israeli political spectrum called for cunning and subversiveness?

"I can manage without an assistant cameraman who isn't one. Let Yosef give his attention to minding the vehicles, Dov," said Chaim.

Kate poured herself some tepid tea. "So there'll be no more slashed tyres, you mean?"

"What else?"

What else? Everyone present, including Kate, could not but be apprehensively aware of their own mortality. That any one of them could end up on a mortuary slab, as Aviva had, if a time bomb, or whatever, was secreted in the vehicles.

It was necessary for Kate to control a shiver when Dov

then told her that he and she had an Independence Day date in Jerusalem.

"With whom?"

"I'll tell you on the way there, and promise you'll find it worthwhile." He turned to Shmuel, who now had a notepad and pen in his hands. "Since my car is a write-off, I'll need a replacement. Another Volvo will be fine. It shouldn't take too long for you to get me one. In the meantime, hire me a self-drive. I'll want it here tomorrow morning."

"Will you want me to drive you and Kate to Jerusalem?" asked Shmuel, scribbling busily.

"That won't be necessary."

Like it or not, Kate was due to be penned in alone in a car with Dov Goldman. But he could hardly pull up at the roadside in broad daylight for another sexual exercise. And if he so much as put his hand on her knee, he would be made to wish he hadn't.

When Dov excused himself to go to the bathroom, Avrom, again the spokesman, thanked Kate for "pulling Dov out of it". Since as a result she now had something to thank *them* for that she wished hadn't happened, it was difficult for her to muster a smile, though she found it amusing that the minute Dov was gone from the room, the new, in-cahoots relationship between her and the crew – which could prove useful – had emerged.

It struck Kate then that human nature being what it was, any group of people minus subterfuges would be hard to find, be it a social circle, or colleagues. Behind-the-back conversation *and* manipulation went on in Kate's office; including some of Ferdie's staff expressing doubts about his editorial judgements, which they would certainly not have said to his face. And who knows what they weren't saying to Kate's?

The possible permutations for intrigue in whatever hierarchy were fascinating. Kate had heard on the grapevine that the bloke one rung down from Ferdie had invited the paper's editor to a dinner party, and if that wasn't manipulation—

Kate glanced at Avrom, now talking earnestly to Chaim; and so quietly neither Shmuel, still making notes, nor Kate, could have overheard. For all Kate knew, Avrom could be privately plotting the downfall of the man who'd recruited him, a practice even more common among activist groups than in every other sphere. Dov had displayed that he could be soft-centred, and Kate hadn't forgotten the hint of ruthlessness she had sensed in the lanky bloke from Chicago.

Avrom was too immersed to notice Dov re-enter the room. Not so Chaim, who interjected into whatever Avrom was saying, "We were just getting a few technical details sorted out for tonight's shoot, Dov."

"No need, I guess, to bore Kate with them," Avrom added with a smile.

"And we'd better warn Kate to watch out for her clothing tonight — " Shmuel put in.

If they'd issued that warning to her last night, it might have stayed where it was – on her body. "What on earth do you mean?" she asked, carefully not looking at Dov.

"On the Eve of Independence Day, how some of the teenage generation celebrate is by spraying everyone within sight with that foam you can buy in aerosol containers," Chaim informed her.

"The same kids, no doubt, who spray-paint graffiti on walls," Kate said with a smile, "and I've noticed that Israel is no less subjected to that genre of art than my own country. But there's one piece of graffiti I've kept noticing on our travels that has to mean something, or it wouldn't be all over the place. It isn't just a random daub — "

What had she said? The proverbial pin could now have been heard to drop.

But Dov, caught off guard though he was, said glibly to the others, "I think Kate must mean that thing with the cupped hands." He hoped Chaim, who had designed it, would forgive him for putting it the way he'd had to!

"That's the one," said Kate, "and the hands are black."

154

What did this lot privately call themselves – the Black Hand Gang? No, melodrama was far removed from the man whose depths Kate was trying to plumb. But that graffiti had to be theirs, and what it represented was Kate's first real lead, as opposed to just following her nose until it hit something concrete as at last it had. Contrary to the physical equivalent of that metaphor, however, Kate's nose had remained undiminished.

"I recall there being some Hebrew words, between the cupped hands," she went on, "but I was of course unable to decipher them."

"If you'd mentioned it before, we'd have gladly obliged," said Dov. But why had she mentioned the graffiti now? Another trick out of the box of them he wasn't sure there was? And perhaps, now, the guys would heed the cautioning he'd given them before she arrived for the meeting.

He gave them a verbal signal that he intended brazening this out. "Perhaps we should tell Kate, first, what a stir the graffiti she's noticed is creating here – since she wasn't in Israel when it all began — "

"Get a foreign observer's reaction, you mean?" Avrom came in on cue. "Like in the film."

"When all what began?" said Kate. "Are you telling me the graffiti is some kind of campaign?"

"A very clever one," said Dov.

Ego again, since he had doubtless planned it.

On that score Kate was wrong. Chaim, who had once worked in advertising, was responsible not just for the design itself, but for borrowing an idea from a poster campaign he had recalled being highly successful in Britain.

"A pair of hands flanking a slogan doesn't strike me as anything special," Kate led them on.

"And with that I'd have to agree," Chaim answered, "if the graffiti had first appeared the way it looks now. What's excited everyone's interest, Kate, is that it didn't. You're too young to remember this, but when I was young and still living in England, big posters appeared one day on all the billboards, with 'White Rain Is Coming' written on them. There was no clue to what the product was, and it excited people's curiosity."

While Dov wished Chaim would get on with it, and cut down on extraneous detail, the cameraman paused to smooth his beard and give Kate a smile.

"When I got home from work one evening, my sister informed me that 'White Rain' was here. The last word on the poster had been changed, but nobody yet knew what 'White Rain' was. It turned out to be a shampoo, and she, like many other women, rushed out to buy it."

"Was it a good shampoo?"

"I didn't ask her. But the point of the story, Kate, is the same psychological approach – and it's working – is being employed in the graffiti campaign you noticed. First the hands appeared. And later the slogan."

"What does the slogan say? 'Doomsday is coming'?" Kate had barely managed to keep her tone from sounding sardonic.

"That sort of slogan wouldn't rate a second glance," said Avrom, "everyone would just dismiss it as the work of some weirdo."

It was Dov who finally supplied Kate with what she was impatient to know.

"What it says is, 'Take Your Life In Your Own Hands'."

"People are still waiting to find out what it means," said Chaim.

An incitement to revolution? Or to drastic change of some kind . . .

"Is Israel due for an election?" she inquired.

"When there isn't one looming, there's invariably reason for one to be hovering," Dov answered dryly. "And you're doing your sprained ankle no good by unnecessarily standing, Kate," he digressed.

She had risen to gaze thoughtfully through the window.

"I'd rather you sat down," he added when she made no move to do so.

156

Did he think what she'd let him do last night meant he now owned her?

"Okay, so you don't care about your ankle, but I don't enjoy addressing your back."

"Sorry about that, but *I'm* enjoying the view."

What the crew would make of the exchange, which had about it the overtones of a lovers' tiff, Dov did not allow himself to dwell upon.

"I'm also musing on what that slogan would mean to me if I saw it in my own country," Kate returned them to the subject they must have been relieved to assume she had dropped.

"And what did you come up with?" Dov was constrained to ask.

"I should probably think it *was* the ravings of some weirdo since, leaving God out of it, my life is already in my own hands."

"But in Israel, Kate, God can be left out of nothing," Dov informed her. "Rabbinical law is applied with a vice-like grip. For example, there's no such thing as civil marriage and divorce here, like in any other democracy. Israeli atheists, or agnostics – and our society, like yours, includes both – if they don't wish to be hypocrites going through the motions of a synagogue ceremony they don't believe in, usually fly to Cyprus to get married."

"What Dov is saying," Avrom chipped in, "is that here people don't have the choices they're entitled to. Religion rules across the board, which is fine for those who want it that way."

While Kate went on gazing at the sea lapping the shore, she learned from the men – and with feeling – that the majority of Israel's citizens *didn't* want it that way, but there was nothing they could do about it. Instead, they must knuckle under.

"We do have some Reform rabbis here, but they're not officially recognised," Chaim told her, "and they get given a hard time. Reform Judaism is booming all over the world, and keeping Jews within the fold because of its liberal doctrines. But it isn't allowed to exist in Israel, though increasing numbers of Israelis are turning to it. I'm not one of them, by the way, Kate. The only one of us who hasn't stuck with the traditional is Avrom."

Kate's theory that a Reform Judaism uprising might be in the offing was dashed to the ground immediately it had entered her mind.

"One way of getting you to sit down," Dov said to her, "would be to order you a fresh pot of tea."

"I've been known to drink my tea standing up. May we please continue the discussion? I'm finding it interesting."

He replied, "Since there's little else to add, why don't I give you a brief summing-up – and let me put it this way, Kate," he said tersely. "The vice-like grip I mentioned is increasingly tightening its hold. What I mean is there's more and more legislation that's heading Israel toward becoming a fundamentalist religious state like Iran."

Kate turned from the window, so appalled was she. "Do you really think that could happen?" Of course he did, and it had to be what the group was out to prevent. But it would be interesting to see how he fielded Kate's question.

"Me, I'm just a film-maker. But that's the way a lot of Israelis see it shaping up, and I would sure hate to see my country take that road."

With the ease Kate ought to have expected, and she must go on playing it his way till her delving was completed. She was pretty sure she now knew their goal – but nothing of their plans to achieve it. Would they, when the time came, employ terrorist tactics? Take hostages, and kidnap ultra-orthodox rabbinical leaders? Or worse? Kate thought of the possible contents of the padlocked trunk and managed not to shudder. Nor would she want to see *her* country take that road, but would she resort to violence to stop it from happening?

When, a couple of hours later, Kate watched Chaim and Avrom set up their equipment at Dizengoff Circle, it seeped through to her what her real function with the unit was.

Aviva had arranged for an area to be kept clear for them, and Dov made a point of introducing Kate to the police officer assigned to that duty, whose accent revealed his South African origin.

"Mrs. Starling is travelling the country with us," he added, "and she's finding my project a useful way of adding depth to her assignment."

If that wasn't what Jews called chutzpah, given his *secret* project, and he had said it to a cop – Dov Goldman was a cool customer. And Kate Starling's presence beside him a clever ploy. What you are, Kate, is part of the cover-up. Who'd invite a professional observer along if they were engaged in subversive activities?

Would the time come when Kate had no option but to blow the gaff? Rat on the man who had stirred in her feelings deeper than sex?

Since she valued her own freedoms, how could she not sympathise with his cause? A picture of the Ayatollah Khomeini and his mullahs laying down the law rose before her. Were there really clerics of that fanatical calibre in Israel, and was their power gathering force as Dov had implied?

The crowds had begun massing to watch the ceremony that preceded the night's revelry, and Kate saw the Tel Aviv equivalent of her local bigwigs seated together in readiness beneath the festive bunting visible everywhere.

All that's missing, she thought, surveying them, is a mayoral chain round that fat man's neck – no, one of the others was wearing it. And the women among them were dressed to the nines, like the ladies' committee at an English garden party. Some of the men wore yarmulkes and others didn't, she noticed.

"Give or take the trimmings, what you'll see here tonight goes on all over Israel," Dov told her.

"And the complexities of your society are beyond the understanding of a stranger." Kate glanced toward the

159

bigwigs. "The man you mentioned is a rabbi is sitting there having a chinwag with a bloke whose head isn't covered. You can't expect me not to find that confusing after what I learned from you and the others this afternoon — "

"Israel has more than one breed of rabbi, Kate. If you'd like to meet one of the dangerous kind – though he won't bat an eyelid at the guys and me being bareheaded – you'll have your chance when we're on location in the West Bank. Why don't we rest our legs?"

"My ankle, you mean!"

But when he looked at her like that – Kate averted her eyes from his and walked ahead of him to sit on the chair provided for her beside his.

Meanwhile the crowd had swelled. A plethora of miniature Israeli flags was being waved in the air. Tiny children were seated on adult shoulders. And the sea of faces, not to mention the noise, reminded Kate of her mother's description of Piccadilly Circus on the night the Second World War ended.

"I wouldn't be in the midst of that mêlée for all the tea in China," she said.

"And that's some statement from a tea addict."

They shared a laugh that helped dispel the strained aftermath of last night.

"Nor for all the tea in Ceylon," Kate added.

"It's been Sri Lanka for some time."

"But people still refer to tea from there as Ceylon. At home I don't use teabags, and if I asked at the place where I buy my tea for half-a-pound of Sri Lanka, they'd think I was being facetious. Why are you always trying to get one over me, Dov?"

"Why do you always think that's what I'm doing, Kate?"

More laughter followed, and evoked a quip from behind the camera which Chaim was loading to begin the shoot. "It's all right for some people!"

Avrom said from amid the lengths of cable he was uncoiling, "Isn't it time you two started work?"

160

"Wasn't your intention for us to begin talking to people *after* the ceremony?" Kate asked Dov.

"And the guys know it. They were there at the meeting, like you were."

But Kate had been too preoccupied to take in Dov's instructions for the shoot. Her gaze roved the crowd and stopped short. "I've just noticed some lads wearing white tee-shirts with that black hand graffiti on them, Dov — "

She had almost said "your slogan", and must watch her words when her own guard was down. Her relationship with Dov Goldman, with its two separate levels, was coming to feel like a cross between a balancing act and playing charades.

It must be the same for him, she registered, when he replied casually, "I've seen those tee-shirts all over the place."

Another ploy in the campaign to excite interest. And the revelation of what the graffiti stood for, and who was behind it, would doubtless be timed for when the subversives with whom Kate had unwittingly become involved took action. Given what they had told her, there would be no shortage of support, in a climactic upsurge reminiscent of the women of Britain rushing to buy "White Rain" shampoo.

It was, indeed, a clever campaign, and Kate silently apologised to Dov for presuming his having said so another display of his ego. Credit for its conception was due to whoever devised the poster build-up Chaim had recalled from way back.

But would the climax to which Kate was thinking ahead be allowed to happen? she conjectured with a shiver, as Chaim's camera focused upon the bigwigs and the ceremony began.

Dov had told her that in Jerusalem, President Herzog would head the official ceremony on Mount Scopus; and that the Old City's Jewish Quarter would tonight be the opposite of the quiet enclave it had seemed to her, though the form its inhabitants' celebrating would take was more like a scene from "Fiddler On The Roof", than a twentieth-century rave-up.

The people of Tel Aviv out on the town for *their* sort of rave-up were, however, respectfully hushed during the ceremony taking place in their city. And not just hushed. Kate was aware of a shared emotion, and wished she could understand the Hebrew words to which she was listening.

Then a great shout of joy split the air, as it doubtless had at that moment throughout this troubled land. As if Israel was triumphantly telling the world, "We've survived to enter our fortieth year."

Kate saw paper streamers being hurled in all directions; and that the crowd now stretched from Dizengoff Circle into the thoroughfares flanking it and along Dizengoff Street as far as the eye could see. Some of those watching the filming had party blowers. Children were wielding wooden rattlers like British football fans were wont to do. And teenagers – including one of those wearing a highly significant tee-shirt – had begun spraying the foam Kate was warned by the crew could ruin her clothing. But she wouldn't let that deter her from talking to those lads.

"Ready for the fray?" Dov said with a laugh.

"But let me tell you in advance, I'm not going beyond the perimeter of that crowd."

What a scene! Kate thought as she rose to accompany Dov. Israelis rejoicing as this morning they had stood silently with heads bowed. A transition so remarkable, Kate could not have believed it had she not seen it with her own eyes. But perhaps just another illustration of the will power responsible for there being a State of Israel.

"I can see you're impressed, Kate," Dov said, "and any foreigner would be. But on Tuesday, everyone will settle down to their everyday lives and nothing will have changed."

"Are you referring to what was discussed this afternoon?"

"Among other things. Okay, we're on our way," he called to the crew.

162

Kate put herself ahead of him and made for the lads with the group's slogan emblazoned on their chests. As her own kids had similarly helped boost Bob Geldof's Band Aid – but nobody could question the worthiness of *that* cause.

Her doing so did not surprise Dov, who allowed himself to construe it as a follow-up to what she had learned about the wall graffiti. Though Kate's latching on to it had briefly shaken him, the only way to handle it was as he had and still was doing.

In another way, it was a relief to have opened up to Kate, though she didn't know the score.

Instead of telling her – which professionally she knew – that it was he, not she, who decided whom they would interview, he lengthened his stride, reached the lads as she did, and immediately began chatting to them in Hebrew.

"Thanks for realising I'd want to speak to them," Kate said.

But there were too many things Dov was coming to realise about Kate Starling; including that, pleasant though she was being toward him tonight, it would take more than sending her two dozen red roses to compensate for *last* night.

"They're students, Kate, and say they speak some English – so you won't need me to interpret for you."

Kate gave them a smile and kept a wary eye on the can of foam.

"How nice to meet you," was by now her familiar preamble. "And I have to tell you," she went on, "that being among Israelis on your Independence Day Eve is something I shan't forget. Those are very striking tee-shirts you have on – I wouldn't mind taking one home for my son. Where would I get one from?"

Don't ever forget that snooping is her trade, thought Dov.

"I have not seen them in stores, have you?" a boy trying to grow a beard asked his friends.

"I did not go looking," said the one with his finger on the aerosol button. "Shall we be in your movie, Mr. Goldman?"

"Not if you squirt foam on me!" Dov said with a laugh.

"Didn't you know you can get in trouble for doing what you kids do with that stuff?"

"Once a year, who cares? And the army will soon keep me out of trouble."

A frizzy-haired girl, whom Kate had not realised was with the students, smiled at her and said, "Men might not to remember from where they get things, but me, I do. And how a person they could forget having something for free in Israel!"

The aerosol was then expertly aimed at the tiger's head adorning her own tee-shirt. "Who forgot? Batya, she is a big jumper to the mistaken conclusions," Kate and Dov were informed.

And a big jumper was the size she'd require. Kate forgave herself the pun and watched the girl take a handful of foam from the table of her bosom and plaster it on the offender's head. If Emily and Jason came home looking like these kids would tonight, she'd stop their pocket money for a month.

No, she wouldn't. She would try to remember she was once their age. Meanwhile, on with the delving. "Where *did* you get the tee-shirts from?" She smiled at Dov. "I really would like one for Jason. He likes the unusual kind, and has one with 'Mothers should be abolished' printed on it – which he expects *me* to wash for him!"

"I should like to have one of them for myself," said the lad with the aerosol, laughing as were his companions.

"But not if this lady was your mother," said the boy standing next to him, responding to Kate's easy manner.

"How nice of you to say that – but you don't have to live with me!"

Dov decided then that there sure was a box of tricks. Kate's next words confirmed that guile was indeed one of them.

"If I take my son a tee-shirt like yours, the one I mentioned might stop being his favourite," she said with a smile.

A boy who had not yet spoken, his hesitant use of English

164

indicating why, then revealed that a man with a carful of the tee-shirts had handed them out to the students outside their college.

"He was the fortunate person not to be trampled under the feet," said the boy with the aerosol. "Batya, she did not manage it to get one," he added squirting foam on the girl's hair.

Kate then found herself with the can in her hands.

"Would you please for a moment to hold it? Mr. Goldman I would not let to have it, he might not to return it to me."

"They've chalked you up as a disciplinarian, Dov."

"Evidently."

"What is that boy doing – ?"

"Taking off his tee-shirt, as you see."

A moment later it was being offered to Kate.

"For your son."

"I can't let you be so generous. He will have to do without one."

The aerosol was taken from her and firmly replaced by the grubby-looking garment. "Please to have it for him. And when you shall see him wear it, it will to remind you of Israel."

A too significant reminder. And with dried ketchup giving it a bloodstained appearance Kate hoped was not a portent.

"It will certainly remind me of how nice your young people are," she said to Dov when she had thanked the boy, and they moved on to talk to some people from whose expressions Dov Goldman's arrival beside them was as though the Messiah for whom the Jews were still waiting had come.

Since they did not speak English, Kate was not privy to his conversation with them, but the sacrilegious thought she had just had led her to ponder if that was how Dov Goldman saw himself. If so, he could be as potentially dangerous as those whom he opposed.

165

Chapter Four

Dov collected Kate from her hotel the following morning in a car she presumed that he or Shmuel had thoroughly checked.

"Shmuel managed to hire you a Volvo, I see," she remarked after they had set off.

"The terrain my work sometimes takes me to, I need a sturdy, reliable vehicle." Dov took the opportunity to say, "There's going to be big trouble for a certain garage mechanic, by the way."

Kate gazed through the window and let the prevarication pass. Until she had proof, it had to be keep your lips buttoned, Kate.

Meanwhile, even Ferdie, who had dealt with stories of all kinds in his long career in Fleet Street, would be sceptical of one based on coincidences, intuition, and a smattering of circumstantial evidence.

"Who do you and I have a date with in Jerusalem?" she inquired. "And why aren't the crew going with us?"

"Avrom has cousins he usually spends Independence Day with, and Shmuel, who has no relatives here, always gets invited to Chaim's."

Dov lit a cigarette and said pensively, "For most Israelis this is a family day. All the people you probably noticed walking along with bottles of wine, and candy boxes, are headed for get-togethers."

"You missed out the bunches of flowers." Dov's tone had impelled Kate to turn to look at him. "Who do you usually spend Independence Day with?"

"The people we're now on our way to." But it wasn't like

family, and you didn't stop being a family man because your wife and child were taken from you. "You look very elegant today, Kate, like the women you'll meet at the party I'm taking you to."

"In that case, by chance I haven't let you down. I thought it was going to be work." Kate had at the last minute decided that the day was too hot for jeans, and had put on a simple grey and white cotton dress. "Not that *I'd* call what I'm wearing elegant," she added.

"On most women possibly not. And what made you think it was work?"

"You didn't tell me it wasn't."

"Please believe the omission wasn't calculated. But would you have come if you'd known?"

"Probably not."

"I don't hear you asking me to turn around the car."

"Since we're already on our way, I shall make the most of an opportunity to meet some more Israelis."

"You never relax, do you?"

"I'd say that makes two of us." How could they, in the circumstances, relax with each other?

Dov said telepathically, "Today I'd like us to try to. What I'd also like is for you to give me another chance. I've been musing about that straight talking you did, on Saturday night."

Kate was surprised he'd had time to. But she knew from her own experience that personal matters had a way of remaining side by side with other preoccupations, however important the latter might be. Her remembrances of Moscow included battling to set things right for little Yuli, while simultaneously pondering her situation vis-à-vis Calvin.

"Who in the hell does she think she is? I thought," Dov went on.

"Well, you would, wouldn't you?"

"But where is that going to get me with a woman like you?"

"You choose your tactics according to the woman, do you? And that confirms what I said."

"All technique and no tenderness, is what you *actually* said."

"Or words to that effect."

They had left Tel Aviv behind and were now on the highway to Jerusalem, Kate again gazing out of the window so Dov would not see her expression.

"There seem to be more military vehicles around today than I recall noticing when I made this journey by sharut." A day of coincidences that weren't coincidences.

"Independence Day is also a time when resentment is liable to burst forth like pus from a boil," Dov replied. "And I, for one, am able to understand why for some of our Arabs, seeing us celebrate it is too much for them to bear."

Dov negotiated a bend in the road, and wished it were as simple for Israel to steer a safe course to resolving the insoluble problem that the Holy City epitomised. Insoluble because, whatever came or went, a lasting peace was impossible with Jerusalem emphatically part of Israel. One thing about which Israeli opinion *was* united was that such it would remain.

Kate had again turned to look at Dov and briefly her treacherous feelings had their way with her. How easy it would be to slip into the clutches of this man. But that hadn't yet happened to Kate, nor would she let it.

"In the Old City," he went on, "when sometimes I'm walking past Arabs lounging in their doorways, I see them looking at me with hooded eyes and it isn't because they envy the Savile Row suit I might perhaps be wearing."

"This is the first time I've seen you wearing a suit," Kate remarked. "And you like our British tailoring, do you? I'd have thought the best tailors in the world were right here," she added with a smile, "given the legendary association between Jews and that trade."

"A legend born of the times when tailoring was one reliable way a Jew could make his living, and if he had nimble fingers he was more fortunate than those gifted only with the brains to be what they never became. How would they have found the money for an education?"

Dov put out his cigarette and smiled. "But my father, who never experienced poverty – the Viennese and German Jews were streets ahead of their Russian and Polish brethren in that respect – once said that tailoring was the perfect trade for our people, since a man could just pocket his thimble and tape measure, and flee, whenever it was again necessary for him to move on."

"If that's a joke, I have to say I don't find it amusing."

"Well, you're not Jewish, are you? And not only is much of our in-humour based on truisms, it's invariably a joke at our own expense that we wouldn't appreciate if an outsider made it. Back with the tailors, Kate, sure we have good ones in Israel, and I don't get all my suits made in London. But next time I do, and I fly over for a fitting, I'll give you a call."

"Meanwhile I'm in *your* country," she parried, "and you were telling me why there are so many army vehicles around today."

"I thought I'd more than implied why," Dov said as some jeeps overtook them, "but if you'd like it in black and white – well, some people spend today picnicking in parks, or other public venues. At some places Members of the Knesset will take the opportunity to combine watching some folk dancing, or whatever, with putting in an appearance to do them some good at the next election. What I'm saying, Kate, is incidents are not unlikely, and police and military presence a useful deterrent."

What a way to have to live, thought Kate. Not just with the hovering threat of another war, but with the uncertainty that taking your kids to a park on a national holiday was safe.

"But where there's sure to be trouble today," Dov went on, "is the location we'll be at the week after next. I can't say that any of us is looking forward to that shoot. If you've never felt tension before, you sure will in the West Bank."

"Are you trying to scare me? If so, you're succeeding!"

"All I'm doing is preparing you. But before then you'll have a very different experience. When we shoot some footage at the kibbutz where I was born and spent my youth."

"I'm sure I'll find that interesting."

And Dov's mother would find Kate interesting: the more so if she detected her son's *special* interest in a gentile woman, he reflected with some trepidation.

"Are you planning to shoot in Gaza, too?" Kate inquired, overly aware that the word unavoidable in the film industry was right now one with fearsome connotations.

"How could the doc. I'm making be complete without Gaza? But the West Bank is scheduled first. And when you're in those territories, Kate, no strolling the streets alone, or you might not return."

Gooseflesh rose on Kate's arms.

"Like you did the night we stopped over in Nazareth," said Dov.

"How did you know that?"

It was a night when they had all retired early, but Kate had found her room stuffy and gone out for a breath of air.

Dov's reply was light. "You'd be surprised what I know."

Oh no I wouldn't. Kate's mind swooped back to the "coincidences" that had preceded their first meeting. Seeing Dov in the Bazaar, a girl on each arm. His being at the Holocaust Museum when she was. His presence beside the desk when she got back to her hotel that evening. Though the explanation for the knowledge he'd just revealed could be simply that he had seen her from the window of his room, together with the rest it smacked of Kate's being under surveillance. It occurred to her now that the group might have already established a lower echelon of activists, one of whom was assigned to watching Kate's movements. That Dov himself had not done the tedious job of tailing her before making the offer, but had prearranged with whomever to be kept informed so he could pop up here and there as he had, and eventually call her with that corny opening gambit, "We really must stop not-meeting like this!"

The tailing, however, had to have an additional purpose, and what could that be but Dov Goldman's having Kate Starling checked out, lest she have contacts in Israel that could do his cause no good? The offer would not then have been made.

Kate gave Dov an angry glance, which fortunately he did not see, since she intended to go on using *him*. When had she stopped thinking of him as Goldman, and begun thinking of him as Dov? Whenever, it marked the moment when he had scored on one level, though she was determined to win on the other.

And here we go again, she reflected wryly, doing our balancing act. The attraction between them pulsating as it had from the first and intensified by the close confines of the car, Kate still hoping that all it was for her *was* physical attraction, and sure that was so for him. And each with a purpose unrelated to what we feel.

As on her previous ride to Jerusalem, Kate was affected by the majesty of the terrain, which last time had set her thoughts on a biblical track that had not yet encompassed Samson and Delilah. A woman now dead, whom Kate had not then known would enter her life, had later introduced that theme; one increasingly credible as the days passed by, given Kate's duplicity.

Make up your mind if Dov believes himself Samson reincarnated, or the long awaited Messiah, Kate! "You didn't finish what you were saying about the West Bank," she prodded him from wherever his thoughts had strayed.

"We do seem to digress with each other, don't we?"

How Kate would put that, was that they stepped back and forth from one level of their relationship to the other. And if one of us comes a cropper, it isn't going to be me.

"There's something else we digressed from," Dov said, "and I'll get back to it in a minute. About the West Bank, fireworks and not the celebratory sort are anticipated there

171

today. Some of the militant settlers who've established a presence there intend an Independence Day march that will be to the Arabs who watch it incendiary to say the least."

"It certainly sounds like lunacy," Kate agreed.

"Which many here think applies to them putting themselves where they have. Their literal interpretation of the Bible is as big a snag to a peace process as the PLO's attitude."

Dov paused reflectively. "And if what we glibly refer to as the territories were to be bartered for peace — well, our government would then be faced with having to forcibly uproot their own people. Some have now lived there for two decades, and all of them would lay down their lives for Judaea and Samaria."

Kate visualised the settlers being dragged from their homes, and the bricks and mortar bulldozed to rubble in their presence. She did not let herself dwell on the possibility that this might have to be done at gunpoint.

Her reply to Dov was, "The picture you just painted is unthinkable in a democracy. And I wouldn't like to be an Israeli soldier ordered to do what could be necessary."

"One way and another, Kate, some have already had a taste of it. The function of the IDF is no longer exclusively the defence force those initials stand for, I regret to say. In the Yom Kippur War — "

"Was that the 1973 one?"

"None other, and Israel the aggressor. A role few Israelis, in or out of uniform, find palatable. And viewed now – that war, I mean – by most as a misjudgement that blotted our copybook."

That has to be why it's rarely mentioned, Kate was thinking when Dov referred to another such blemish.

"As for the massacre a certain Israeli hawk allowed the Lebanese Christian Militia to perpetrate on their own soil – there was an outcry in the streets here about it, and our cheeks haven't stopped burning with shame."

Kate glanced absently out of the window as they drove

past the disused military vehicles now a memorial to the battle for Jerusalem, which the young girl in the sharut had pointed out to her, and said after a pause, "I doubt there's a country in the world with nothing to be ashamed of."

"But an extra dimension is attached when the country is Israel," Dov replied.

"Why should it be?"

"We're Jews, aren't we?"

"A chip on your shoulder, Dov, if I may say so."

"And not without reason. An outrage, believe me, is a bigger outrage if Israel commits it. If you can supply a better explanation for that than mine, let me know."

They fell silent until they reached the outskirts of Jerusalem and entered a suburb where an estate of mellow stone homes was set, terrace upon terrace, in the hilly terrain.

Dov pulled up the car to allow a family, whose appearance implied their religiosity, to cross the road, and Kate remarked, "That couple look like teenagers dressed up in their grandparents' clothes." But the girl was pregnant, and two small children were helping the boy push a pram.

Dov told her that youthful married couples of that ilk made their homes in closed communities with their own kind. "And what it amounts to," he added wryly, "is perpetuating the ghetto existence the rest of Jewry struggled to escape from."

Another paradox among the many Kate had observed. "What category of Israeli would they fall into?" she inquired.

His response was rueful. "Since every category has its subdivisions, I long ago lost count. And before we arrive at the party I'm taking you to — "

"Let me thank you now for thinking of it."

"Cut the formality, Kate, and let me say what I tried to before we began grasshopping to other topics. I didn't sleep a wink on Saturday night — "

Nor had Kate, but he wouldn't have the satisfaction of learning it.

"After you left," he went on, "well, I began seeing what you'd meant – The women I've known since I was widowed expected no more of me than I did of them, and I never allowed an affaire to last long, lest the woman *began* expecting more."

He paused to light a cigarette – given the subject, a humiliating reminder for Kate that he had stood smoking between her legs. And if he thought the line he was now handing her the route to positioning himself there again —

"What I'm saying is I'm not the kind to feign tenderness — "

"And you certainly didn't with me."

"Look – this is going to sound terrible to you, Kate – but having sex long ago became for me no different than eating a meal when I'm hungry."

"I could have told you I got that impression and saved you a sleepless night of self-examination."

"Since I already knew it, that wasn't what the self-examination was about. The big question was how had I got that way? Do you know what used to happen to ponies when they were used in coal mines, Kate?"

"They went blind. What has that to do with this?"

"From not using their sight. And I can't think of a more fitting parallel for what I think's happened to me."

Dov turned the car into a leafy avenue, pulled up, and said after a silence during which he sat gazing through the windscreen. "I have to make this clear to you, or I won't enjoy the party."

"That's a good enough reason, I suppose."

"But not the sole one. Technique without tenderness you said. But like the ponies not using their sight and ending up blind, tenderness toward a woman is long gone from my life."

Since he had not turned to look at her, it was necessary for Kate to address his profile.

"Are you telling me you've lost the emotional capacity?"

He switched his gaze from an unoccupied Ford parked

ahead of them to Kate. "I'm asking for the chance to prove it isn't irretrievable."

"With me as the guinea pig? No thanks."

"Please don't do this to us, Kate."

"I wouldn't constitute refusing to collaborate in your experiment detrimental to myself. You certainly have a nerve, Dov, and — "

The rest of Kate's sentence was, like her feeble protest on Saturday night, cut short by a kiss. But this time she mustered the strength to push him away.

"Please, Kate. I need you."

Both his words and his tone surprised Kate into letting him gather her close. Nor could she stop herself from putting her arms around him.

Though Kate's heart was thudding, at that moment desire was absent and she knew it was the same for Dov. As if his unexpended emotion had begun pouring forth once he'd pulled the self-imposed stopper out. And what else was the two-way feeling now flowing between them but what Kate would rather it were not?

They were still quietly holding each other when two sets of youthful parents went by, casting censorious glances at the spectacle within the car and hurrying their respective offspring out of corruption's way.

"What must they think of us, Dov?"

"Probably that we're residents of Tel Aviv who should be arrested for sullying their neighbourhood."

And if Dov's worst fears weren't prevented from materialising, such was the sort of country Israel would be, he wanted to add. But there were thoughts he couldn't share with the woman with whom he now knew he wanted to share everything. The irony was if she weren't a foreign journalist, he wouldn't have made use of her and found himself in this situation.

"What are friends of yours doing living in this neighbourhood?" Kate asked, since she couldn't imagine them being older versions of those disapproving youngsters.

"They don't," Dov replied. "We were early, so I took a detour."

"And we shall now probably be late."

They exchanged their first smile of rapport, then Kate disentangled herself from his embrace.

"I had better fix my hair."

"But how lovely you look with it disarrayed."

While Kate searched in her bag for a comb, Dov started the car and returned them to the main road, where more young families, some with their elders accompanying them, were strolling along.

"This district of Jerusalem is Mea Shearim," he told Kate.

"And I couldn't help noticing how happy its inhabitants seem. No – happy isn't the right word, it implies they all have smiles on their faces. It's just something about them. I think untroubled fits the impression I got."

"Well, they've given themselves into God's keeping, haven't they?" said Dov. "And that's fine by me. Like I said, I'm a tolerant guy. The little boys will grow up to want no more from life than their fathers and grandfathers do. Studying the Torah is a thriving industry here."

"What a way to put it!"

"But in effect true. The government not only sponsors it, but considers it of such priority, Torah students are exempted from military service – though there's a Yeshivah in the West Bank where they don't choose to be exempted."

"Is that the Hebrew word for a rabbinical college?"

It struck Dov then that it wouldn't be easy for Kate ever to stop feeling an outsider in Israel. Learning Hebrew would help, but in other respects —

"The students don't necessarily become clergymen," he explained. "In Israel, studying the Torah is considered an end in itself and some devote their entire lives to it."

"How do they support themselves and their families?" Kate wanted to know.

Dov now felt as the crew sometimes did when conversing with Kate, that she was interviewing him for her articles.

But she was too, the woman who could be to him, if he let it happen, both lover and friend. Since friendship implied trust, for the foreseeable future, however, the completeness he yearned for was out.

"You said the government sponsors what we're discussing. Does that mean the students get a grant?" she prodded him while fixing her smudged lipstick.

"Sure. And some who made aliyah from wealthy families are helped out by their parents. But most of the colleges were built with money provided by orthodox philanthropists, mainly American. At the other end of the pole, a fairly recent addition to the Jerusalem downtown scene is an Institute representing the Reform Judaism that doesn't officially exist here."

"Who put up the money for that?"

Why don't you just drop by there and ask them? Dov almost said. But when would she, now, have time to? Though accepting his offer was providing insights she might not otherwise have gained, he hadn't until now given a thought to the detailed information a journalist required; or to the necessity for its accuracy. He hadn't cared a damn about her assignment.

Dov then came face to face with his own ruthlessness, as Kate had, before accepting the offer, with her own ambition. Okay, so he would try to be more helpful to *her* work. But let's not forget that you're still not sure she isn't on to you.

Thus the two continued what Kate had reflected was their balancing act, the more precarious now for the feeling they had let flow between them.

"I can't tell you the exact source of the cash for that Institute," Dov replied to Kate's question, "and I think what it's actually called is the Hebrew Union College, probably because Reform is under the same umbrella with Liberal and Progressive Judaism."

Kate had been briefly immersed in her personal misgivings and said, collecting herself, "I didn't mean for you to have to rack your brains, Dov."

What he had actually been doing was subjecting himself to some more self-examination. "You're welcome to *pick* my brains, Kate."

But unfortunately not on the matter that yawned like a cavern Kate must somehow cross. Meanwhile, while wishing Dov's arms were still around her, she went on discussing religious philanthropy, which was as good a topic as any other right now, and learned that the college under discussion would doubtless have been erected via money from an American benefactor.

Dov capped this with a dry remark and a smile. "I can imagine Jerusalem's overwhelmingly orthodox Jews walking past that place as if it isn't there."

"What you mean is they hope, if they don't acknowledge it, it will go away — "

"What it stands for, too."

But once something has taken root it was there to stay. Did that also apply to affairs of the heart? Kate asked herself, aware that though hers had stopped thudding, what Dov had stirred in her was still disturbingly there.

They had just driven by the King David Hotel, and Dov, still penitent about not having considered Kate's assignment, told her that the hotel had been the British army's headquarters at the time when the advent of the State of Israel was hastened by Jewish terrorists destroying the headquarters with a bomb.

"Would you have agreed with such tactics?" she took the opportunity to ask him.

"Since I was just a schoolkid at the time, I'm not in a position to be judgemental now," he replied.

And employed his own tactic of changing the subject, thought Kate when he began talking about the party his friends always gave on Independence Day.

"The buffet will be loaded with goodies and the wine will flow, Kate. So why not put away your invisible notebook when we get there and enjoy it?"

"Since I'm here to report my impressions," she said

returning his smile, "I'd be falling down on my job if I did as you've requested. What sort of people, in addition to the elegant ladies you mentioned, shall I be rubbing shoulders with?"

"I suggest you wait and see. And it isn't a by-invitation date, it's open house for any of their friends who can make it."

Kate's reaction to that was, "The hostess could find herself with leftover food, or not enough — "

"Since she's the kind who goes over the top with everything, the latter couldn't happen."

"And the leftovers, if there are any, could of course go into her deep freeze," Kate revealed the domestic aspect of her womanliness to Dov. "Is she a career woman?"

"She's a highly successful lawyer, Kate."

"And is the host in the film business, like you?"

"No, his work is more in his wife's line. He's a police inspector."

Kate did a mental double-take.

"We served together in the '67 war and stayed in touch, though we afterwards went our very different ways."

Very different indeed. Nor would Kate put it past Dov to exert his charm to infiltrate the police force. How far had the network she had initially thought just a small group by now spread?

Wide enough for the identity of the man behind it to have leaked to whoever thought it necessary to cut him down, Kate privately reiterated her fears while he turned the car into the grounds of an imposing block of flats and parked it.

"I wouldn't have thought a police inspector's earnings sufficient for him to live in a place like this," she remarked casually. What a good actress she had found herself capable of being.

"But this one is married to a lady of means," Dov replied. "When I first met Yaacov and Naomi, she was still a student, and they were living in a one-room apartment smaller than the bathroom they now have. Naomi knew what she was doing when she chose commercial law for her speciality."

Dov got out of the car and came to open Kate's door for her. Was he going to leave it here unattended? So the two of them might be victims of failed brakes, or whatever, on the way back to Tel Aviv?

Kate was distracted from her anxiety by Dov's then taking from the car boot the biggest box of chocolates she had ever seen, and that too matched his image. "If you're making such a magnificent gesture," she said with a laugh, "you might have had the box gift wrapped."

"Where I bought them, they'd run out of fancy paper."

"And would they, anyway, have had a sheet large enough?"

"Okay, so I spare no expense on those I care about," Dov defended his extravagance. And if he ever bought Kate a ring, it had better be one of her choosing, he thought, as her presence beside him in this peaceful grassy setting, the sun shining beneficently upon them, briefly allowed him to cast aside all else.

Kate, however, was more aware of the sun's heat. "If we don't go in, those chocolates will melt, Dov."

An indication of how practical Kate was and he was not, right now, being. Dov Goldman had no time to fall in love, and certainly not with a woman he didn't trust – but that didn't mean he hadn't.

As they made their way to the apartment building, feet crunching on sparkling white gravel, Kate noticed that one of the several parked cars was occupied by a young man reading a newspaper. If he was still there when they emerged, it could mean he was minding Dov's car. Conversely —

Dov took her arm and gave her a smile, cutting short her gory conjectures. Whatever else he was, Dov Goldman wasn't foolhardy. That young bloke had to be one of his operatives. And his beaky profile was vaguely familiar . . .

They were riding in the lift to the penthouse when Kate

dredged from the motley recollections of her day alone in Jerusalem, visiting the Garden of Gethsemane, and the stillness of that quiet haven being suddenly shattered by some Italian tourists. A large party, and all of them gabbling away, as they brushed past her while she stood looking at the ancient olive trees. Trailing along behind them had been beaky-face, whom Kate had assumed was one of them. Oh yes, Kate had very definitely been tailed before the offer was made to her!

She stemmed a resurgence of the anger that had gripped her in the car, when that probability had occurred to her. Kate had been under constant surveillance in Moscow and had not anticipated being prey to that treatment – or its effect upon her – ever again.

How dare Dov Goldman have a British journalist tailed! Stay cool, Kate. But if it wouldn't put paid to her own close surveillance of him and his Black Hand group, she would have it out with him here and now. And sooner or later, she would have to contrive to do some tailing of her own.

Meanwhile, the heck with it, she would try to enjoy this party, she resolved when they joined the noisy throng in an apartment whose spaciousness and lavish furnishing implied that the hostess believed in living up to her income.

A panoramic view of the Old City was visible through a picture window spanning an entire wall. Sofas and armchairs of soft white leather were companionably grouped, though most of the guests were standing in clusters, glasses of red wine in their hands. Since the carpet, too, was white, Kate contemplated the possible spillage when the party got going. And the collection of modern art with which the walls were adorned gave her the feeling she was attending a preview exhibition in a classy gallery.

Naomi proved to be a petite woman with silver streaks in her short black hair, her vivid red silk dress singling her out from the crowd.

She came to greet Dov, and when he had introduced Kate to her – complete with credentials – gave Kate a somewhat contemplative glance, before making an announcement in Hebrew to her guests.

"What is she telling them, Dov?"

"About you and your assignment. Those who speak English will probably be lining up to talk to you!"

"How very kind of her."

And how crafty of Dov to bring me to a gathering like this.

"That white-haired guy in the corner is a judge," he told her, "and the woman he's chatting to is a government press attaché."

"Are they friends of yours?"

"Just acquaintances."

But their presence confirmed the reason for Kate's, she thought uncharitably. With a British journalist in its midst, Dov's unit couldn't be a cover for something subversive. Had he brought Kate lest any of the influential people here suspected him? Well, the evidence that there'd been a leak was all too real and Aviva in her grave because of it.

While Naomi was asking Dov how the film was going, Kate glanced around at the guests; and if appearances were what they seemed, she'd say that several different strata of Israeli society were represented here. Among the elegant women were some who looked arty, and there were men, too, who qualified for that label. Others, male and female, had the aura of academics. Given Naomi's legal speciality, those who looked like business executives probably were; and her husband's profession allowed Kate to wonder if the two blokes conversing together, who seemed out of key with the rest of the gathering, might be his subordinates, who would rather have spent this national holiday else-where.

"My husband, he is in his study taking the telephone call," Naomi told Kate.

"When was there ever a party when Yaacov didn't spend most of it on the phone?" said Dov with a smile. "And not just at his own parties, Kate. He does it at mine, too."

"But Kate, she shall to meet him soon. I shall go now to

tell him we have with us a distinguished guest from Britain. Please, now, the both of you to have some wine and also some food."

"Some of the men are wearing yarmulkes on their heads," Kate observed as they went to a table groaning with goodies as Dov had promised.

"In Israel, why would that surprise you?"

"I somehow got the impression that the people you mix with weren't in the least religious."

Dov handed her a plate – which she recognised as the Rosenthal china she couldn't afford.

"The only answer I can give you to that, Kate, is I'll mix with anyone who's prepared to mix with me. And wearing a yarmulke doesn't in every case signify intolerance."

He carved a slice of the giant turkey for her, and watched her help herself from the vast assortment of salads, adding tersely, "Unfortunately, Israel doesn't equate with this gathering."

Kate thought it time to lighten up. "What did you do with your magnificent gesture?"

"I left it on the hall table."

"How will Naomi know it's from you?" Silly question!

"It's where that thing she calls a sculpture was standing, and the thing is now on the floor. That's an annual joke between Naomi and me, she knows what I think of her taste in modern art."

Dov filled his own plate and glanced at the walls. "I couldn't live with those paintings, could you?"

"No, as a matter of fact, though they must have cost the earth."

"Some of the artists are present, Kate, so let's be careful to keep our opinion to ourselves!" he said with a laugh.

"You hadn't struck me as a man who'd spare another's feelings."

"But you don't yet know me, do you?"

With that, he led her into the midst of the throng, some of which had now spilled over on to the terrace outside the picture window, and Kate began to enjoy what was to prove a stimulating afternoon.

One in which she became aware that Dov – since many greeted him as they would an old friend – mixed with people of all shades of opinion. Kate noted, too, that though these were hotly expressed and debated, rancour was absent.

When a professor whom she learned was active in the Peace Now movement was referred to in his presence as an "Arab-lover", Dov smiled and said to her, "This is typical of Israeli get-togethers, Kate. Every citizen is an armchair politician, a philosopher too. Did you expect the professor to sock the other guy?"

"Since he's a peace activist, not really."

Kate was then engaged in conversation by a woman doctor, and subjected to a quizzing about Britain's National Health Service.

"Is it true they are shutting the hospital wards for lack of finance?"

Kate set aside loyalty to her country and told the truth, after which she was cornered by a Member of the Knesset wanting to know why the *Guardian* had lost sympathy with Israel.

"What makes you think it has?"

"As well as to speak some English, I am able to read it. And for what other reason would the British Jews of my acquaintance have said to me that they no longer take that newspaper?"

"I've always had a lot of respect for the *Guardian*," Kate replied.

She was told with asperity by the leathery-complexioned old man, "And once I agreed with you, as did my British friends."

"Lost sympathy" was how he had put it. But where, in Kate's profession, did impartiality begin and end? It was that for which her training had taught her to strive and sometimes, like the position in which she now found herself vis-à-vis Dov's cause, no simple matter. A journalist was just a person with sympathies and viewpoints, like the public whom their occupation empowered them to influence.

"May I get for you some more wine?"

"No, thank you."

"Our Israeli wine is not to your taste?"

This conversation was beginning to feel like an inquisition. "It's delicious, but my head is already swimming," she said with a smile. Dov was no longer at her side, nor was he within sight. How was she, without appearing rude, to escape from her inquisitor?

"I understand you have here visited an absorption centre."

"I was actually visiting a Russian friend."

"Who has told to you that they are feeling depressed?"

"She appeared to me to have good reason to be."

"And that you shall print in your paper?"

Kate was finally rescued by her hostess, who took her arm and led her to an unoccupied alcove – well, unoccupied except for another of the sculptures like the one in the hall, only this one was taller than Naomi and resembled, if on a larger scale, the Lego structures Kate's son had put together when he was five.

"You and me, Kate," said Naomi, "we have not yet had the little chat."

Kate's instinct told her she was about to receive another warning-off. Was Dov having an affair with his friend's wife? Kate wouldn't put it past him. Or, at the very least, that a past affaire he had brushed off, and Naomi hadn't, was responsible for Kate's now being surveyed from head to toe by this striking-looking woman lawyer.

Naomi fingered one of the jet earrings that matched her necklace and the ring on her little finger. "I do not know how to put this to you, Kate — "

But she was going to.

"Dov Goldman, he is not the one-woman man — "

"Since my relationship with him is professional, why tell me?" Kate prevaricated.

"There is no such thing as only professional, when the man is he whom we are discussing, and the woman she is one like you. Beautiful – and for once I am able to compliment him – also intelligent."

Almost, if not quite, a repetition of Aviva's anxiety. The Samson and Delilah theme.

"I am not myself in love with Dov, as you are possibly thinking," said Naomi. "Yaacov, he has been all-in-all to me since the day, in our youth, when we met. And I to him. That is never going to change."

Then the reason for Naomi's concern had to be Aviva's reason minus the jealousy. Which indicated how widespread was Dov's underground network. And Kate now had no doubt that it did indeed include her police inspector host who, as far as she knew, was still closeted in his study. She had yet to be introduced to him.

"What I am telling to you," Naomi resumed, "is, in addition to that you could get hurt, the project Dov he is now working on, it is of importance not just for himself, but for Israel."

Well put, thought Kate. And the double entendre contained in it extended – if you were in the know – to Kate's being told she could get hurt. "I'll bear in mind everything you've said," she replied, feigning a smile.

"And I have for you a message from Dov. He has received a telephone call on a matter necessitating his immediate return to Tel Aviv. But he wishes you to continue sharing our Independence Day celebration, and will send for you the car to return you to your hotel."

Kate's first reaction was, Which of the crew had died a violent death? Her second was fury. How dare Dov Goldman abandon her among people she didn't know, and without a second thought!

Kate spent the evening alone in her hotel room, beset by anxiety and anger in equal measure. While part of her continued to seethe about Dov's not having given her the option of returning to Tel Aviv with him, her concern grew, lest Aviva's fate had befallen another of the unit.

Had she known Chaim's phone number, she might have dialled it, to make sure his home hadn't been blown up, with him and Shmuel in it.

But how many evenings had she, by now, spent pacing the floor, or gazing pensively into space, her thoughts centred upon Dov Goldman and the repercussions of the man he was?

Was that man a visionary, or a manipulative power-seeker? Whichever, he had become for Kate two men. One the public spellbinder and private philanderer. The other the man who had held her close in a parked car in Jerusalem that afternoon.

She stopped herself from calling his suite at the Dan, and when by midnight she had not heard from him went to bed, if not to sleep.

The phone on her bedtable rang at five a.m.

"Hi, Kate, it's Shmuel."

"What're you doing disturbing my slumbers?" she lied.

"Dov's just decided we're heading for the kibbutz two hours from now. He asked me to let you know."

Nobody was maimed or dead. Dov's abrupt departure and this dawn phone call were just his usual treatment. When Dov Goldman beckoned, everyone ran to his bidding. And Kate Starling, her delving not yet completed, had no option but to join them.

How could she be in love with such a man?

PART FOUR

CHAPTER ONE

Leah Goldman was seated on her verandah, her pensive gaze spanning the valley betwixt the Golan Heights and Syria, when Dov took Kate to meet her.

When she rose to embrace her son, Kate saw that she was a tall woman, and with the sturdiness that bespoke her pioneer youth. There was about her too something of the quality – enhanced by wispy hair scraped back into a bun – of Golda Meir who, like Dov's mother, was of the generations whose bare hands had laid the foundation for what was then but a dream.

Golda had risen to be Prime Minister and, thought Kate, would've had to have been not just a strong woman, but an ambitious one. Another Maggie Thatcher. Though Kate had not yet exchanged a word with Leah Goldman, she sensed that hers was the selfless inner strength without which the land now Israel would not have been transformed from a near-wilderness.

Though the emotional reunion between mother and son lasted no longer than a minute, Kate had time to cast her eye at the steep incline above which the small bungalow where Dov was raised was situated. Was that the once-rocky climb his father had to make with a young wife in labour in his arms? And had the tent Dov was born in been pitched where the house now was?

The verdant environs, and the kibbutz itself – a place of well-laid pathways, with a tranquil rose garden, and a sizeable swimming pool – were hard to relate to the thoughts Kate had just had. And what was it but a microcosm of the achievement against the odds Kate had observed on all sides?

Whatever the rest of the world finds to criticise about Israel, they should also take off their hats to her, Kate was thinking when Dov said "Sorry about the hiatus, Kate! Mother and I haven't seen each other for some time."

"My son is a busy man," Leah said with a smile. And after Dov had introduced them, "So you have come to Israel to afterwards tell the world what you think of us?"

A remark that, given Kate's final thought, seemed somewhat uncanny. It was, however, the same reaction to Kate's assignment as Barbara's mother-in-law had expressed. As if Israelis assumed their country to be ever on trial. The chip Kate had told Dov was on his shoulder, and he'd replied it wasn't without reason. Were there grounds for it? Kate had to admit that possibility, but thought the Jewish psyche, born of their history, equally responsible.

"I told you where we'd find my mother, didn't I?" Dov said with a laugh that hid the sadness seeing her alone on her verandah always evoked in him.

"To sit peacefully and remember, it is one of the pleasures of old age," Leah replied.

But Kate had not failed to notice the bunker dug deep below ground, where young kibbutznik mothers had sheltered fom Arab attack when they were children, still there in readiness should *their* children require whisking to safety.

When they had walked past it, Kate had glanced at its heavy protective cover, and wondered what it must be like to live with that constant reminder. Have to pass it each time you walked to the communal dining room. The kibbutzniks probably didn't notice it. Like people whose homes were close to an airport said you stopped noticing the noise of the aircraft. But all that meant was you were trying not to.

While Dov went inside the bungalow to fetch the jug of iced tea his mother had made before their arrival, and Leah Goldman engaged her in what felt like polite conversation, Kate mused, too, on how Dov had managed to point out the school as if it had no personal significance for him. It occurred to her, now, that tragedy and bereavement, on a level beyond the natural pattern of life, had become something Israelis took in their stride, whatever their private pain; that the hardness many displayed was a personal armour.

Kate was seated beside Leah Goldman on the swing couch suspended beneath a faded striped awning, sharing with her the magnificent view Dov had promised, and registering that his mother's accent had remained, when she spoke English, that of a well-educated Viennese.

It was difficult, however, for Kate to visualise the old lady as a product of that genteel continental background. How had she made the transition from stylish frocks and hats? From the Viennese waltz to the Horah, a robust and noisily executed dance Kate had seen some people enjoying at the Moshav location, their arms on each other's shoulders to form a huge circle, and their voices singing out the words of the accompanying song.

Kate had been surprised to learn from the Rosses that the Horah was often danced at sophisticated Jewish weddings and Bar Mitzvahs in Britain and the States; and that Barbara had once broken the stiletto heel of an evening shoe joining in the dance that had, since the Zionist dream was born, epitomised it, and now its fruition, for Jews everywhere.

Her conjecture led her to ask Leah Goldman if she and her husband had ever considered leaving the kibbutz to make their home in a city.

"Why would we wish to?"

"I've heard that many people do."

"But that is nowadays. And shall I tell you for why?"

The old lady absently twisted her wedding ring, palm upward, and Kate saw the calloused evidence that this was indeed a woman who had worked side by side with the men. Had equality reigned in other respects? Probably; in circumstances when neither male nor female had time for the norms of society. Women's Lib before its time, and on a practical level that brooked no argument. Kate had friends active in the Women's Movement, and smiled at the mere idea of their clearing rocks, not to mention shifting boulders.

"What is there now here for the young to strive for?" Leah Goldman resumed. "It is they who are doing the leaving. For the middle-aged it is now too late, though they still have the years. What they might have done with their brains was set aside because hands were what was then needed."

"Where do the young people go to when they leave?" Kate inquired.

"Some, they join with others, and with new young immigrants, to found a kibbutz, or a moshav, of their own." Leah flicked a fly from the skirt of her shapeless print dress, and remarked that the insects had remained difficult for her to live with. "Others," she went on, "are attracted by the bright lights that were not there to distract their grandparents. In my time, of course, there was not here a city like Tel Aviv. And such a city was not envisaged by me and my friends. Of a nation living together like one big kibbutz, is to describe it to you what we dreamed of — "

The dream again. "I expect you found it hard to come to terms with how things turned out."

Leah's silent shrug said more than words. "A person must live with their disappointments, Mrs. Starling."

"Please call me Kate. Dov is a long time getting that cold tea, isn't he?"

"My son has probably forgotten his errand and is looking through the family snapshot album. There are beautiful pictures in it of his wife and daughter. Of his father also."

Kate opened her bag and showed Dov's mother the snaps of Emily and Jason she had not shown him, nor had he asked to see them.

Leah took her spectacles from her skirt pocket and put them on. "Your girl, she is much like you — " she said scanning the photographs. "But the boy I would not have thought was yours."

"Jason has his father's colouring."

"And your husband, he is a journalist like you?"

"He's a pharmacist, and not my husband any more."

Since Kate was not alone in her endowment with a womanly sixth sense, an alarm bell then rang in Leah Goldman's perceptions. What was there between Dov and this gentile Englishwoman? And was his taking so long to fetch a jug of tea from the refrigerator just putting off telling his mother what she would not wish to hear?

"Please to excuse me," she said to Kate, "I had not noticed there is no ring upon your finger."

But Kate had noticed a sudden change in the atmosphere – as if Dov's mother had become wary of her. Put that together with the old lady's learning Kate was divorced.

Dov then appeared with the tea and some glasses on an ancient-looking tin tray, which he set down on the small, plastic table without apologising for his lengthy absence, and Kate could not but contrast his lifestyle with his mother's.

Indeed, she thought while they drank the cold beverage, and some small talk went back and forth between mother and son, it was as hard to relate Dov to his background as his mother to whence she had sprung. But going up in the world, thought Kate, was more easy to adapt to than settling, idealist or not, for less than you'd once had.

"I am sorry, Kate, that my home has in it only one spare bedroom, or I would ask you to stay, while Dov's unit is filming at the kibbutz, here with him and me."

"That's a kind thought," Kate replied, "but I shall be quite comfortable where I've been accommodated."

Since this was not one of the several kibbutzim that catered for tourists, there was no guest house where the unit could stay under one roof. Dov's being a son of the kibbutz had, however, ensured two bungalows somehow being made available.

Kate had thought – with a resurgence of yesterday's anger – that his being the famous Dov Goldman would doubtless have ensured it anyway.

"How long shall my son be with me this time?" Leah asked him.

"Long enough for you and Kate to get to know each other."

A reply that caused both to sit up.

In the days and nights that followed, Kate allowed herself to be lulled into a sense of well-being she knew could not last. The quiet ambience of the kibbutz, and the friendliness of those with whom the unit ate in the large dining room, were as balm to her soul. Her observing them at work did not give the impression they were putting on a show for the film, or for her. Nor their easy hospitality, when she and Dov drank coffee with this couple or that on their pleasant verandahs, with nought but the sound of a neighbour mowing his patch of lawn disturbing the evening stillness.

Since Dov's mother retired early, after saying goodnight to her there remained some time to while away, before they themselves bade each other goodnight in public, and later came together in Kate's borrowed bungalow. Nor was it, ever again, the coming together their first had been.

Instead, it was as if the time break between their closeness in the car and Dov's taking Kate in his arms the following night had not happened. Though his knocking on her door was not prearranged, opening it to him had seemed to Kate the progression of love to its natural fulfilment.

Since then, she had let herself be carried by its tide toward whatever destiny. She had not felt like this about Alun, in her youth; and her doubt that what she had briefly felt for Calvin, in Moscow, was love, had indicated that it wasn't. And come what may, she thought while Dov slept, his head upon her breast, on their last night at the kibbutz, she would have this tranquil interlude, with the man she loved, to remember.

Though Dov had not told his mother he had finally met Rivka's replacement, the old lady's perception had required no verbal confirmation. Did her son think his mother didn't

196

hear him creep from the house late at night, and return when dawn was filtering in through her bedroom curtains? When he grew old himself, he would learn that elderly people were light sleepers. But it was wisest to pretend deafness; blindness also. From early childhood, Dov had shown himself to have a mind of his own. A loving son, but one who if you told him to do "that" would do the other. Leah was mindful, too, of the unthinkable possibility of a rift with her son in the autumn of her years.

When Dov came to bid her farewell, she would again – but this time on purpose – be where and how he said he always thought of her. Let the picture of his mother on the verandah of the home she had helped his father build, and all that represented, be what brought Dov to his senses. His parents had not been through all they had so there could be a Jewish state, and afterwards devoted their lives to it, for the child born to them in a tent to marry now out of the faith.

Kate was present when that farewell took place, and said to Dov afterwards, "I don't think your mother is too keen on me."

"You're not a suitable prospective daughter-in-law, Kate, and I needn't tell you why."

They were walking beside the rose garden and when they stepped off the path, the sweetness gone from the air, and the unit's vehicles visible, packed and ready to move on, the symbolism of leaving a garden of roses behind her – what else had this interlude been? – combined with Dov's brusque reply, returned Kate full force to Dov's other self, and to her professional obligation. Loving each other wasn't part of the bargain they'd made. Nor would it stand in the way of either.

"We haven't so much as mentioned marriage," she said managing to smile.

"But my mother is no fool."

CHAPTER TWO

The transition from the kibbutz to the West Bank was for
Kate like being catapulted to a different world. One in which
her fears for Dov's safety heightened. Though she knew that
his was not an anti-Arab cause, there was the feel of
departing civilisation for territory in which enemies lurked.

Kate was continuing to travel in the minibus, rather than
put herself through the strain of pretending to Shmuel, in the
close confines of the car, that her relationship with Dov was
solely professional.

If the crew hadn't guessed by now, she reflected as they
reached Bethlehem, they were dafter than Kate thought
them. But she and Dov were keeping to themselves how they
felt about each other. As if it were too private and precious to
share with others.

Or is it that we know there's no future for us together? she
was thinking when Yosef cut into her musing.

"We are now to pass by the Tomb of Rachel, Kate. She
who has died in childbirth and was too the favourite of the
wives of Jacob," he added in his pedantic English.

"The youngest and most beautiful of the Matriarchs is
how the guide books put it," Chaim chimed in.

"And I guess the ladies queuing outside the Tomb would
be mainly childless pilgrims, waiting to pray there for
fertility," said Avrom.

Kate had time to scan the queue, as they passed by, and
saw that some of the women looked European, and were
smartly dressed. Such was the powerful mystique of the Holy
Land, people were drawn here from the far corners of the
earth to pray at its shrines.

"An outrage is always a bigger outrage if Israel commits it," Dov had declaimed, and had attributed it to the Jews still being viewed by the rest of the world as different. Since God had deemed them His chosen people, how could they not be seen as different from others? thought Kate. And their promised return, triumphant if bloody, to where the shrines of three religions were, not be under the rest of the world's microscope? It wasn't just Jews whose faith emotionally involved them with this land, and that was never going to change.

Kate's own sense of the mystical was jarred when later she entered the Church of the Nativity and was unable to relate the humble circumstances of Jesus's birth to the staginess imposed upon the grotto, framed as it was by red curtains complete with gold-fringed pelmet, and resplendent with silver whose pièce-de-résistance was a big glistening star set into marble flooring.

Her kids always had a make-believe Star of Bethlehem at the top of their Christmas tree, but Kate hadn't expected to see one when she gazed upon His actual birthplace.

Outside, the unit was filming the comings and goings of the assorted pilgrims, some of whom Kate passed in the vast, pillared Basilica as she made her way out of the church; and most wearing sweaters, which Kate too had learned was necessary inside the cool interiors of the shrines.

She removed hers, and put on her sunglasses, before going to join the men. As usual, fascinated onlookers had gathered, and some were being urged by their tour guides to return to their buses.

"Why are you filming this shrine?" she asked Dov, when he paused in issuing an instruction to the crew.

"Hang on a minute, Kate," he replied, and said to Chaim, "Can you also include the lady buying the rosary from the Arab vendor?"

More than the minute he had promised ticked by before Kate heard him pronounce, after peering through the camera, "Okay, it's a take. Also a wrap," he added, lighting a cigarette.

"The answer to your question, Kate, is that for Christians, this shrine is where it all began."

"I can't argue with that."

"But you would if you could," he said with a laugh. "Any *more* questions?"

"Yes, as a matter of fact. Where does the lady buying a rosary from an Arab fit into that?"

"I shot that for quite a different reason," he replied. "What it illustrates is how the spiritual and the material are intertwined, even in the Holy Land, and that nobody has any scruples about making a living from selling artefacts for a religion they themselves don't espouse."

Kate recalled Charlene, the transvestite, saying this, if less succinctly. But Charlene hadn't limited his cutting remarks to Arabs. "That includes the Jewish jewellers who sell gold and silver crosses, doesn't it?" she felt constrained to say to Dov. "But do you intend including Jews in this aspect of your film?"

"Why wouldn't I? I'm not doing a whitewashing job, which would do Israel more harm than good when the doc. is networked worldwide. I have never thought that God left out the Jews when he was doling out human nature."

"So your cynicism extends even to your own people?"

"Cynicism, Kate, is unproductive and I've never lumbered myself with it. In case you hadn't realised it, a pragmatist is what I am. Israel's thriving tourist trade would be a lot less so if those who wouldn't otherwise set foot in the Jewish State didn't come to visit their own religious shrines. If you'd like proof, we overheard someone say so this morning, and fortunately Avrom picked up his voice — "

"Fortunately? What are you going to do, Dov? Use it to load your argument?"

"What do you think my argument is?"

"That the rest of the world doesn't give a damn about Israel, but your country is nevertheless still here to tell the tale."

"Clever girl! But that isn't an argument, Kate. It's a

statement. One, however, that won't be said in words, and if foreign viewers conclude from the film what you have in advance, Dov Goldman is as good a director as he thinks himself."

Kate's feeling for him enabled her to smile at what would have once seemed another distasteful display of his ego. "If the cap fits, they can wear it, you mean?"

"And the same goes for the Israeli viewers who will see themselves – what's that English expression?"

"Warts and all. How shall you and I explain this little tête-à-tête to the crew?"

"They've seen me soothing troublesome females before."

"Troublesome, am I?"

More than she knew. And right now, Dov was resisting the urge to kiss the tip of her sunburned nose.

"Our next location will be where you start paying attention to the warning I gave you," he said to her. "That I don't want you wandering off on your own. In Hebron we'll be attempting to shoot some footage in the produce market, and — "

Kate had come to see his bossy manner with her as the protectiveness it was, and cut him short. "Don't worry about me, Dov. I'll stay glued to your side."

He called to the crew, who were now loading the equipment, "Okay guys! Let's get the show on the road."

The same breezy words he always used; as if we weren't headed for where anything could happen, and frequently does, thought Kate.

Nor could the PLO leader's reunification with the Palestine National Council have failed to fuel the fire. Kate recalled seeing Yasser Arafat on TV, leaving the meeting that had allowed an exultant smile to bely his usual bland demeanour.

While Kate stood waiting, arriving and departing pilgrims jostling around her, the Arab vendor selling rosaries on her left, and the birthplace of her own religion behind her, she rethought what Dov had said to her during their exchange about his film. Until now, she had viewed the making of it as no more than a cover for his subversive activities. A means by which the group could tour the country mounting support for their cause – though Kate had still to find out *how* they were doing so. The wall graffiti, and the free tee-shirts, had to be but a part of it.

Was the film a statement from the man plotting to avert what he feared was his country's destiny? "A statement" was what he had called it – and hadn't he said that it was up to its audience to conclude what they would?

Since resentment of religious strictures, the effects of this on people's everyday lives, had cropped up over and again in the interviews already on film, it wouldn't be necessary for Dov to load the argument. That the Jewish State was being torn apart by the very reason for its existence already seemed unarguable to Kate, and it had struck her that some Israelis seemed as concerned with that as with the Arab threat with which they must also live.

A sickening illustration of the Arab case in human terms awaited her when the minibus passed by the notorious Dahaishe refugee camp, on the Bethlehem-Hebron road.

Kate was prepared for seeing the IDF soldiers beside the gates. But not for the squalor visible through the high, wire fence, or the women and children watching from within.

The hostility on some of those kids' faces must've been imbibed with their mothers' milk, Kate thought. But they were probably born in that camp. For those people misery was a way of life.

"I shall never get that picture out of my mind," she said when they had left the camp behind. "How can you blokes bear knowing it's there?"

Avrom replied, "Believe it or not – I guess most foreigners wouldn't – our government's attempts to improve conditions in the camps are foiled by the refugees' refusal to cooperate."

"Would *you* be prepared to cooperate with people you saw as your captors?" Kate flashed.

"In an ongoing situation, and if it would make life less

squalid, probably. The more so if I had a wife and kids. Efforts are made to find work outside the camps for the men, Kate, but few accept it, and not because they're lazy. Every camp has its PLO spies and troublemakers, and the refugees are scared to be seen cooperating with Israel even in their own interests."

"What Avrom's telling you," said Chaim, "is that for the camps not to be the propaganda weapon they've become wouldn't suit the PLO."

"Who would not be satisfied to get back the territories," Yosef declared, "but would then want for themselves Jerusalem – an aim which the refugee problem is so conveniently masking.

"The blood bath that would ensue from such a confrontation I do not care to contemplate," he went on chillingly, "but the Arabs have many more friends at the UN than Israel has. It would not be them whom the world it would blame."

"Like the world hasn't bothered asking why the rich oil states don't put their hands in their pockets to alleviate their brethren's poverty in the camps," said Chaim.

Avrom added tersely, "I guess what it'd take for them to do so is some sort of headline-making flare-up when their charity would serve to emphasise what's seen as Israel's total lack of it."

"Meanwhile," said Chaim, "prosperous Arabs are living in luxury close by the Dehaishe camp – did you notice those beautiful homes, Kate? Turning a blind eye to their own people's plight just down the road. It beats me how they can. And you asked how *we* could bear knowing the camp is there! The answer is the average Israeli wants none of this."

"But the average Israeli isn't the sort we'll be meeting at our next location. I'll be interested to hear their views."

"Which they'll express to you in a way that'll make you think butter wouldn't melt in their mouths," said Avrom, "in other words, in the manner of the righteous. There are, however, among them and their kind, people prepared to commit murder in God's name."

"Some, though it's remained unproven, already have," Chaim chipped in.

Kate was horrified. "Among them and their kind, you said, Avrom — does that mean the militant settlers in the territories?"

"Not just them," he replied. "Others believe as they do. That Israel was destined to be a Jewish theocracy and nothing and nobody must stand in the way of that coming about."

Kate could not but relate this to her lover's determination to *stop* it from coming about. And to one attempt on his life already having been made. Such fanaticism not only knew no bounds; it would not pause to differentiate between Arab and Jew, but ride roughshod over whoever blocked its path.

While Kate tried to put these thoughts from her mind, Avrom said on a lighter note, "If you fancy buying some souvenirs, or jewellery, there's a good store in Hebron. And you could interview the counter clerks about how they're enjoying living in the West Bank!"

"I don't need an excuse to do a bit of shopping," she answered managing to laugh.

"But Avrom forgot to mention to you that the store, though it's open for business, has its windows shuttered and IDF soldiers patrolling outside, like everywhere in Hebron," Chaim supplied.

Kate's apprehension was mounting by the minute. "Is our stopover hotel in Hebron?"

"Is she kidding?" Avrom said to Chaim, and to Kate, "It sure isn't. Given how the Palestinians in the territories feel about Israel, there's no guarantee an Israeli film crew would live to see tomorrow dawn. And for another thing, no place in Hebron would have us, since the Park Hotel was hoodwinked by a certain clerical gentleman into letting him and some other people celebrate the Passover there in 1968, after which the hotel couldn't get them out."

"Avrom is referring to Rabbi Levinger — " said Chaim.

"I find it hard to make myself mouth his name!"

"Whom some think responsible for changing the course of Israeli history," Chaim finished his sentence.

"That is sure how posterity could see it," said Avrom. "As the ideology being put out by another of our too-well-known rabbis will surely be recorded as the ravings of a Jew with Hitlerite tendencies. The guy I just referred to managed to get himself elected to the Knesset, by the way, Kate."

"How could a Jew have Hitlerite tendencies?"

"By being prepared to apply the notorious 'final solution' to the Arabs if necessary. And I have to tell you that's a school of thought — thankfully limited to the very few — expressed by some of our so-called men of God."

"What's this other rabbi's name?" Kate inquired for future reference.

"Kahane. But those two are just dangerous oddballs," said Chaim. "A bigger worry is the ultra-orthodox parties holding the balance of power, and what some of their supporters are capable of."

Another oblique reference to the risk Dov was taking, and Kate allowed herself to envisage a man wearing a yarmulke and prayer shawl doing what had been done to the Volvo's brakes. An act of violence she still found difficult to associate with devoutness. But Aviva's death was proof that Dov represented a serious threat to those whom he opposed – and what were the lengths to which they were prepared to go but an extension of the special dispensations from God they believed that their own piety had bestowed upon them? Entitling them to themselves break the sacred Sabbath laws in order to stone the vehicles of those who drove on the Sabbath.

That this went on in Israel was fact, and if you convinced yourself that everything you did was for God . . . Well, that had to be why fanaticism knew no bounds. In Iran an entire nation believed that their marching through the streets chanting "Death to Israel" was on behalf of Allah. Right now, Kate would have liked religion wiped from the face of the earth!

Avrom returned her to a more mundane plane.

"Back with our stopover, Kate, we'll be staying in Kiryat Arba. That's the settlement that sprung from Levinger's craftily establishing a Jewish presence here."

"Does he live there himself?" Kate wanted to know. "I wouldn't mind meeting him — "

Avrom replied with asperity, "No, he prefers to live in Hebron, and be the red rag to a bull that he is! Since he enjoys airing his views to the press, if he's in town while we're here, you could get your wish."

Kate then learned from Yosef that they would be staying in a private house.

"Shmuel, he has the friends like him from Brookline, USA, who have agreed it for Dov to rent from them their home."

"Dov made it worth their while to take a short trip," Chaim explained to Kate, "which isn't that uncommon in the film industry."

"But the usual reason is that the house is an ideal location," said Avrom, adding a humorous reminiscence about a woman vacating her home while her husband was abroad, and his returning to find the place full of people and equipment.

"But wait for the punchline, guys – they were shooting a bathroom scene, and he said to the Hollywood star in the bath, 'Excuse me, I'm having my favourite fantasy.'"

Kate then found herself with three men laughing their heads off, and it struck her that she hadn't before seen them as they momentarily were; released from the tension that had surely worsened for them since Aviva met her death.

How they could go on with what they were doing was to Kate not just remarkable, but indicative of their determination to set right what they thought was Israel's major ill. But since Israel was a democracy, what was there to stop Dov from speaking out? Why had he gone underground?

For a reason you'd rather not contemplate, but must, Kate. There were people who would brook no interference in what they thought right for the Jewish State.

Kate emerged from those frightening thoughts as they entered Hebron, and put a smile on her face. "Dov said something about *attempting* to shoot footage in the market – What did he mean?"

"That where we shoot, and if we do, is dependent upon the mood here today," Avrom replied, "also on if the IDF think it advisable. In addition to the obvious, Kate, the time of year is dicey. It's Ramadan, and I guess the Arabs get extra touchy from having to fast."

"I haven't been here too often," said Chaim, while Yosef nosed the bus into a line of vehicles heading as he was for the town centre, "but whenever I am, it comes back to me that in the forties there was a massacre of Jews here — "

"Aren't the Jewish settlers afraid there might be another?" Kate asked.

"Not so you'd notice it," Avrom said cryptically, "but could be they've learned to live with that possibility."

"How they've also learned to live is in a fortress," Chaim added, "but Kate will see that for herself."

Yosef then lost patience with the traffic hold-up and turned into a side street little more than an alley.

"Are you out of your mind?" Avrom said to him, "or have you just forgotten this is the territories?"

"I would not be so foolish as to enter the Casbah," Yosef answered, "but Dov he will be tapping the foot — "

He stopped speaking and pulled up with a squeal of brakes as an Arab leading a mule appeared from a yard, to cross the street.

"If you'd kept going you could've made it!" said Avrom edgily.

"Who is the driver here, you or me?"

"But look what's happened now!" exclaimed Chaim.

The animal was displaying its fabled characteristic, blocking the street despite the Arab's efforts to push it forward.

Kate noted the stick in the man's hand. "If he whips it, I'll — !"

"You'll stay right where you are," said Avrom.

Meanwhile, as if from nowhere, some men and boys had gathered to watch the spectacle – and Kate was all too aware that the minibus was part of it. The seedy-looking buildings on either side were tall enough to have shut out the sun, and a feeling akin to claustrophobia joined her apprehension.

An excitable clamour might have been expected, but the opposite was the case. Silence, made ominous by remembrance of what could happen in the West Bank to vehicles with Israeli number plates.

"Any chance of your backing to where we came from?" she asked Yosef.

It was Avrom who replied, "If there were, do you think he wouldn't have? What the mule is doing here, a truck is now doing at the top end of the street!"

A swarthy face then appeared at Kate's window and her heart turned a somersault – or so it felt.

"Do not turn to look at him," Yosef instructed.

"I already did."

Chaim forced a chuckle. "See anything in his hand, Kate? A rock, for instance?"

"All I saw was decayed teeth." And a baleful stare. Sweat had broken out on Kate's forehead, and it wasn't from the heat. She reached out and honked the horn, startling the mule as it did her companions and the Arabs.

"Now why didn't I do that sooner?" she said as the animal went on its way.

"I myself would not have dared," said Yosef, "and Dov he would say it unwise."

But panic had put Kate's finger on the horn. "Probably, but it worked and we're out of there," she answered as they left the traumatic incident behind.

When finally they alighted from the vehicle, Dov thundered, "Where the hell have you been?" Interpreted by the men as impatience, Kate knew it was relief that she was safe.

"Proving that short cuts can turn out a time-consuming journey," she said, "and I'm now looking forward to seeing the Tomb of the Patriarchs," she added giving him a smile.

Dov simmered down. "While we're setting up outside, Shmuel will escort you."

Reminding Kate yet again that protecting her was for him a top priority, though what he thought could befall her here, and with two IDF soldiers standing by . . . The situation of the Tomb was nothing if not tranquil.

As she and Shmuel walked together beside the mosque that housed the revered remains, he told her that in Byzantine times the Christians had roofed over the walled compound erected by Herod the Great.

"What they actually did, Kate, was turn it into the Church of St Abraham, which had in it a special area for Jews to pray in."

"And after it became a mosque, was the same privilege accorded your religion and mine?"

"I'm not too well clued up about your lot. But I do know that for centuries Jews weren't allowed any further than partway up the entance stairway. And it's only since the occupation that pilgrims of whatever persuasion may enter the prayer hall."

When they reached the entrance, a tall Arab, hands devoutly clasped and a smile on his pock-marked face, addressed Kate.

"Welcome to the Tomb of Ibraham, lady."

"Ibraham to him, and Abraham to me," Shmuel whispered as they mounted the stairs, "and I guess that sums it up."

And between them, the Bible and the Koran had a lot to answer for, thought Kate.

In the prayer halls where the tombs were sited, she found herself affected by the atmosphere. Shmuel too, she noted.

"This is one of Jewry's most hallowed shrines," he said

quietly, "like Hebron is one of our four holy cities. In the Patriarchs' time it was known as Kiryat Arba. That's why the place we'll be staying in was given that name by the settlers."

Those who, in God's name, laid claim to land the Arabs who lived here believed Allah had meant them to have. How was a conflict of passionately held ancient beliefs to be resolved in twentieth-century political terms?

Later, after lunching on pitta bread and houmus from a stall in the square, Kate saw the passion upon which she had ruminated graphically displayed.

The crew had just set up the equipment on the edge of the market, when an elderly Jew buying vegetables clutched his side and slumped to the ground.

Kate was hastening to his aid, when Dov pulled her back. "Get the camera rolling, Chaim!"

Before Kate had time to tell Dov what she thought of his callousness, the market was full of uniforms and every Arab in sight being hustled away.

"What the heck is going on, Dov?"

"The old man was knifed. Didn't you see the guy standing beside him run away?"

She felt the colour drain from her face. "I just saw him slump and thought he'd fainted."

"But *I* saw the flash of steel."

Kate turned her head and saw an ambulance pull up.

"Are you getting this?" Dov said to Chaim. "The military haven't had time to tell us to leave yet, so let's make the most of it, guys."

A stretcher was now being rushed toward the limp figure on the ground, over whom some IDF men were hovering anxiously.

"Why would that old gentleman risk shopping in a market full of hostile Arabs?" Kate voiced her thoughts. "It doesn't make sense."

"Nor does how the families from Kiryat Arba flock here on

210

Friday mornings, buying in for the Sabbath," Dov replied. "I'm told the produce is good, and could be the old guy's wife said 'go buy me some carrots'."

"Another 'could be'," said Avrom, "is they're not going to let the Arabs' hostility scare them off and have it seem a weakness. Who knows how those people's minds work?"

The passage of the stretcher-bearers with their frail burden, and flanked by armed soldiers, was sufficient to momentarily silence Kate and her male companions.

They watched the ambulance speed away, then Kate went with Dov to speak with the IDF officer.

"He told me, when I asked if it was okay to shoot some footage, that getting our equipment smashed up was no skin off his nose," Dov said as they walked toward him. "And when I mentioned a British journalist being with us, he said he came from Liverpool."

Kate would have known that from his accent, when he said to her, "Shalom! That incident must have been interesting for you to witness."

"Also distressing. Is that old gentleman going to die?"

The young officer took off his glasses and contemplated them pensively, before looking at Kate with myopic blue eyes. "For his sake, his family's, and my own I hope to God not. If he'd just got his finger jabbed, all hell could be let loose by retaliating settlers."

While Dov asked him a question, Kate noted a weariness emanating from him, and would not wish to be in his shoes. Did enforcing Israel's seemingly endless occupation of the territories go against the grain for him, as the crew had said it did for many of the IDF? Presumably they were also empowered to deal with the retaliations the officer had mentioned, take whatever came from both sides.

"I'd strongly advise you, Mr. Goldman, not to attempt further filming in Hebron today," he said.

"And tomorrow?"

"Volatile situations have to be played by ear."

As Kate knew too well. "But I would like to interview

Rabbi Levinger," she said, "and that won't involve filming."

"He's away on one of his frequent demonstrations," the officer replied. "And now, if you and Mr. Goldman will excuse me, this is going to be one helluva day!"

With that, he strode off.

"What did he mean by that, Dov?"

"At the very least, they'll be up to the neck in questioning the Arabs they rounded up, Kate."

"At the very least? Does that imply there could be some beating up? Some of the pictures of that sort of thing, in British papers — "

"Do they also publish pictures of the other side of the coin?" Dov cut in. "Like the little Israeli kid found in a West Bank cave dead, and with his head bashed in? The beating up you referred to, Kate, is unlikely to take place in a military headquarters during a questioning session. It happens, when it does, in the thick of things, and provocation is the reason for it. I make no excuses for the violence itself. But a soldier is just a human being in uniform, and in that respect the IDF is no different from any other country's military."

"That was quite a speech, Dov." Kate glanced around the deserted market, the colourful produce heaped high on the stalls, but not a soul in sight.

While the crew were loading the equipment into the minibus, their sweat-streaked shirts now a familiar sight to Kate, she moved closer to Dov, affected by the sudden stillness, and by the absence in the street of all but the IDF.

"There'd be no grounds for rounding up Arabs who weren't in the market. Where has everyone gone to, Dov?"

"Home to lock and bolt themselves in, I guess. That officer wasn't exaggerating when he mentioned retaliation, Kate. Whole Arab villages have been known to get wrecked after an incident like this."

Kate recalled Chaim having mentioned "retaliating settlers", a snippet of information she had mentally filed without envisaging the reality. "An eye for an eye, you mean?"

"As the Bible has it."

She gazed down at some rotting apples littering the pavement. "When your wife and child were killed, did you want to kill those who did it?"

"I don't waste my time on futile thoughts and actions, Kate."

Kate looked up and met his gaze. "But revenge is an instinct — "

"Then it's one I don't have. Move it, you guys!" he called to the crew. "Let's get the hell out of here."

"Am I to take it we're leaving the West Bank?" said Kate. "Because I'm not ready to, Dov. If I hadn't joined up with you, I'd have come here by myself — "

"Another reason I'm thankful we did meet," he said quietly.

"But that doesn't change what I said. And I wouldn't mind visiting that store Avrom said is on the main street."

"Okay, Kate. We could use some light relief, let's have ourselves a shopping spree."

Thus it was that Dov bought Kate a ring in Hebron.

The store, as Kate had been forewarned, was shuttered, but open for business via an adjoining snack bar, a cheerless little place in which a man wearing a yarmulke was behind the counter lethargically wiping some glasses.

The crew, except for Yosef who had remained with the vehicles, sat down at a table, and Kate stopped herself from advising them to drink their beer from the can, since the cloth the man was using looked none too clean.

Who do you think you are, their mother? she thought wryly while following Dov into the shop. Well, there were certainly moments when those blokes stirred the mother hen in her, though she'd known them for just a short time. A short time in which much has happened, and the set-up isn't the everyday sort, Kate. There are things you know about them that have set you worrying on their behalf, as you would if you saw friends at home taking risks that weren't your business, and you just had to watch it happening.

There was too the increasing feeling that the group was a bunch of amateurs out of their depth in dangerous waters.

A summation that didn't, however, fit Dov Goldman whatever the situation.

Dov had walked ahead to the far end of the store, leaving Kate to admire some of the turquoise and submarine-blue glassware tourists were advised to buy in Hebron. But nowadays, how many would risk coming here?

Trade had to be bad. But the middle-aged Israeli chatting to Dov across the counter seemed markedly placid. Which didn't jell with the word "retaliation". Did that civilised-looking man applaud those acts of revenge? Whether he did or not, he and all who had settled in the territories were bracketed together, though it was doubtless just those who were by nature hotheads who went on the rampage.

When Kate joined Dov, he switched to her language, and as always, after Dov had introduced her, she received the Israeli greeting whose literal meaning continued to be elusive.

"Shalom."

"You don't seem too busy today," Kate said conversationally.

The man's reply was a shrug, and Kate glanced around at the motley display of goods. Candlesticks and Chanukah candelabras. Prayer shawls of the drab sort she saw old men wearing beside the Western Wall, and white satin ones bordered with blue. Silver and brass ornaments, with Hebrew words engraved upon them. Bookmarks and picture postcards. And yarmulkes of all descriptions.

Those heaped on the counter had Stars of David embroidered on them. But there was no shortage of that Jewish national emblem in this store, whose presence in Hebron must be to the Arabs as bellows to a smouldering fire.

"Are you scared of being here?" she asked bluntly.

214

Again she received a shrug. "It is God's will for me to be here, as the Bible says."

Back with the Bible, thought Kate. "Have you heard yet what happened today in the market?" she said and was surprised by his seeming able to shrug off that, too.

"Another incident, so what can you do? Last week, one of the IDF boys who keeps watch around here was saved by another from having his throat cut."

"But if no Jews had settled in the occupied territories, the IDF wouldn't have to risk their lives protecting them, would they?"

"And Judaea and Samaria," said the man, "would have remained an amputated limb."

"Which you believe the settlers have sewn back where it belongs?"

You're good at your job, my love, Dov wanted to tell her, but trying to provoke this guy will get you no place.

The man was now polishing his spectacles on a spotless handkerchief, his plump face creased into the holier-than-thou smile all too familiar to Dov, in whom his kind of Israeli aroused pity and frustration rolled into one. The former because their lives were restricted to the narrow horizons their piety imposed. The latter because they weren't open to argument, as if their path were preordained.

There would, however, be room for them, as for all kinds, in the truly free society Dov and the group were working to attain, he was thinking, when the man replaced his spectacles on his nose and said to Kate, with the air of one who has been carefully deliberating, "I could not have put what you just said better than you did. And what you have to understand is that Israel needs all her strength to continue the fight between Gog and Magog that it is God's will for His chosen people to do."

Gog and Magog? thought Kate. Where am I? Back in the dark ages? Did this bloke really believe the Israeli-Arab conflict was a battle to the death between good and evil?

215

Apparently he did. For him and his kind politics entered into the matter no more than did the national boundary lines on the map.

"Do you think there will be some sort of backlash, after the incident in the market?" she asked him.

"If there is, it must be seen in the context of what I have just said to you."

Kate now knew the answer to whether or not he would applaud it.

"Who is it," he went on, "who puts bombs in our bus stations, I ask you? Who was it who near to the Western Wall brought tragedy, not too long ago, to young Israeli soldiers on their proud graduation day?"

Kate brought from her mental filing cabinet a news item she had seen on TV at home. "Who was it who tried to blow up that mosque in Jerusalem?"

"That too must be seen in context," was the pat reply.

Not pat, smug, Kate registered. But wasn't smugness believing that all you did was right? "Well, thanks for letting me in on your views," she said politely.

"They are not my views, young lady, but God's will."

And Kate could imagine him and his wife saying that to each other, and believing it, if one of their grandchildren got blown up along with a school bus. Though grief would rack them, it would all be put down to the fight between Gog and Magog.

Her gaze again roved the goods on display, from one religious artefact to another, past the cheap-looking knick-knacks, and settled upon something that resembled a nightdress case.

"Is that circular satin thing with the embroidery on it what I think it is, Dov? If so, I might buy it for my mother — "

"I doubt if your mother would find a matzo-cover useful, Kate!" Dov laughed when Kate told him what she had thought it was.

"Could I look at one of those traycloths?" she asked.

"It isn't a traycloth, Kate. It's a 'chalah' cover."

"Oh. My friend Barbara's got one, she had it over the loaf when I was there for a Sabbath Eve dinner."

"But one from Hebron, she would be pleased to receive and to use," said the man hopefully.

"It was my mother for whom I was looking for a suitable gift — "

"Then you need look no further than our magnificent local glassware."

While Kate was inspecting the selection quickly put before her, Dov thought, not for the first time, how far removed was her gentile background from his Jewish one.

He watched her select a small piece for her mother, and when the man said to her, "Nothing for yourself also, from Hebron?" it was Dov who replied.

"Yes, we'd like to see some rings."

While Kate was getting her breath back, and Dov equally surprised by what he had heard himself say, the man led them to a jewellery showcase.

"Please to follow me."

A second later, they were gazing down upon a glittering array, neither having recovered their equilibrium. Dov had rushed them forward to a moment he had not anticipated coming so soon. And Kate had not allowed herself to look ahead.

When her tongue stopped feeling paralysed, she was prohibited by the man's presence from expressing her feelings. But what were her feelings? Her mind returned to Dov's interpretation of his mother's reserve toward her. And her own reply, that they hadn't so much as mentioned marriage.

Nevertheless, when a man gave a woman a ring, it meant something more significant than Kate was right now prepared to contemplate, she was thinking when Dov looked into her eyes, and memories of their intimate moments returned to her.

Recklessly, she cast thoughts of the future aside. "Diamonds aren't my style, Dov. May we look at some less showy rings?"

Dov was not surprised that her choice was a single pearl in a simple gold setting. She had unhesitatingly tried it on the fourth finger of her left hand, and after the man removed the price tag, it was Dov who, while the bill was being written, replaced it there.

Why can't I hear invisible violins playing? Kate thought as they left the store. Instead, her happiness was marred by a distant drum. Warning her that sealing their love with a ring made it none the less love without trust. There was, too, the old superstition, "Pearls for tears", which Kate had forgotten until now.

While the crew admired the ring they thought she had bought — or did they? — the position in which she now found herself finally hit her. Mad about a man with whom she was being as deceitful as he with her. In the thick of a situation so complex, and liable to become more so, there was no way of foreseeing how it would end.

Some minutes later, Kate was dismayed by the unit's arrival at Kiryat Arba, where it was necessary to pass through a guarded checkpoint in order to enter. She remembered Chaim's making a remark about the people here living in a fortress, but the actuality came as a shock.

"What happens at night?" she asked her companions in the minibus. "Do the guards shut those great big gates and lock everyone in?"

"How else would they lock possible intruders out?" Avrom replied.

"But I have to say I don't like the idea of being locked in!" said Kate. "Not one bit."

"And you haven't even seen the wire fencing yet," said Chaim. "But since you're in Israel to record your impressions, Kate, you are now seeing an aspect of Israeli life that would probably make your readers' hair stand on end."

"Well, it wouldn't be anyone's idea of feeling free, would it?" she answered as they drove past a space between two

218

blocks of terraced homes, and the fence to which Chaim had referred enhanced the fortress ambience. Complete with barbed wire.

"You won't hear the settlers complaining," Avrom told her.

"But don't bother adding, Avrom, that they put up with it for God's sake."

"Okay, you've got the picture, Kate. But we shan't be here too long. If Dov's advised no shooting footage tomorrow, he may decide to call what we shot in the market a wrap, and leave."

"Did you get on film, Chaim, how the Arabs were hustled away – as well as that old man being carried off on a stretcher?" Kate inquired.

"I am getting the feeling," said Yosef, "that Kate she thinks the Arabs they have a case."

And Kate the feeling that Yosef alone, among the men, had little if any sympathy for them. But he'd lost his brothers in the conflict, hadn't he?

"Those who were taken into custody after the incident, they will by now have been released," he told her, "except if some are known to be troublesome."

"But Dov saw the one who did it run away — "

"A night in jail will be a deterrent for others of his kind," Yosef answered, "and houses will still be being searched for him. But now, Kate, I shall give you the small tour of Kiryat Arba, before we shall come to the home of Shmuel's absent friends."

Chaim said with one of his throaty chuckles, "By the time we get there, Shmuel will have the tea made, Kate!"

The men had sensed Kate's low spirits, and were trying to cheer her up. "I could use a nice cup of tea!"

"Any little thing we can do for you, I guess you only have to ask," said Avrom.

A touching moment for Kate, and once again it was necessary to remind herself that these friendly blokes were a bunch of subversives, amateurs at the game or not.

But she wasn't going to let herself think about what might be in the padlocked trunk.

Instead, she gave her attention to the suburban homes by which they were passing, terrace after terrace of them, and reminiscent, with their gardens and garages, of the housing estates inhabited by young-executive families in England, the layout designed to hug the steep hillside where Kiryat Arba was sited. The opposite of what the word "settlement" conjured up, thought Kate. In one way, if in no other, the settlers had conformed to modernity.

"These homes wouldn't be cheap where I come from," she remarked, noticing that more were being built, as they reached the end of a terrace and Yosef turned the corner. "What do Shmuel's friends do for a living?"

"I think he said they both work in a bank," Avrom supplied.

"Is Kiryat Arba big enough to have a bank?"

Kate then learned that many of the settlers commuted to jobs in Jerusalem or Tel Aviv.

Yosef pointed out the school, which Kate would have known was one, since some young mothers were collecting their children.

Afterwards, she was shown the sizeable building that housed the synagogue, and the college whose students of the Torah were renowned throughout Israel for their eschewing exemption from military service – which Kate thought unsurprising, given their choosing to study among the militant settlers.

"And now for a peek at busy downtown Kiryat Arba," Avrom quipped, as they skirted a small square, its sole inhabitants a man clutching a grocery bag, and three young mothers gossiping beside their parked prams.

How those mums could accept their kids being raised penned in by wire fences, and all the rest of it, was beyond Kate's comprehension. But they had probably been raised here themselves and had known no other way of life.

When they arrived at the house, Shmuel was frying onions in the kitchen, and Dov gone.

"I thought it'd better be me who burns my buddies' pans!" he said rushing back to the cooker, after letting them in. "Dov said not to let you cook supper, Kate. Since we're now into a heavy schedule, he wants you to take a rest."

And what Dov wants, Dov gets! "Where has he gone to?"

Fortunately, Shmuel was concentrating on the sizzling onions, and the others standing behind Kate in the kitchen doorway, or they would have read her feelings in her face.

"All I know is someone called him when we got here, and he left soon after. We're to meet him tomorrow, in Qalqilya. When I've made the spaghetti sauce, Kate, I'll make you some tea — "

"Stop behaving like a host, Shmuel. This isn't your house and I'm capable of making my own tea."

A moment of silence followed – and if they hadn't guessed before who had bought Kate's ring, they surely would now. Why had she allowed herself to behave like the let-down female she felt?

She pulled herself together and made tea for all of them. While they drank it, she voiced her fears as casually as she was able to.

"Dov doesn't usually drive himself, does he?"

"Oh, didn't I mention it?" said Shmuel. "Someone came by to pick him up. I put the Volvo in the garage is why you thought he'd taken it – to leave space for the bus on the drive."

And if Kate was going to be worried stiff whenever Dov wasn't with her, she would end up a head case. It wasn't just his peremptory treatment, his not waiting for her to get here before leaving, that had made her lose her cool.

"Would you blokes mind if I didn't join you for supper?" she said, feigning a yawn.

"She doesn't fancy my cooking!" said Shmuel.

"Sleep is what I need, right now." Though she was unlikely to get a wink.

"Whatever you feel like doing, you do," said Chaim.

221

"Which is Kate's room, Shmuel? I'll carry up her holdall for her."

"Dov said give Kate the master bedroom."

She mustered the good grace to let Chaim take her bag upstairs, though its weight was light, and took a shower while still trying to calm herself. Another miserable night thanks to Dov Goldman! Which didn't stop her from climbing into the lonely double bed – in a room that might have been furnished by Habitat – with his ring still on her finger, and his face before her when finally she fell asleep.

CHAPTER THREE

Dov walked into the living room of the small apartment and smiled at the eager young faces that met his gaze. Some looked in their twenties. And others in their thirties, which was young to a guy who wouldn't see fifty again.

A hush had followed his entrance, and the burden of his responsibility brought an ache to his throat. More and more couples like those in this packed room were looking to him to ensure them and their children a future free of the religious oppression they feared.

Like the academics he had met with, they and their kind were the life blood of the movement, to whom its aim was as deadly serious as to Dov and the group. And soon it would not be an underground movement, but a new political party whose voice could not be ignored.

While he drank the coffee someone had put before him, aware of the respect with which he was being regarded, his eye roved the gathering.

"Please don't sit silent on my account," he said with a laugh. "I'm just taking a breather after my journey."

"And we appreciate your coming, Mr. Goldman," an earnest-looking fellow seated cross-legged on the rug replied.

Dov noted that two of the men had on yarmulkes, a sight that gladdened his heart, since their pledging themselves to the cause whose name was tolerance boded well for the Israel he wanted.

The vivacious girl in the white dress and her husband were Sabras, whose home this was. Present, too, were immigrants from Britain and the States, who hadn't settled in Israel to end up living under a holy yoke. It was to lend their strength to the Jewish State that they had uprooted themselves and come here. But the increasing number of those returning whence they came was a source of concern to a country desperately in need of new immigrants.

Dov could pinpoint the moment when the seeds were sown for the double life he had been living for more than a year. He had gone to Chaim's twentieth wedding anniversary party, last spring, and had left it a changed man, stopped in his tracks by something Chaim's nephew had said.

Dov, Chaim, and Avrom were standing together on the patio, watching some of the guests dancing, and Dov remembered wishing he'd brought a woman along. How the one he now thought of as *his* woman had reacted to another of his sudden absences he wouldn't let himself conjecture. All would soon be out in the open.

His thoughts returned to that April evening. Chaim's nephew coming to stand beside his elders and saying grimly, "The way things are going, Israel could eventually be a country where men and women dancing together is forbidden, and I'm not waiting for it to happen. Nor are some of my friends."

Chaim had said after a pause, "Are you telling me what I think you are, Yigal?"

Dov would not forget Chaim's expression. This was his sister's son, and very dear to him.

"But it wasn't my intention to spoil this evening for you by telling you now. I just couldn't contain myself," Yigal replied.

"I don't believe this," said Chaim. "As far back as when I came to London for your Bar Mitzvah, you told me it was your dream to live in Israel. When you made aliyah, your mother blamed it on me — "

"The dream's gone sour, Uncle. Like it has for a lot of people. The crowd I mix with are fed to the teeth with how things are, and it's getting worse. And I'm not referring just to the maniacs who chuck stones at our cars when we drive on Shabbat. My neighbour, who's joined a Reform congregation, told me the Boy Scout troop his lad joined — the kids are all from Reform families — has been refused the funding and a place to meet that Tel Aviv offers other troops in the area — ”

“Since you're not Reform,” Chaim cut in, “what's it to you?”

“Can't you see the writing on the wall, Uncle?”

Suddenly Dov had, and all too clearly. As if a flash of lightning had struck him, and he had said quietly, “There's more likelihood of what you fear materialising, Yigal, if your sort throws in the towel and leaves.”

“My neighbour said that when I told him I'd decided to. But if he wants to wage a war he can't win, that's his privilege. I'm taking my wife and kids back to where religion isn't just another word for power politics.”

Yigal had left them digesting the import of his bitter words, and Chaim exclaimed, “A nice anniversary present I just got!”

“But I have to tell you,” said Avrom, “that your nephew's reason for leaving Israel scares the shit out of me.”

Dov said thoughtfully, “But Yigal's neighbour *isn't* leaving, is he? And there must be a lot more like him — sickened by what they see happening to Israel and not prepared to let it.”

A pause had followed, and Dov recalled listening to a few bars of “I'll do it my way,” — a Sinatra tape was providing the dance music — before astounding his friends.

“Okay, so there's no shortage of people fed to the teeth, like Yigal said, with how things are. I've made up my mind to spearhead the opposition and I want you two with me.”

Dov's thoughts were returned to the present by his young hostess at a gathering that proved how right he had been.

“More coffee, Mr. Goldman?”

“Yes please, Chavah.”

“Chavah and I couldn't believe it when we were told today that the movement leader is you,” her chubby husband said.

"Well, you'd better believe it! And let me thank all of you here for getting together at such short notice. My identity is at this stage, however, to go no further."

"We were told that, too," said Chavah.

"And I'm sure I can trust you," Dov replied while Chavah poured more coffee for him and the man Kate had dubbed "beaky-face", who had ferried him from Hebron and was now seated at his side.

"Without the small committees like yours up and down the country," Dov told them, "the movement wouldn't now be strong enough to be a force that has to be recognised."

"And there's no need to explain why you kept us in the dark, Mr. Goldman," said a tall blonde leaning on the wall beside the door. "If the opposition there'll be had come before you got organised, the graffiti campaign, and all that, wouldn't have had the extra interest of nobody knowing who's behind it — "

"Exactly," said Dov, imagining the reaction of these nice young couples to learning his identity had leaked to someone who had then wanted him dead.

"But very soon we'll hold our first public rally," he went on, "at which I'll be the speaker. The press will be there to hear our aims and ideology. From then on we'll be a political party, with a registered office and a paid staff. It's arrangements for the rally that I want to discuss this evening."

"Will it be in Tel Aviv?" asked Chavah, whisking away his ashtray and replacing it with a clean one.

"It will be in Jerusalem."

Dov saw them catch their breath. As if he'd told them he was entering the lion's den, which in effect he was. But what better show of strength than bearding it on its own ground?

Chapter Four

Kate could not bring herself to greet Dov when he rejoined the unit in Qalqilya. They were early, and he a few minutes late, which enabled her to see him alight from a car and its driver – beaky-face! – speed away.

She plunged the hand with Dov's ring on it in her pocket, her expression stiff, as he strode toward her. Why can't we be just any old couple in love? Instead of having to hide it from those around us, and keep things hidden from each other.

Treading carefully, not to mention being suddenly hurtled from their loving relationship to their other one, as Kate was when she found Dov gone yesterday, was tearing her nerves to shreds.

"Okay, folks," Dov said briskly when he reached them, "let's get set up before the fun begins."

While Yosef told him that the minibus had been stoned by angry Arabs as it entered the city – a frightening experience for Kate – Dov wanted to take her in his arms and tell her he hadn't meant to upset her. The look on her face had stopped him from saying so much as "Good morning" to her – and since arranging the rally entailed his appearance at countless more gatherings like last night's, he was headed for a rough time with the woman he loved – who was far too perceptive to fall for the line he hadn't bothered handing her to explain his sudden absences.

Kate's not questioning him had revived Dov's feeling that the professional snooper she was had smelled something fishy and was biding her time. And once the Party was publicly launched, she would surely berate him for not giving her paper a scoop. All Dov could hope in that respect was that she'd forgive him if she got an exclusive on the inside story.

"You told the crew to get set up before the fun starts," Kate harked back. "What are you expecting to happen that you haven't filled me in on?"

"The first thing you need to know is that Qalqilya was, until recently, a thriving, and – give or take the odd extremist – peaceful little town," Dov replied.

Kate cast a glance at its main street, where pedestrians were few, the shopkeepers seated in their doorways illustrating that the cash wasn't exactly rattling in their tills; and the glances they gave an IDF foot patrol tramping by indicating who they blamed for it.

She then learned from Dov that Qalqilya had been unique in the territories for its citizens making the best of the ongoing occupation.

"Until a pregnant woman from a nearby Jewish settlement was killed, and her husband and kids badly burned, when a petrol bomb was flung at the family car," Dov went on.

"We were fortunate the minibus was only pelted with stones," Kate said with a shudder.

"The unprecedented violence here is now tailing off," said Dov. "But avenging settlers doing their worst – and they weren't from where the dead woman lived – triggered off a spate of it that went on for weeks. Qalqilya became just another typical West Bank town, and the fragile good relations it had with its occupiers could be gone forever."

"Is that how long the occupation is going to last!"

"That has to be how it looks to the Arabs, Kate. And the territories seem to me more potentially explosive each time I set foot in them."

Dov lit a cigarette and added, "But I imagine that by now you've got the picture well enough to realise it isn't the black and white one it seems to the outside world."

"Was it ever Israel's intention to withdraw?"

"That's a question a lot of Israelis would like answered,

228

Kate. But whether it was or not, if it were to be done now, the government would have a militant settlers' uprising on their hands, and even the ultra-orthodox Bible believers who don't live in the territories would probably rush to join it."

Were they shortly due to have a vastly different uprising on their hands, with Dov Goldman leading it? Kate cast that thought aside – and its accompanying prickle of fear for his safety. She still didn't know exactly what he planned to do, but the mounting tension she sensed in him told her it would be soon.

Later in the day, after interviewing some of Qalqilya's civic dignitaries – who struck Kate as sincere if worried men still trying to make the best of things – Dov told her that he would not be going with the unit to their next location, but would spend the night in Tel Aviv and meet them in Beer Sheba tomorrow.

The sweetmeats Kate had politely eaten with the Arabs, while Chaim's camera rolled, rose in her gorge. Another of Dov Goldman's disappearing tricks! But it wasn't one yet. Okay, so the half of him who was leading an underground movement had to do what he must. But the other half was Kate's lover – and she would use that to try to tail him.

"If you don't mind, Dov, I'll do what you're doing. I have some things to do in Tel Aviv."

"Fine," he replied, "though it'll add the extra travelling that in my opinion you could do without."

"Please allow me to decide what's best for myself."

Kate saw Chaim exchange a glance with Avrom – but they were probably getting used to Kate being frosty with Dov.

Nor did Dov blame her for it, or relish having to say to her, "I shan't have time even to take you to dinner, Kate. The meeting I'm going to could go on into the small hours."

If that was his way of letting her know they wouldn't be sleeping together, Kate had got the message she'd been about to send him. Nor had she failed to note that when Dov mentioned a meeting, Chaim gave his attention to his camera, and Avrom to his sound equipment.

"I shall be busy myself," she replied.

If it meant Kate's loitering outside the Dan until Dov emerged from it, however long, tonight she'd find out where he went to. There were usually taxis waiting outside the big hotels, and she envisaged herself leaping into one and saying melodramatically, "Follow that car," wearing her dark glasses and with a scarf covering her hair.

"Would you mind, before we set off, Shmuel, calling the Yamit to see if they have accommodation for me?" she requested.

"Dov asked me to arrange that they would any time, Kate."

"How very nice of him," she said trying not to sound sarcastic.

The journey to Tel Aviv could not have been comfortable for Shmuel, who was left to make conversation with two people who had nothing to say to each other that could be said in his presence.

When they arrived at the Yamit, Kate paused there no longer than it took to sign in, dump her holdall in her bedroom, and do the necessary to avoid recognition. She had not long to wait outside the Dan, nor was the "Follow that car" routine required. Dov emerged without Shmuel and set off on foot along Hayarkon Street.

Fortunately, Kate's sunglasses were the kind that adapted to whatever degree of light or shade, or she would surely have been groping her way along the shadowy side streets that were Dov's route to Dizengoff.

At last she had the satisfaction of doing to him what he'd done to her, to check her out. Why wasn't she enjoying it? The time when she would have was gone. Before she began loving him and fearing for him.

On Tel Aviv's busiest street, it might have been difficult for Kate to keep him in sight, but he had unwittingly done her the favour of wearing the light-coloured overcoat he had worn on the night he came looking for her in the cafés on the seafront.

A chill wind was again blowing tonight, but Kate had eschewed the red leather jacket that had kept her warm that night, lest it catch his eye, and had only a sweater around her shoulders.

She stopped beside a shop window when Dov halted and scanned a door as if he was looking for an address he hadn't previously visited. Apparently he had found it. Kate allowed a couple of minutes to pass by after he entered, before crossing the street and seating herself at a pavement café from which she could maintain her watch.

Though she wasn't hungry, she studied the menu and ordered a meal, not caring what she ate – but why let Dov Goldman do her out of having dinner? – her conflicting feelings in keeping with her illogical thoughts. It was not just Dov with whom she was angry, but with herself. He had conned her into a position no woman would envy, but as things now stood it was odds-on which of them would win first prize for treachery.

An hour later, Kate withdrew that thought. The winner would definitely be Dov. She had ploughed her way through a generous serving of fried chicken and chips and was digging into a mound of ice-cream when he emerged from the doorway across the street. With him was the transvestite with whom Kate had shared a sharut to Jerusalem.

Kate was momentarily too stunned to have tossed the money for her meal on the table and resumed tailing Dov. Instead, she watched the two stride side by side toward Dizengoff Circle. Charlene's enormous feet shod in the same gold court shoes he had worn that day, and the outsize gold plastic bag again swinging from his hand, Kate registered with the part of her mind that wasn't still trying to take in the depth and breadth of her lover's duplicity.

If she had learned nothing else from following Dov tonight, the wide-ranging support for his cause, and the lengths to which his operatives would go to further it, was now evident. Charlene was a far cry from beaky-face. Put that together with Naomi and her husband, she a lawyer and he a police inspector, and a computer would tell you what Kate's brain had already told her.

But when would the crunch come? And what form would it take?

Kate paid her bill and left the café, wishing she were anything but a journalist. She hadn't been sent to Israel on a hard news assignment, but was following up a hard news story that would get her a page one by-line, in addition to the feature articles she was here to write.

Was it worth what she was going through? And was Dov Goldman worthy of being given Kate's heart? Worthy or not, he'd got it, and suddenly the whole thing was too much for Kate. What she needed was a respite, however brief. Somewhere to run to.

She returned to her hotel and made a telephone call.

"Mrs. Ross?"

"It's Kate Starling, isn't it? I recognised your voice, dear — "

"I'm sorry to call you so late at night — "

"That's quite all right, dear. I don't go to bed early, only my husband does."

"I'd like to take you up on your invitation. Would it be inconvenient if I took a cab and came now?"

This girl has a problem, thought Mrs. Ross. "The bed in my guest room is always made up, dear. I'll have the kettle on when you get here and we'll have a nice cup of tea together."

Mrs. Ross's motherly presence was as reassuring as hearing her voice on the phone, and her home a comforting place to be; a haven in which Kate could put herself back together.

She awoke next morning in the sunny guest room to the sound of birds chirping in the trees outside the lattice window, and lay gazing at a framed picture of the Queen with her corgis, on the dressing-table, on which the old-fashioned lace runner and a china crinoline lady enhanced the atmosphere of this room being like a bit of England.

Kate visualised Mrs. Ross carefully packing her treasures, mementoes of a chapter she was ending to begin a new one where it seemed so many Jews of her generation chose to end their days. In the land not yet theirs when they had put their pennies in the blue and white JNF box.

The story Mrs. Ross had told Kate of those long ago days had come to seem ever more meaningful as the depth of feeling Israelis had for their country, despite internal strife, was over and again graphically displayed.

What but that had driven Dov to the hazardous measures he was taking to halt Israel's slide to where he feared she was heading?

Kate switched her thoughts to her children, whom she had not called for almost a week. Emily and Jason were probably right now having their usual morning row about which of them occupied the bathroom first, and while they ate breakfast there'd be the squabble about whose turn it wasn't to feed the cat. No, their gran would pander to their laziness while Kate was away, and tell them she would do it.

What sort of woman are you? Taking off and leaving your responsibilities to your mum? Again the guilt Kate had suffered since putting herself first assailed her. But her mother was happy being needed, and the kids spoiled rotten. The heck with guilt that sprang from Kate's own childhood memories of Mum always being there when she got home from school. She'd call the kids tonight.

Where would the film unit be then? Still in Beer Sheba? Kate had lost track of the schedule, as she'd lost count of the times Dov had suddenly gone off. Or gone missing without a word of explanation.

As for Charlene turning out to have been a "plant", part of the checking-out preamble to Dov's using Kate – seeing them together had sent her spinning full circle back to the coincidences that weren't coincidences.

Charlene must have waited to get into the sharut Kate was heading toward, or perhaps – what did the mechanics matter? What mattered was that Kate was in love with the schemer who had engineered everything, unable to put him from her thoughts and conscious that his ring was still on her finger. But still with her too was the feeling that theirs was an affaire that belonged only in the present. Like there was to this entire episode an ominous sense of living for the moment, and at a whirlwind pace from which Kate had been impelled to flee.

But this time it was Kate who had done the disappearing trick, and Dov who would do the worrying! When Kate felt ready to return to the fray – and given her instinct that the crunch would not be long in coming her respite had better be brief – she would call and leave a message for Dov at the Dan.

Meanwhile, she would make the most of the peace and quiet, in Mrs. Ross's kindly company. Try to separate her emotions from what she was in Israel to do.

Breakfast with Mr. and Mrs. Ross on the terrace proved Howard's father to be a man of few words, and Kate got the impression that anything his wife did was fine with him. Also that he was not unaccustomed to rising in the morning to find a guest in his home who was not there when he retired last night.

Mrs. Ross confirmed this, while pouring coffee for Kate. "How did you sleep, dear? The last occupant of my guest room told me the bed was too comfortable, whatever that means! We often put up young people from London whose family have given them our phone number, just in case, when they visit Israel."

"Too comfortable means you don't want to get out of it," Kate said with a laugh.

"Eat up your scrambled egg, dear. I've made you Howard's favourite breakfast. Barbara says that me cooking for him in the mornings, when he's here, is a rod for her back when they go home. But what are mothers for?"

Kate thought Barbara would correct that to, "What are mothers-in-law for?"

But Kate was enjoying being mothered by the woman her

friend couldn't get on with, and allowed herself to be plied with food, while Mrs. Ross chattered on and Mr. Ross read his paper.

"That's a lovely ring you're wearing, dear," said Mrs. Ross. "I don't recall you having it on when you were here with Barbara."

Nor had Mrs. Ross failed to notice that the ring was on Kate's engagement finger. Was the girl's strained air, and her coming to stay at a minute's notice, due to a quarrel with a man? Kate Starling, though a girl was what she seemed to an elderly woman, was Barbara's age or thereabouts, not one of the kids who rang up out of the blue when they needed a free hotel.

"I acquired it very recently," was all Kate was able to say. Had there not been the other level to her relationship with Dov, so bruised and battered were her feelings, she might have found herself pouring out her troubles to Mrs. Ross, though not in Mr. Ross's presence. But what were Kate's troubles due to, if not that other level, where menace continued to be waiting in the wings?

Mrs. Ross saw Kate shiver. "If you're feeling a bit chilly, dear, borrow my cardigan. It's here behind my chair — "

"I'm fine, thank you."

"Just so long as you don't catch a cold while you're staying here. Barbara would never forgive me. I wouldn't wear that ring when you're washing up, dear, even the best of pearls can get scratched."

Mr. Ross then departed the table and Kate burst into tears.

"That's quite all right, dear. You have a good cry. Get it out of your system — "

"The trouble is – I – can't — "

Mrs. Ross rose to come and pat Kate's shoulder. "Here, take my hankie, it's quite clean — "

"I'm sure it is," Kate managed to say while dabbing her eyes with the immaculate lace-trimmed square. "I shouldn't be behaving this way — "

"But we can't help our feelings, can we, dear? And your own mum isn't here to comfort you."

If Kate's mother saw her in the state she now was, she wouldn't believe it. Kate wasn't in the habit of going to pieces. It had taken Dov Goldman to reduce her to the vulnerable woman she hadn't thought herself.

"Feeling better, dear?" said Mrs. Ross when Kate blew her nose and her offer to wash the handkerchief had been refused.

"Yes, a little." Tears were an emotional release. But what did they do for the problems still with you?

"My husband will be out all day," Mrs. Ross told her, "something to do with the synagogue committee, I think. I never know how he spends his time, but as long as he's happy, I am."

"Don't you get lonely, here on your own?"

"Well, how I look at it, dear, is why should I? Before he retired, he was at work all day, and I was on my own then, wasn't I? Why should retirement have to be any different? I enjoy my housekeeping like I always did, and without a man under my feet, which is what I keep hearing from my women friends who aren't widows."

"You're quite a philosopher, Mrs. Ross."

"That must mean that philosophy is common sense. Now, what would you like to do today, dear?"

"Whatever you'd have done if I weren't here."

"The kind of guest I like, but I don't get too many of them! You can help me clear the breakfast table, Kate, and afterwards the living room will get its usual dusting."

By mid-afternoon, participating in Mrs. Ross's homely routine had restored Kate's equilibrium. Since today was Friday, there was the Sabbath Eve meal to prepare, and Kate found herself peeling carrots for the stew Dov had called tsimmes, while Mrs. Ross dealt with the chicken she would roast to eat with it. She was watching Mrs. Ross prepare the chopped liver when the doorbell rang.

"Would you mind seeing who it is, dear?"

But Kate knew before she opened the door. Nor did she bother asking Dov how he had found out where she was, which was just part of the mechanics that by now seemed unimportant.

While they stood regarding each other, Mrs. Ross appeared in the hall and after a moment thought it time to break the silence.

"Why don't you invite your visitor in, dear?" she felt able to say since Kate hadn't slammed the door in his face.

After introducing them, Kate said stiffly, "I've been working with Mr. Goldman on his current film project, Mrs. Ross."

And that's not all, that kindly lady thought. "And I'm sure you have things to discuss," she said. "You two go and sit in the living room, and I'll make some afternoon tea."

"The afternoon tea would be very nice," Dov replied, and Kate saw Mrs. Ross succumb immediately to his charm, but who didn't? "But I can't stay too long. I actually came to collect Kate."

The nerve of the man! "That was thoughtful of you," she said, "but quite unnecessary."

Mrs. Ross departed to her kitchen and left them to it.

When they had seated themselves in the living room, Kate said conversationally, "Afternoon tea is a British institution."

"And the whole world knows it. Don't behave with me as you would with a stranger, Kate."

"If we're going to talk about behaviour, there are comments I could make about yours."

Dov had no option but to let that pass. "Why did you run out on me?"

"Let's just say I felt like a change of scene."

"I see."

A pause followed during which Kate kept her gaze on a vase of flowers, and Dov's remained riveted to her.

"A break was all you intended, then?" he said eventually.

"If you mean was I thinking of severing our agreement,

237

why would I do that when it suits my purpose as well as yours?"

"Look – I don't have time for this! Are you coming with me now, or aren't you?"

"Why should I?"

"Because I need you."

"But something else you don't have time for is me. Or why, aside from your unexplained absences, would I have the feeling I'm sharing you with something more important to you than I am?"

A loaded question if ever Dov had heard one, and he had better not let himself be lulled by love into forgetting that his beloved was a professional snooper.

"I do have an additional important project under way," he replied. "It will shortly be completed, and there are many last-minute matters I have to attend to."

The crunch was definitely due. "Is it anything I might find of interest to my assignment?"

"May we get back to us, Kate?"

"Are we an 'us'?"

"Well you're still wearing the ring I put on your finger. Come with me now, Kate. Please."

If he had sent Shmuel to fetch her, Kate would have dug in her heels. But he had come himself despite the pressure he had just implied.

"All right, Dov. But I'd appreciate it if you'd try to be a little less peremptory toward me and a deal more considerate."

"And I, Kate, if you would bear with how I have no choice but to be at this particular time."

A reply that had about it the ring of destiny. And "chilling" was the word for its effect upon Kate. That Dov thought himself singled out for a historic purpose had never been more plain to her than it was now, and Aviva's biblical analogy returned to her. Hadn't Kate already begun doing to Dov what Delilah did to Samson when she cut his hair? What was his coming to get her but a sign that his strength to concentrate on what he must had weakened? How shrewd Aviva had been.

When later they were in the car and on their way, Kate asked more lightly than she felt, "Where are we off to, now?" and added to Shmuel, "I had the idea that Dov was driving himself today, or you'd have been welcome, I'm sure, to have tea with us at my friend's house."

"That's okay, Kate. I ate an apple. And it's nice to have you back. The other guys missed you, too. And where we're headed is again to Dov's house. On Sunday we're scheduled to shoot footage in Haifa. But Dov's giving us tomorrow off, so we'll be able to unwind."

Who was Shmuel trying to kid? Himself, or Kate? And the man beside her was the human equivalent of a coiled spring. "I need you," he had said to Kate. But what could she do for him other than be there?

Three weeks had slipped by since a car crash intruded on their last stopover at Dov's house and the mounting tension began. How, in that short while, could love have bound them together as it had, though there remained between them a divide neither could cross?

Since Kate was in no mood to chat, she was thankful that Shmuel had fallen silent. Though Dov seemed to have forgotten her presence, so preoccupied was he, his hand on hers assured her that he hadn't, and she tried to give her mind to planning the introduction to her series of articles. In which her involvement with the leader of an underground movement played no part.

That night, Dov came to her room and made love to her with an intensity that told her he had feared that he had lost her, and though no words passed between them, Kate knew how much she meant to him, as he to her. That each had met what could be called their "Waterloo", rendering them so vulnerable to each other, and yet so completely entwined, that death was what it would take to prise them apart.

When she awoke the next morning, Dov was gone from

her bed and from the house. But unlike the last time, none of the crew had accompanied him. They were eating breakfast when Kate entered the kitchen, clad in her dressing-gown.

She managed to sound casual. "How come you didn't drive him as usual, Shmuel?"

"He said he didn't need me to, and that he wouldn't be gone too long."

"But you did inspect the car?" Kate was unable to stop herself from asking.

They were all eating cornflakes, and put down their spoons. Then Avrom said, "What happened with the other brakes has sure put us all on edge."

"If I'm included in that, yes, it certainly has. Did you, or didn't you, inspect the car, Shmuel?"

"As it happens, I was in the bathroom, Kate. Well, coming out of there when Dov was about to leave – that's when he said he wouldn't need me — "

A miserable morning was spent by all, since Kate had set the men worrying and her own anxiety was plain. They surely knew as well as she did that Dov's preoccupation was such, he wouldn't be thinking of his own safety. The more chagrined was she, therefore, for giving the blokes a hard time, when Dov breezed into the house at noon, bearing a takeaway lunch for everyone and flowers for Kate.

With his arrival the mood changed. The crew were relieved, and Kate euphoric that Dov was safe and seemed briefly lighthearted. If this was his last fling before the crunch, Kate would enjoy it with him.

They ate on the terrace, laughing, talking, and drinking wine. An onlooker would have thought them people without a care in the world. Almost, thought Kate, as if we're on an artificially induced "high". Later, she was to think of it as the "high" before the fall.

They spent the afternoon lounging in the shade of the gnarled old tree. When night came, Kate left the men to their apéritifs and went into the house to prepare the meal she had promised them.

"What can I get you to drink, Kate?" Shmuel asked when she returned.

"Where's Dov?"

"He fancied a stroll before dinner."

"And you lot let him go alone?"

Again it was Avrom who replied. "Dov doesn't need a minder, Kate."

They knew damn well he did.

"I said to him, Kate, that I too would like the stroll, but he refused me to join him," Yosef then revealed.

"Like everyone else," said Chaim, "Dov sometimes prefers his own company."

And thought himself well able to manage without a minder. "All right, Shmuel, I'll have that drink. A gin and tonic, please."

Chaim then attempted some light conversation. But the day's bonhomie had crumbled to an anticlimactic low.

As time ticked by and Dov did not return silence reigned on the terrace. When his absence stretched for an hour, foreboding entered the atmosphere.

"Has he ever done this before?" Kate demanded.

Avrom replied, "Not when he's said he's going for a walk."

"And I don't see him forgetting I'm cooking a meal for us."

By now, Kate didn't give a damn if the crew thought she feared Dov had been mugged, or had guessed she was on to their activities.

"It's past ten o'clock!" she exclaimed glancing yet again at her wristwatch. "And don't tell me I'm making a fuss. You're as concerned as I am. Why are you just sitting there?"

Avrom rose from a wicker chair and put himself in command of a situation he would prefer not to think of as an emergency.

"Take the car, Shmuel, and Yosef will go with you to look for Dov. I'll go make some phone calls and Chaim can keep Kate company."

Kate and Chaim did not exchange a word after the others had departed, Kate pacing the terrace, and the cameraman fidgeting with his beard.

"Who did you call?" she asked when Avrom returned shaking his head.

"Everyone I could think of who Dov might've dropped by to see, which isn't too many. In Haifa he doesn't socialise, Kate, he comes home to rest."

"If you didn't call the police and the hospitals, I will."

The men exchanged a glance. Then Avrom replied, "Dov wouldn't want you to do that, Kate."

Kate didn't bother asking why not. "And what shall you do if Shmuel and Yosef can't find him?" she flashed.

"May we leave that in abeyance?"

By midnight, the others had returned grim-faced, and from then on Kate's pacing was non-stop.

"Shall we try your tea remedy?" said Shmuel.

She stopped short and whirled around to face him. "How will us sitting drinking tea help Dov?"

It was time for her to do some straight talking.

"There's something I had better tell you. I've known all along that this was no ordinary film unit, and it was my intention to write for my paper – when I could prove it – exactly what you lot are up to. I think Dov suspected that – and it's possible he warned you. But none of that matters, now. All I want is for you to get off your butts and do something."

A silence followed. Then Kate said, "I understand your hesitating to tell the police Dov is missing. But since they don't know about his subversive activities — "

Avrom cut her short. "When I made the calls I mentioned, Kate, I also put out some alarm ones to friends who are strategically placed. If they can't find out where Dov is, nobody can. Publicising this, at this juncture, could wreck everything Dov's worked for, and I'm asking you to accept that."

"*What* juncture?"

"You guessed the wall graffiti was ours, didn't you?" said

Chaim. "Well, it's no longer just painted on walls, Kate. Yesterday, posters went up, with the same logo on them, announcing a public meeting, but without yet revealing where it'll be held, or the date."

"And the day after they hit the streets, Dov disappears! Put together with what was done to his car brakes — "

Kate went to the trolley and poured herself a gin without the tonic, to anaesthetise the feeling threatening to tear her apart.

When the silence following her outburst lengthened and deepened until she could bear it no longer, she left the men to their private thoughts and went to her room to be alone with hers, the scent of Dov's aftershave on the pillow beside her, and engraved upon her mind remembrance of how they had last night lain together, no words necessary between them, their love saying it all.

When the telephone shrilled through the house, Kate was by the window watching the sunrise, and could not bring herself to pick up the receiver on the bedtable.

She forced herself to go downstairs, where Shmuel sat weeping at the kitchen table and the rest of the men seemed turned to stone. This was how Kate would remember them. Not as a group of subversives, but as Dov's friends when they learned he was dead. There was no need for them to tell her that her lover was gone from her.

Chaim saw her knees buckle and caught her. "Get some brandy, one of you — "

"I don't want brandy! I want Dov. I loved him, and he loved me."

Nobody spoke until Chaim had settled her in a chair. Then Yosef said quietly, "I was perhaps the only one of us, Kate, who did not notice what was happening to you and Dov under my nose. But I am glad for him that it did happen. So long he went without love."

"How could you have known that?"

"I guess we all knew," said Avrom, "that contrary to appearance Dov was the one-woman kind of guy."

"And sometimes," said Chaim, "when he was at my house, I'd see him looking at my wife and me together with sadness in his eyes."

Kate thought of Leah Goldman whose son was her life and envisaging the old lady's grief fired her with anger. "Between us we must raise an outcry! Get me the details and I'll call my paper — "

Chaim put a kind hand on her shoulder. "Another Jew found dead in the West Bank, Kate, isn't world-shaking news. That was where they found Dov."

"But what we have to ask ourselves," said Avrom, "is how did a guy who went for a walk in Haifa end up in an alley in Nablus?"

"He sure didn't walk there!" said Shmuel. "He would've had to be transported. By people who didn't mind breaking the Sabbath so nothing will change in Israel. And clever enough to make his murder look how it does."

If you're that sure who did it, why don't you go get them! Kate privately shrieked. One of Dov's wisdoms stopped her from saying it. Revenge was futile. Hitting back at the assassins wouldn't put an end to what they represented.

"Would you mind telling me what's really in that padlocked trunk?" she asked his friends. "It crossed my mind that could be where you kept your arsenal — "

The men looked shocked.

"You thought we were terrorists? And after the nice way we treated you?" Chaim said before letting her know that the trunk's contents were as benign as she had let herself hope.

"Propaganda material – and paper weighs heavy – for a public rally in Jerusalem that now won't take place," Avrom capped it. "Okay, Kate, we were playing crafty, we had to, but we were playing clean. We knew the opposition was unscrupulous, is why we went underground. But I have to say the significance of the failed brakes came as a shock. That was when we realised they would stop at nothing — "

"Or this time next week," Shmuel cut in, "Dov would've been the leader of a party that could have brought sanity to a political arena where it's sure gone missing. The wind of change our country needs in every way."

Kate wanted to apologise to her dead lover for believing him capable of the violence that had cut him down. And while she sat, dry-eyed, her hands covering her face, rocking herself back and forth such was her sorrow, she thought too that her loss could be Israel's loss. Who was there to carry forward the surge that Dov Goldman had inspired?

In Israel's religious climate, it had taken a very special man to get this far. But when the whole story was revealed – and Kate would ensure it – there were those in his own country who would view that man's timely removal from the scene as God's will.

MAISIE MOSCO